HIGH PRAISE FOR ROBERT J. RANDISI!

"Another winner. Keough is tough, obsessed with his job, righteous, and surprisingly mischievous."
—*Booklist* on *Blood of Angels*

"[Randisi] doesn't waste a phrase or a plot turn…. His prose is supple and never flashy."
—*Publishers Weekly*

"A skilled, uncompromising writer, Randisi knows which buttons to press—and how to press them."
—John Lutz, author of *Single White Female*

"Randisi knows his stuff and brings it to life."
—*Preview Magazine*

"Randisi has a definite ability to construct a believable plot around his characters."
—*Booklist*

"This is the hard-boiled detective story as it ought to be: tough, fast, savvy, with a touch of sentiment, but without pretension and fake moralizing. Enjoy!"
—Dean Koontz on *No Exit From Brooklyn*

THE VOICE ON THE PHONE

Busby handed the phone to Keough, who propped himself on the edge of the desk, putting his hand on her shoulder to keep her where she was.

"This is Detective Keough," he said. "Who am I speaking to?"

"You know who this is, Detective," the man—Gabriel—said. "Are you a member of the task force?"

"I am working with the task force," Keough said, "but I'm a member of the Federal Serial Killer Task Force."

"That sounds very important," Gabriel said. "A nationwide task force to search for serial killers?"

"Yes."

"And that makes you an expert?"

"Of sorts."

Gabriel sounded amused. "Tell me: Do you believe I am who I say I am?"

"And who is that?"

"I am Gabriel, the man who killed those three girls."

"Three?"

"Yes," Gabriel said. "I am not responsible for the fourth. Do you believe me?"

"I do."

"Completely?"

"Yes."

"Then you have to tell them," he said. "I did not kill that fourth girl."

"But you are going to kill another one, aren't you?"

"Yes," Gabriel said without hesitation, "of course I am...."

Other *Leisure* books by Robert J. Randisi:

Thrillers:
EAST OF THE ARCH
CURTAINS OF BLOOD
BLOOD ON THE ARCH
IN THE SHADOW OF THE ARCH
THE SIXTH PHASE
ALONE WITH THE DEAD

Westerns:
THE FUNERAL OF TANNER MOODY (anthology)
LANCASTER'S ORPHANS
MIRACLE OF THE JACAL
TARGETT
LEGEND
THE GHOST WITH BLUE EYES

ROBERT J. RANDISI

BLOOD OF ANGELS

LEISURE BOOKS NEW YORK CITY

This is for Marthayn,
certainly my Guardian Angel for the past ten years.

LEISURE BOOKS ®

December 2004

Published by

Dorchester Publishing Co., Inc.
200 Madison Avenue
New York, NY 10016

Originally published as *Arch Angels* by Thomas Dunne Books, an imprint of St. Martin's Press.

ISBN 0-8439-5476-0

BLOOD OF ANGELS

Prologue

Little America, Wyoming
November 2003

JOE KEOUGH HAD his hand on his gun when Harriet Connors stopped in front of him.

"Don't shoot," she said, "it's just a damn jacket."

"Sorry." It was an old habit, something he did on a stakeout, touching his gun, making sure it was there if he needed it. He looked at the jacket Harriet Connors was wearing. "It's very nice. Fits you good."

"I think so, too," she said, looking in one of the mirrors. "And you can't beat the price."

Keough looked through the window that separated them from the hotel lobby. They were in the Little America gift shop, and the smells from the restaurant across the way were making his stomach growl. The complex not only housed the gift shop, restaurant, and hotel but also an arcade and convenience store in another building, and a gas station. This was the flagship of the Little America chain, having opened sixty years ago. It was one-stop shopping, everything and a room. But he and Harriet weren't looking for any of that; they were looking for a man.

"Don't you want to know how much it is?"

"I'll bite," he said. "How much?"

"Thirty-nine ninety-five," she said. "I'm going to buy it."

"Go ahead, it's your money."

"In fact," she said, "I'm going to buy it and wear it now."

"Harriet," he said, "we're really not here to shop, so why don't you be quick about it?"

She pulled off the price tag, kept the jacket on, and went looking for a salesclerk. She was only gone a minute before she came running back, a sheepish look on her face.

"What's wrong?"

"I read the price wrong," she hissed at him. "It's a hundred and thirty-nine ninety-five. I missed the one!"

"How could you miss a one?" he asked.

"Jesus," she said, "I almost embarrassed myself. I was going to tell the clerk that I wanted it, no ifs, ands, or buts, and I was going to pay cash. But a hundred and thirty-nine . . . for fleece? I mean, it's pretty and it fits good, but it's only fleece."

"So put it back."

"I pulled off the price tag," she said urgently. "How do I put it back?"

"Put it in one of the pockets and hang it back up," he said. "It's just a price tag. If anybody says anything, show them your badge. We're the police."

"Oh, that's right."

While she put the jacket back, Keough checked the lobby again. There were two windows to check in at, with a computer at each one. A girl manned each station, but neither of them was the one they were looking for. They needed the girl who had been working last night. She was supposed to be coming in soon. One of the girls on duty now would give him the high sign when she showed up.

"Okay, I put it back," she said, standing next to him. "Nothing yet?"

"No, and I'm getting hungry."

"We can eat," she said. "Just tell your girlfriend where we'll be."

Keough didn't have to think about it very long. His stomach made a sound they both heard. "Okay. Wait a second."

He walked around from the gift shop to the hotel and stopped at the nearest check-in station. The girl there was just handing a guest his key—a real, honest-to-goodness metal key.

"She hasn't come in yet," the pretty blonde said. She appeared to be in her twenties and her name tag read CANDY.

"I know," he said. "My partner and I will be in the restaurant. Will you come in and get us when she gets here?"

"I'll send her in instead," she said. "I can cover for a few more minutes so she can talk to you."

"I'd appreciate that," he said. "Thanks."

"No problem, Mr. FBI," she replied.

"I'm not the FBI," he said, but she wasn't listening. Nobody ever did.

He turned, rejoined Harriet, and walked into the restaurant with her. A hostess showed them to a table by a window. Outside, the snow was coming down harder, and the windows were fogged. A waitress appeared promptly because there were only a few tables occupied. They each ordered iced tea and she gave them time to look at the menu.

"You know," Harriet said, holding it in her hands and regarding him over the top of it, "this could be very romantic, if we weren't waiting for a serial killer to show up."

"I have to thank you for going along with me on this, Harriet."

"You're my partner," she said. "Why wouldn't I go along?"

"Because nobody else agrees with me," he replied. "They agree with the FBI profiler."

She shrugged. "I haven't worked with that particular profiler before. I've been working with you for months, and you've been right most of the time."

He didn't bother pointing out that he'd only been wrong once in all that time.

"The profiler says the guy's working his way back to Cheyenne, where he started," she said, "and you say he's going to be here. That's only a difference of a couple of hundred miles."

"The profiler's wrong."

"I know," she replied. "That's what you always say. The thing that gets me is that you're usually right. How do you do that?"

"Instinct," he said. "Profiling is not an exact science, and it's something that's learned. You can't learn instinct."

"I'm learning that the longer I work with you."

Actually, they were 150 miles east of Salt Lake and 300 west of Cheyenne. Basically, they were in the middle of nowhere.

The killer had already taken women to four hotel chains along I-80 between Salt Lake and Cheyenne and left the girls behind—dead. The information they had showed he usually stayed in the room with them two to three days. Everything in Keough that was a cop told him this was the killer's next stop. Candy had told them that when she was leaving work last night, she thought she'd seen someone fitting the description they gave her, but she didn't know what room he'd gotten, or if he'd checked out in the morning. That's what the other girl was supposed to tell them.

"I'm having the home-style meat loaf," Harriet said. "It'll make my father turn over in his grave."

"Why?"

"He always told us kids never to order meat loaf in a restaurant. 'You don't know what they put in it,' he'd say."

"I love the way you portion out these tidbits from your past to me."

"We're partners," she said, "not lovers. You don't need to know everything."

He looked across the table at her, not knowing how to respond. Harriet was a good partner, but she wasn't lover material. She was a little older than he and on the heavy side. Well, not so much heavy as kind of . . . boxy.

"You're a good partner, Harriet."

She stared at him, and for a moment he thought she wasn't going to take the compliment.

"What are you going to have?"

"Chicken-fried steak."

They were almost through with their meal when a dark-haired girl walked in, looked around, and then made a beeline for their table. She was the opposite of Candy in that while she had a rather homely face, her skin was absolutely radiant.

"Are you the FBI people?"

Rather than argue, Harriet said, "Yes."

"I'm Mary Louise," she said nervously. "Candy said you wanted to see me?"

"Yes," Keough said. "Sit down, please."

"Am I in trouble?" she asked apprehensively.

"No, honey, not at all." Harriet reached out to take the girl's hand to reassure her. "We just want to ask you a few questions about a man you may have checked in last night."

"Then you can go back to work," Keough added.

Relieved but still somewhat suspicious, the girl finally sat down between them.

"This is the man we're interested in," Harriet said, putting a composite sketch in front of her. It had been done on a computer and was fairly clean. "He would have come in with a woman, probably with red hair."

"I remember him," the girl said excitedly. "He came in about this time last night. He had a girl with him who was wearing a bad wig. She looked young enough to be his daughter."

"This is important, Mary Louise," Keough said. "We need to know what room you gave him, and whether or not he checked out today."

"I can go and check right now."

"Would you do that?" Harriet asked.

The girl got up and hurried out.

"Could we be this lucky?" Harriet asked.

"Lucky?"

"Okay," she said, "if it is him, then it means you're that good. If he's still here, then we're lucky."

Keough nodded his agreement with that statement and popped the last piece of steak into his mouth.

Mary Louise came rushing back, out of the breath, and said, "He hasn't checked out."

"Did he write down on the registration card what kind of car he was driving?" Keough asked.

"A Toyota Camry," she said, showing him the card. "Maroon."

"Okay, Mary Louise," Keough said, noting the room number—112—on the card, "you can go back to work now. It's important you don't say anything to anyone about this."

"B—but. . . . who is he?"

"Don't worry," Harriet said. "Just go back to work."

"A—all right."

"And thank you," Keough said.

She nodded and hurriedly left the room. Harriet took out her cell phone.

"What are you doing?" Keough asked.

"Calling for backup."

"Backup is three hundred miles away, remember?"

"What about the locals?" she asked.

"No time," he said. "We'd have to identify ourselves, explain why we're not the FBI, and who we really are. . . . That girl may possibly still be alive, because they've only been here one night. We have to move now, Harriet."

She glared at the phone in her hand, as if this were all its fault, then put it back in her coat pocket and said, "Okay. Let's do it."

The maroon Camry was parked several spots down from room 112. This late at night, most of the parking spots were taken. There was plenty of cover for them to use to get across the parking lot. Lampposts partially lighted the way, but for the most part, they were in shadow.

"If he's been in there with her since last night, she's bound to be in bad shape," Keough said.

"What are you saying?"

"If this is our guy, we don't want to lose him. We don't want to get involved in a hostage situation. I'm saying we take him no matter what's going on in that room."

"So we give the girl up in order to get him?"

"Harriet," he said, "let's just not lose him."

She hesitated, then said, "All right."

Together, they moved to the door of room 112. He stood to the left, she to the right. They'd done this before; they knew who would go in low and who would go high.

Keough was about to knock on the door, when a voice and a flashlight came from the parking lot.

"Hey, you there! What are you doing?"

Keough and Harriet turned in the direction of the voice. Whoever it was shone his flashlight right in their faces.

"Turn that light off!" Keough hissed.

"I am the manager here," the man said, coming closer and getting louder. "Who do you think—Are those guns you're holding?"

Before Keough could answer, three quick shots sounded from inside the room. The bullets punched holes in the wooden door—and into the manager, who happened to be standing in the line of fire.

"Damn it!" Harriet said. "Let's go."

Keough nodded. He took a breath and stepped in front of the door without giving a second thought to whether or not more bullets would be forthcoming. He slammed his foot right next to the doorknob, and it gave and slammed open. He went in low while Harriet went in high, and they found themselves face-to-face with the Interstate Killer.

He was not a tall man, but fairly slight, so he was mostly hidden behind the girl he held in front of him. The problem was—as Keough had pointed out—he'd had her since last night, and she was pretty far gone. He was having trouble holding her up with his left hand around her waist while holding his gun in his right hand.

"Stop there!" he shouted. "I'll kill her."

Keough didn't feel they had time to hesitate. The potential hostage situation had to be defused immediately, before it could develop. The girl kept slipping down, revealing more of the killer's face and head before he hitched her up again, but she was not small and his arm was growing tired. Keough knew the man would kill her before he'd drop her, so Keough caught his breath, waited for her to slide down again. Even as Harriet called out his name, knowing what Keough was thinking, he went ahead and took the shot. . . .

One

JENNY DOBBS HAD no idea how close she was to dying. She thought it was just another day in her eight-year life, but Gabriel knew better. He also knew when, where, and how the girl was to die. Gabriel knew everything. He knew that eight years old was not too young, because when he was eight, he'd wanted to die. If only he had, he would not be here now, getting ready to take the life of Jenny Dobbs.

This would be the first. The boy was perfect. In fact, the child was almost too pretty to be a boy, but that was what made him so perfect. Sariel had picked Brian Andrews specifically because of his looks. There was an almost cherubic quality to the boy's face, to which his curly blond hair added a golden halo.

He would be the ideal first victim.

Keough's concentration was on his kite when a voice from behind broke in.

"Most people I know would be in a bar," Harriet Connors said. "You're out here in College Park flying a kite."

He turned his head to look at her, then quickly turned his attention back to the black-and-orange kite, which stood out starkly against the blue sky.

"How did you find me, then?"

"I know your hobby," she replied, "and this is the closest place to our office to fly a kite. It wasn't hard to spot the only man who was doing it while wearing a suit."

College Park was about five miles from the White House, but it was an easy one-mile walk from the nondescript office building where the Federal Serial Killer Task Force had offices. Since FSKTF was an unwieldy acronym for the unit, most of the members simply called it the FSK.

"So why would I be in a bar having a drink," he asked, "or flying a kite?"

"I'm sure you heard," she said, "or read the headlines."

She held out a copy of the *Washington Post*, the headline of which read TRISTATE SERIAL KILLER GETS DEATH PENALTY. He didn't have to look at the paper in her hand, though. She was right. He had heard, and he had read the newspaper.

"So?"

"So you were right," she said, "again."

"And everybody resents me for it, right?" He meant the other members of the FSK, a collection of detectives culled from law-enforcement agencies all over the country. Harriet Connors had recruited him a year ago from his last job, which was with the St. Louis Police Department. Since that time, they'd been partners, and the number-one team in the unit. Harriet was the number two in the unit overall, and she had chosen him to be her partner because she thought he had the best mind of any detective she'd ever met.

"I don't know who resents you," she said, "but I know who doesn't." She put the paper down at her side. "You're the best partner I've ever had, Joe, and the most intuitive detective I've ever known. I'm proud of you. Because of you, we put another one away, and they sentenced him to death."

"Good for us," he said. He took a box cutter from his pocket, waited until the kite was on an upward swoop, and then quickly cut the string.

"I'll never understand why you do that," she said, watching as the kite sped away on the wind, "spend money on a kite and then cut it loose like that."

He turned and looked at her full-on for the first time. He'd been noticing over the past few weeks that she'd changed. She'd dropped a lot of weight and was dressing differently, no longer wearing clothes that were designed to hide her body. She'd always been a handsome woman, not what you'd call pretty or even feminine, but that had started to change. She'd even done something to her hair and was using more makeup. The effect was startling. She looked like a different woman, and the word *handsome* no longer applied.

"It's cathartic."

"And you need catharsis?"

"On occasion."

"Because of this?" she asked, indicating the newspaper.

"You think I needed to fly a kite because a scumbag we put away got sentenced to the needle?" He smiled and shook his head.

"Then why?"

He stared at her for a moment, then said, "I'm not sure."

"You've been here a year," she said. "You haven't unpacked; you don't have a girlfriend, or a favorite restaurant or bar. . . . You're not happy, are you?"

"Who's happy?" he asked. He cut her off before she could pursue that line further. "Come on, let's walk back."

"Good idea," she said. "The director wants to see us."

He still couldn't get used to the "director" being his superior. He was used to his bosses being "Sergeant" or "Lieutenant" or "Major." "Director" made him think of Hollywood. But he wasn't just a cop anymore; he was a fed—a dreaded fed. Never thought he'd see the day, but then, his life seemed to be full of upheavals these last few years, going from New York to St. Louis to Washington in what seemed to be a blink of an eye, not to mention being on-again, off-again with Valerie. And then there was the diabetes. . . .

"What's he want to see us about?"

"He didn't say."

They walked awhile, squinting into the sun. It was warm—too warm. There weren't any seasons anymore. There just seemed to be two months of winter, and then heat. At least there was enough wind to get a kite into the air.

"You don't really think they hate you, do you?" Harriet asked. "The other members of the unit?"

"No," he said, "I don't."

"They envy us maybe," she said, "and our clearance record, you know?"

"I know."

"And I'm well aware our record is due largely to you."

"Harriet—"

"No, it is," she said. "I know that, but I don't care."

"It's a job, Harriet," Keough said, "a job we do well together."

"Yes, we do."

As they were approaching their building, he said, "Have I told you how good you're looking lately? I mean, not that you didn't look good—I mean—"

"Thanks," she said. "I've been working out. It's . . . it's nice of you to notice."

"Yes, well . . . I did, I did notice . . . but then, I'm a master detective, remember."

She just smiled.

Two

THE DIRECTOR OF the FSK was Gregory Wallace, a former federal prosecutor, who'd been the first choice to run the unit. But he was a lawyer, not a detective or investigator of any kind. All members of the unit had known who the director would be when they'd agreed to accept an appointment, but hardly any of them liked it. There were also members of the unit—men—who didn't like the idea that Harriet Connors was the number two.

As far as Keough was concerned, he didn't care who was number one or two—that all sounded very Austin Powers to him anyway—as long as he got to do what he did best—put killers away.

He and Harriet entered Wallace's office and were invited to sit down. Wallace was a perpetually well-groomed man in his late forties—never had a hair out of place. His contact with the other members of the unit was usually through Harriet, or occurred during a staff meeting. Keough found it curious that he had been invited into the director's office at all.

"You're both to be congratulated," Wallace said. "Your latest got the needle."

"We heard," Harriet said. "There was something else you wanted, sir?"

"Yes, there was," Wallace said. "Harriet, Joe, you are the best team I've got. I think we all know that either of you would have been a better choice to run this unit than I was."

"I'm not sure we all agree on that, sir," Keough said. He had never lusted after the top position in any unit he'd served in. For him, being a boss and collecting a larger paycheck—and pension— was never what it was about.

"I appreciate that, Joe," Wallace said. He mistook Keough's disregard for being in charge as an endorsement. Keough let it go at that. Harriet Connors didn't speak, and Keough knew that was because she agreed with Wallace.

"That being said," Wallace continued, "there are three matters on my agenda I need to discuss with you. First, there's a possibility that we could be opening another office."

"Where would that be, sir?" Harriet asked.

"In the Midwest. The exact location is not set yet—in fact, the idea is not set, either, but I've been asked to suggest someone to run the office if and when it becomes a reality."

Keough hoped the director was not going to offer him the job. He would rather have the offer go to Harriet. As Wallace's second, she was the obvious choice.

"I'm going to suggest that you, Harriet, head that office," Wallace went on, "and I assumed you'd want Keough to be the number two."

Keough remained silent and waited for Harriet to answer, but before she could, Wallace spoke again.

"You're a fine team and I don't want to break you up."

"We appreciate that, sir," Harriet said, then amended her statement. "That is, I appreciate it. Whether or not Joe wants to accept such an appointment is up to him."

"I'll give you both time to discuss it," Wallace said. "Now the second item on my agenda. I'm sending the two of you to the Midwest to look into a series of child murders."

"Where, exactly?" Keough asked.

Wallace passed two plastic file folders over to their side of the desk. Keough picked up the blue one in front of him, and Harriet took the red one set in front of her.

"Chicago," Wallace said, "and St. Louis. Seems there's a killer loose in each city, strangling children."

Keough opened his file and looked at the first page.

"Little girls in St. Louis," he said, looking at Harriet. "Three so far, since February."

She looked up from her file and met his eye. "Little boys in Chicago. Also three, same time frame."

"Not only that," Wallace said, "but each of the murders took place two to three days apart—and by that I mean a St. Louis murder, and then a Chicago murder—and vice versa."

Keough looked at the director.

"Who goes where?" he asked.

"I want you to coordinate," Wallace said. "Work the two cases together. One of you can go to St. Louis and the other to Chicago, but stay in touch. Use anyone else from the unit as you see fit. There're only about four or five hours separating those two cities. I want to know if we've got one killer traveling up and down I-Fifty-five, or two killers with a similar MO."

"Who goes where?" Harriet asked again.

"I'll leave that to you," Wallace said, "but Joe, you came here from St. Louis, and Harriet, you're from Chicago originally, aren't you?"

"Yes, sir," Harriet said. This was something Keough had not known before.

"Seems logical to me, then," Wallace said, "but as I said, I'll leave it to you."

"Sir," Harriet said, closing her file, "the question of a Midwest office . . ."

"Will be settled by the time you return," Wallace said. "I'll need a recommendation from the two of you as to where the office should be set up—St. Louis, Chicago, Jefferson City, Springfield, or somewhere else. I'll need that recommendation regardless of whether or not you two end up in that office. Understood?"

"Yes, sir," Keough said, and Harriet nodded. "But you said there were three items?"

Wallace frowned. "The third is not so pleasant."

Keough looked down at the folder he was holding, thinking that the second had not been so pleasant, either.

"There is also a possibility we may be disbanded."

"What?" Harriet said. "After only a year? Our record is impeccable."

"It's just being discussed," Wallace said. "Nothing's been decided yet."

"But . . . why?" Harriet asked.

"We were formed just before nine eleven," Wallace pointed out. "Apparently a lot of the funds originally meant for us are being diverted to the Office of Homeland Security."

Harriet opened her mouth to argue but then closed it again immediately. What argument could she offer?

Wallace stood up. He was of medium height, but he presented a commanding presence nevertheless—one that had served him well in the courtroom.

"Agent Connors, Detective Keough."

They stood, as well. Keough had requested that he continue to be addressed by his last rank, "Detective," rather than as "Agent" Keough. He was the only member of the unit to have made that request.

"Go to work on these murders and consider the possibility of a Midwest office. Leave the other matter to me."

"Yes, sir," said Harriet.

"Good luck," Wallace said, shaking hands with both of them. "Make the travel arrangements in the usual fashion and I'll sign your vouchers."

"Yes, sir," Harriet replied.

"By the way," said Wallace, "the other members of the unit have been told nothing about the possibility of being disbanded. Please don't discuss it with them."

"No, sir," Harriet said.

"And the other matters?" Keough asked.

"At your own discretion," said Wallace.

"Thank you, sir," Harriet said.

"I'm hoping this is one killer with a fast car," said Wallace. "Maybe he'll even crack himself up on the highway."

"That would be . . . convenient, sir," Harriet said as she and Keough left the director's office.

Three

HARRIET STAYED BEHIND to make the travel arrangements while Keough went to a nearby bar to wait for her. It was filled with Washington types, both male and female. Harriet was right when she'd said he wasn't happy. He didn't have a woman in his life, and he didn't have a favorite place to eat or drink, and this was the reason: He hated Washington types. They were self-important assholes who kept their cell phones on audio, rather than on vibrate, to make sure that everyone could hear how important they were, and then they talked loudly enough for everyone to hear their business. The women were just as bad as the men, so he did not have a female friend, or any male ones, for that matter. It had taken him a year just to get the other members of his unit to stop rolling their eyes at him because of his techniques, and his inability—or unwillingness—to believe in what had already become accepted and traditional profiling. He did not believe that serial killers were, for the most part, people with a disease, any more than he believed that addictions such as alcoholism or smoking or overeating were a disease. He believed that all of these things were conscious life choices and that most people were unwilling to pay the price for making them.

He did not fit into the Washington picture. Even though he enjoyed his job, he hated living in Washington, and maybe a midwestern office was just the thing for him—if the unit was not disbanded altogether. If he admitted it to himself, sometimes he missed St. Louis. He didn't miss New York, but he kind of missed the Gateway City.

"There's the man of the hour," a man's voice said.

Keough turned his head, saw Agents Lou Savarese and Lenny Pickett approaching. Pickett had come to the unit from the Pittsburgh Police Department, Savarese from the investigative arm of the New Jersey State Police.

Pickett had the largest collection of socks Keough had ever seen. The man never seemed to wear the same ones twice, and the gaudier the better. Keough wondered if the man had found some treasure trove of colorful socks on the Web. Maybe eBay?

He couldn't see Pickett's socks as the men approached, but he could see the malicious glint in Savarese's eyes.

"Lou," Pickett said from behind his partner, but the bigger, older man ignored him. Savarese was in his forties, thickset and swarthy, looking like he'd just stepped out of an episode of *The Sopranos*. Pickett was slighter, pale, almost timid, except for when he was working. Then he was very methodical and assertive. But the only interesting thing about the man seemed to be his taste in socks.

"Got another one, didn't you, Dee-tective?" Savarese said, moving to stand next to Keough at the bar. "Another one of your boys got the needle, huh?"

"They're not my boys," Keough said.

"Oh, sorry," Savarese said. "It's just that you seem to have so much in common with them. How else would you be able to track them down so well?"

"That's why they call me a detective, Lou," Keough said. "I detect. You should try it sometime."

"Where's your girl today?" the Italian asked, ignoring the remark.

"If you're referring to my partner, she'll be along any minute.

Since she's second in command, you better be ready to say 'Yes, ma'am' and 'No, ma'am.'"

"Yeah," Savarese said, looking at his partner, "like I'd treat that cu—uh, excuse me," he said to Keough—"that dyke like my superior."

"I wouldn't let her hear you call her that, Lou," Keough said. "She'd probably break your jaw."

"Hey, Agent Harriet Connors is lookin' kinda good these days, don't you think, Lenny?"

"Why don't you lay off, Lou?" Pickett asked.

"Lay off? Whataya mean? All I'm sayin' is that suddenly she's startin' to look like a fox." Savarese looked at Keough. "Any idea why that is, Joe? Maybe she's gettin' some? Maybe some man finally got her hooked on dick, huh? Who do ya think that could be?"

Keough had heard enough. He put his drink down and turned to Savarese, who straightened up and sneered into Keough's face.

"You boys got a problem?" Harriet Connors asked.

Savarese looked over at Harriet. From the look on his face, it was obvious he was wondering how much she had heard.

"Me an' Joe?" he asked. "What kind of problem could we have? Lenny and me, we were just congratulating Joe on you and him closin' another one out, Agent Connors. No harm in that, is there?"

"Lenny," Harriet said, "why don't you take your partner to another bar and buy him a drink, huh?"

"You tellin' me to leave this one?" Savarese demanded.

"Lou," Harriet said, facing him squarely, "I'm kicking your sorry dago ass out of this bar. You got a problem with that?"

Savarese stared at Harriet for a few moments, then back at Keough, who was breathing hard. If Harriet hadn't come along, he'd have taken a long overdue swipe at Lou Savarese. His intention would have been to bloody the man's nose, causing him to bleed all over his silk T-shirt and gold chains. Savarese always looked like a refugee from a road show of *Saturday Night Fever*.

"Nah, I don't have a problem, Harriet," Savarese finally said. "I got better places to drink anyway."

"Come on, Lou," Lenny said. "Let's go."

"Yeah," Savarese said, "let's get out of here. It's startin' to smell . . . queer in here."

As Savarese turned, Keough stepped after him, reaching out to grab his shoulder to turn him around. Before he could do it, though, Harriet Connors grabbed his arm.

"Let it go."

"We've been letting things go with him for months, Harriet. He doesn't belong in the unit."

"I know that, Joe," Harriet said. "He and Lenny haven't closed out a single case, but it's not Lenny's fault. Just remember that the director recruited him personally."

"That's something I'll never understand," Keough said. His heart rate was dropping back to normal and his hands were no longer clenched into fists. "You ready for a drink?"

"I'm ready for a big one," Harriet said.

They carried their drinks to a table. Keough recognized a senator to his right and a congresswoman to his left. Somewhere behind him, a cell phone was chiming, this one playing the call to the gate at a racetrack: *Da-da-da-dadadada-dadadada-da-da-da-daaaaa*.

"You don't have to do it, you know," Harriet said, and he realized she'd been speaking to him.

"Do what?"

"Defend me, especially against an idiot like Lou Savarese."

"I wasn't defending you," he said. "You're my partner. I was standing up for you. There's a difference."

"There is?"

"Yes."

"So it wasn't because I'm a woman?"

"No," he said. "You're a woman second, and my partner first."

With a wry grin, she said, "I'll try to remember that. Let's take a look at these cases."

Four

AN EIGHT-YEAR-OLD GIRL had been strangled in St. Louis on February 7. She had apparently been abducted after leaving her school, in between the time she had been dismissed and the time her mother had arrived to pick her up. Her mother claimed to have been only five minutes late. But that had been enough time. The girl's body was discovered two days later, after an intensive hunt for her.

Three days later, an eight-year-old boy had been strangled to death in a suburb of Chicago. The boy had apparently been permitted to walk the four blocks between home and school alone, and it was during this walk on the afternoon in question that he'd been taken. His body had been discovered three days later in a nearby lot.

The following month, the pattern emerged, only this time a boy had been taken and killed in a Chicago suburb first, and then a girl in St. Louis two days later. And then, in early April, it had happened again, St. Louis first, and then Chicago.

"The Chicago papers are calling this one the 'Chicagoland Killer," Harriet said. "When did they start calling it 'Chicagoland'?"

"Maybe around the time they started calling New York 'The Big Apple,'" Keough said, staring down at his file. "They were calling it that when I moved to St. Louis." He looked up at her then. "How come you never told me you were from Chicago?"

"I did."

"You didn't."

She scowled and said, "Okay, maybe I didn't. That wasn't a very happy time for me."

"Your childhood?"

"Childhood, teen years," she said. "I was . . . a fat kid." She said it as if that explained everything—and maybe to someone who had also been a fat child, it did. He let it go.

"You want to switch?" he asked. "I'll go to Chicago and you go to St. Louis?"

"That would be counterproductive," she replied, mustering every ounce of logic she could. "You know St. Louis; I know Chicago. Besides, you've got contacts in Missouri."

"Okay, then," he said. "Another drink?"

"One more."

Keough got them each another beer.

"How does this sound to you?" she asked when he returned.

"Like two killers."

"Not one going back and forth?"

"That," he said, "would be counterproductive."

"Would it?"

"Why run back and forth like that?"

"So you think it's more likely we have two killers targeting children the same age at the same time?"

"Boys and girls," Keough pointed out.

"Same age group," she pointed out in turn, "eight to ten."

"Wait a minute," Keough said. He opened his folder. "Eight, nine, and ten." He looked across the table at her. "Yours the same?"

She opened her folder, then nodded. "Yes. You think that's a pattern? They're going after an eleven-year-old this month?"

"Next month," Keough said. "We still have a few days of April to play with."

"Jesus," she said, "if they're not caught, they'll work their way up to teenagers soon."

"Two killers," said Keough, "following the same pattern. Could that be a coincidence?"

"One killer, driving back and forth, like the boss said."

"Or two killers," he said, "acting together, staying in touch with each other."

"They'd have to have personal knowledge of these kids," Harriet pointed out, "to know exactly how old they are."

"That means parents, or teachers. . . ."

"Counselors, caregivers . . ."

"Could be domestics. . . ."

Harriet sat back and closed her red folder. "So it could be anyone."

"What else is new?" he asked. "You got us both flying into O'Hare?"

"Yes," she said. "I thought you'd want to rent a car and drive the route from Chicago to St. Louis."

"Good thought."

"How do you feel about going back to St. Louis after a year?"

He left his blue folder on the table and sat back, shrugging.

"Come on," she said. "You hate Washington. Maybe going back to St. Louis will make you want to stay there."

"We could recommend the new office be opened there."

"If there is a new office. If not, you could always go back there."

"To work? Not likely."

"Why?"

"I like to move forward."

"So if we're disbanded, you'll look for work somewhere else?"

"Maybe I'll go private."

"You? A private eye?"

"Consultant," he said.

She looked surprised. "You've given this some thought?"

He finished his beer and said, "I always have a contingency plan. What are you doing tonight?"

"Got a date."

"Another one? Third time this week, isn't it?"

"You're keeping track?"

"I just notice things."

"Well, I have had three dates this week, but not with the same guy."

"Playing the field."

She stood up, then picked up her purse and slung it over her shoulder.

"I have this new body," she said, "and I'm going to enjoy it."

He opened his mouth, but she snapped, "Don't say it!"

"I wasn't going to say a thing."

"I'll see you at the airport in the morning. Our flight leaves at nine A.M."

"Better make it an early night, then."

As Harriet left the bar, Keough decided to have one last beer before heading home. Harriet certainly had changed during the year they'd been partners, but one thing had stayed the same: They worked together well. He hoped that losing weight, working out, everything she'd been doing over the past few months, was making her happier.

As far as going back to the Midwest, and St. Louis in particular, he wondered if the visit would do anything to cure his own recent malaise. No, not recent. He had not been happy since arriving in Washington, and the passing months had changed nothing. He enjoyed working with Harriet, and took pride in their clearance record, but that was about it. He needed a change, and maybe a return to the Midwest—and maybe the opening of an office there—would be it.

He decided against another drink, paid the check, and left the bar. He went back to the apartment he had not yet started to think of as home—and maybe never would.

Five

WHEN THEY FINALLY reached their seats in coach, Harriet said, "You know, flying stopped being fun even before nine eleven. It used to be exciting. I remember that when I was a kid, people used to get dressed up to fly. A few years ago, it seemed that people started traveling dressed in whatever they were wearing when they fell out of bed that morning. And the food! Don't get me started."

"Fine," Keough said, "I won't."

"It doesn't bother you?"

"It didn't," he said, "until I took this job. I've flown more in the past year than I had the previous five. And I never liked flying, so before or after nine eleven makes no difference to me. It's always been tedious."

They fell silent for a while, each doing whatever they could do to get comfortable. Luckily, they were sitting two abreast and not three. Harriet had taken the aisle seat. The first time they flew together, Keough had learned that this was the only way she could fly, sitting on the aisle. He didn't mind the window seat. He was happy as long as he didn't have to sit between two strangers.

They didn't speak again until after takeoff, when Harriet said, "So what do you plan to do?"

He looked up from his in-flight magazine and asked, "About what?"

"Washington," she said, "the job. You've been antsy ever since you moved. You need to change you life every few years, is that it?"

He returned the magazine to the pouch attached to the seat in front of him and turned toward her.

"You know, I never used to change my life that much from year to year. Okay, I got transferred a few times with the NYPD, but there was never anything life-altering until that Kopykat case. After that, my life just seemed to have been in turmoil from year to year. Moving to St. Louis, transferring several times while I was there, the whole diabetes thing, and . . . and everything else."

"Valerie?"

He hadn't been referring to Valerie—or any other woman—but he let her go on thinking that. He'd never told Harriet how his last case, the one concerning the serial killer in East St. Louis, had turned out. He had never explained how his young partner had shot the man down in cold blood after he'd been released because of political interference in the case, and he had certainly never told her how he had covered the incident up. He had, however, told her how he felt betrayed by not one woman, but two, when he felt they had both played him for a fool.

That was what she was referring to at that moment.

"Yes," he said, "Valerie and everything else. I don't understand why I've been faced with a life-changing decision each of the last three years or so."

"And then I came into St. Louis and gave you another one."

"You gave me an opportunity, Harriet, and a good one. But now . . . I seem to be doing it again. Trying to make a decision that will change my life."

"It's not you," she said, touching his arm, "it's just . . . life. Look what we're faced with now. Moving to the Midwest to man a new FSK office—if there is even still an FSK unit when this is all over. Not your fault, Joe, and sure as hell not mine. If this unit folds, we'll both have decisions to make."

"I understand how life has a habit of throwing you curveballs," he said, "but lately I just seem to be . . . flailing away."

"I'm not a baseball fan," she said wryly, "but I think I get the analogy."

"I don't know," he said, straightening in his seat, "maybe a move back to the Midwest would be good for me."

"Could you move back to St. Louis? After what happened?"

"It would probably be better than trying to move to Chicago and starting over."

"So you'd suggest St. Louis for the new office?"

"I suppose," he said. "But what about you? Wouldn't you prefer Chicago?"

"No," she said, firmly shaking her head, "I have no desire to move back to Chicago after all these years. No desire what-so-ever."

She'd always been pretty tight-lipped about her past, and even though they talked easily about his life, he'd never felt the need to pry, so he didn't start now. She put her seat back and closed her eyes. He reached once again for the in-flight magazine to give the crossword a try.

They both dozed until some time later, when Harriet said, "You know, I've been taking a course."

"Hmm?"

"A course, to be a better investigator."

He opened his eyes.

"You're a great investigator, Harriet," he said. "Who could you possibly take a course from?"

"Don't laugh, okay?"

"Okay," he said, steeling himself.

"A psychic."

He turned his head and looked at her.

"That's interesting."

"You didn't laugh."

"Why would I laugh? Why a psychic?"

"I want to be . . . open to everything. You are probably the most intuitive detective I've ever seen. I mean, the number of times you went with your gut and were right is astounding."

"Those are just . . . hunches, or feelings."

"It's more than that," she said. "You should go to this course with me. The woman who conducts it is amazing."

"How so?"

"She introduced us to something called remote viewing," Harriet explained. "It's visualizing with your mind's eye, which I think you do."

"How does it work?'

"Well, there are ten of us in the class, all detectives from different departments and agencies. She held up an envelope in front of the class, asked us all to close our eyes and concentrate, and draw on a piece of paper."

"What did you draw?"

"A pagoda."

"A what?"

"A pagoda," she repeated. "You know, a Japanese—"

"I know what a pagoda is, Harriet," he said. "Why did you draw it?"

"Because it was what I saw."

"What did the other people draw?"

"One man drew a fence, another a field; a woman drew a big rock."

"And then what?"

"And then the instructor opened the envelope."

"So who was right?"

"When she unfolded the paper inside, it was a drawing of a field with a fence, a big rock . . . and right in the center, a pagoda. We were all right."

"So you all have the power?" he asked. "ESP?"

"Not ESP," she said. "Remote viewing, using your mind's eyes. And I suppose everyone has it to some degree."

"It sounds interesting," he said sincerely.

"You have to go with me one day, Joe," she said, squeezing his arm. "You'd amaze them!"

"Maybe not," he said. "A lot of times, my mind is just a blank."

"Like when?" she asked in a "yeah, right" tone.

He put his head back, closed his eyes, and said, "Like now."

After a moment, she said, "Well, at least you didn't laugh."

"You're my partner, Harriet," he said. "I'll never laugh at you."

"I appreciate th—"

"I'll laugh with you," he went on, "but never at you."

He didn't open his eyes, but he knew she was laughing.

When they touched down in O'Hare, they went to the nearest car rental counter and rented two vehicles. He was going to drive to St. Louis directly from the airport.

"Sure you don't want to check in with the Chicago PD with me?" she asked.

"Chicago's going to be your part of this case," he said. "I'll get started in St. Louis."

"Be careful driving," she said. "What is it? Four or five hours?"

"Depending on how fast you go."

"I wonder," she said before they parted company, "if you'll pass the killer along the way?"

"That would be a hell of a coincidence."

"And I know how much you hate coincidences."

It was one of the very first things she'd ever learned about him.

Six

KEOUGH WAS SURPRISED at the depth of emotion he felt when he came within sight of the skyline of St. Louis and the Gateway Arch. He was at once elated, and nervous. Butterflies invaded his stomach as he was reminded of his last experiences here, and yet he felt great pleasure just at seeing the Arch rise majestically above the city of St. Louis, and the Mississippi.

When he left New York, it had been under untenable circumstances. It was virtually impossible for him to have stayed there, and to continue to work for the New York City Police Department. His departure from St. Louis had been, however, a voluntary . . . banishment. He'd punished himself for what he had envisioned as a grave transgression against his nature, which was to enforce the law. However, if he'd truly wished to punish himself, wouldn't he have left law enforcement entirely? As he pondered it now, moving to Washington to work with an elite serial killer task force had hardly been any penance at all.

Crossing the bridge, he studied Busch Stadium, which he understood would soon be torn down to make way for a new home for the Cardinals baseball team, and the hotels that dotted the downtown area. He eschewed the more expensive places to stay and steered his rental car toward the Drury Inn. He could have found even cheaper lodgings, but he preferred to stay downtown.

He parked the car in a municipal lot and carried his single bag with him to the hotel. In the lobby, once he'd checked in, he grabbed a copy of the *St. Louis Post-Dispatch* just to see if the paper had anything about the murders in it. He scanned it when he got to his room, but there was nothing about the killings in this edition.

Harriet had told him she would be staying in a Days Inn in downtown Chicago. Apparently, they were both trying to save the unit some money. Since she knew in advance where she'd be staying, she had given him the number. He dialed it, but, as he had expected, he did not find her in. He left her a message, telling her where he was staying and leaving her a number. That done, he sat down with his file and checked to see who was handling the cases.

The responding detectives to all three cases were different, but since the murder of the third child, a task force had been set up, and all three detectives were working together under the command of a sergeant named Dan Henry. The name was familiar to Keough, but at the moment, his memory could not supply him with a face, or a point of reference. What the file did provide him, though, was a phone number, so he dialed it and asked for Sergeant Henry.

A gruff voice answered. "Henry here."

"Sergeant, my name is Detective Joe Keough. I, uh—have we met before?"

"Once," Henry said, "last year, before you left St. Louis. It was at some political function you were attending with the mayor."

Before leaving St. Louis—before working with Marc Jeter to catch a serial killer in East St. Louis—Keough's life had become a string of meaningless political gatherings while working in the mayor's office.

"Where are you calling from?" Henry asked.

"Here, in St. Louis."

"I heard you were with some kind of serial killer task force," Henry said. "What brings you here?"

"I think you know."

"Well," Henry said, "I knew somebody was coming; I just didn't know who."

"Can we meet and talk about these murders?" Keough asked.

"The feds are coming in to take over, huh?"

"Not take over," Keough said. "Assist."

"You were a city cop for a long time, Keough," Henry said. "First in New York, then here in St. Louis. You ever know the FBI not to take over once they came in?"

"I understand what you're saying, Sergeant," Keough said, "but let me assure you—"

"Okay, okay," Henry said, "you're gonna be different. Do you know a bar called Jimmy Patrick's? Downtown, on Olive?"

"I know it." Patrick's was a cop hangout Keough knew about, even though he hadn't frequented the place very much when he worked here.

"Meet me there at seven tonight," Henry said. "We'll talk then."

"Officially or unofficially?" Keough asked.

"Whatever," Henry said, and hung up.

With the early flight, and gaining an hour from the East Coast to the Midwest, that gave Keough a couple of hours to kill, and he thought he knew how he wanted to kill them.

Seven

ALTHOUGH KEOUGH HAD only been house-sitting the entire time he'd lived in St. Louis's Central West End, it had just started to feel like home to him before he left. Oh, who was he kidding? He only thought it had started to feel like home because Washington never had, and never would.

As he drove through the West End, some of the pleasant hours he'd spent walking the streets there, or stopping in some of the bars and restaurants—like the Welsh pub he'd frequented, called Dressels—came back to him. Finally, he parked in what he thought of as his old parking spot, got out, and walked to the house. As he mounted the front porch and approached the front door, he instinctively knew that the owners had not yet returned from Europe, or wherever their money had taken them, and that no one was living there at the moment. It took only a peek through one of the front windows to see that the furniture he had used while living there had once again been cloaked in sheets. A shame to waste a great old house like this, he thought.

He turned and looked out from the front porch. One of the few friends he'd made while living there—the only friend he'd made on that block—had been the older man who lived across the street, Jack Roswell. They'd played chess and often gone for a beer together, and when Keough discovered he had diabetes, Jack was a help there, too—at least he tried to be. Jack suffered from a bad form of diabetes that affected his feet, and he'd tried to help Keough accept and deal with the fact that he'd contracted adult-onset diabetes. Jack had tried hard, but while Keough was now on medication and did try to stay away from sweets, he still had not fully come to terms with his . . . disease.

He crossed the street to Jack's house and went up the steps to the old man's porch. Immediately, he got the same feeling he'd gotten earlier; he was sure this house was empty, as well. Maybe Jack's daughter had finally gotten him to move in with her and her family. While Jack had loved his grandchildren, and loved seeing them when they came to visit, he was always glad when they went home at the end of the day. But maybe his disease had progressed to the point where he had needed help.

He rang the bell, hoping he was wrong. It would be good to see the old fella again, and maybe get in a game of chess or have a beer and some homemade chips at Dressels. He waited a few moments, then rang the bell again. Finally, he had to admit that his fears had been realized. Jack could have been out, but the truth of the matter was that he rarely ventured far from his house. It was more likely that he just didn't live there anymore.

As Keough went back down the stairs, Jack's neighbor appeared, also descending her stairs. She was an older woman with a red face and white hair, and Keough thought he recognized her, but in truth, he'd interacted with no one on that block but Jack.

"You lookin' for Jack Roswell?" she asked.

"I was, yeah," Keough said, "Do you know if he moved in with his—"

"He's dead."

Stunned for a moment, and then hoping he had heard wrong, he asked, "What?"

"He died," she said, louder this time. She was wearing a heavy coat, even though it was a warm day. She took small steps on legs that appeared to be thickly wrapped beneath some sort of support hose.

"W—when did he die?"

"A few months ago," she said.

"How?"

She shrugged as she made her way down the path to the sidewalk.

"In his sleep," she said. "Daughter came and found him in his bed. Been there for a few days. Lucky for us he wasn't there longer. Dead people start to smell, ya know."

Yes, he knew that very well.

"I meant what did he die of?" Keough asked.

"The diabetes finally got 'im," she said. "He didn't take care of himself, ya know. Probably coulda lived a few more years if he'da taken care of himself . . . ya know."

"Yeah," he said, "I suppose he could have."

She peered at him then and asked, "Ain't you that fella used ta live across the street?"

He stared at her for a moment and then, embarrassed and somewhat ashamed, said, "Uh, no, that wasn't me."

"Just as well," she said. "He was a standoffish bastard, he was . . . ya know."

"Yes," Keough said, "I know," and started back to his car.

He sat behind the wheel, thinking what a horrible friend he was. He'd promised to stay in touch with Jack Roswell, but he never had. Now the old man was dead, and Keough felt a sense of loss that shook him. What of the other people he'd known while living here? His partner Al Steinbach had died of a heart attack before Keough left St. Louis. What about Valerie Speck, the woman he had dated on and off? True, he'd felt betrayed by her in the end, just before he made his decision to move, but if he were to find out that she had died . . . What about Marie Tobin and Kathy Logan, the last two women he'd slept with? Or the mayor, for Chrissake? Was he even still mayor?

And what of Marc Jeter, the last partner he'd had, if only for a little while? After Marc admitted to shooting the serial killer Andrew Judson in cold blood and Keough had covered for him, they had not seen each other again. They'd agreed that Jeter would leave the police department—that actually being the young detective's own idea—but Keough had never checked to see if he'd done so. Jeter had been a pleasant kid with good instincts and a habit of quoting Mark Twain at any moment. What had happened to him? Why hadn't Keough bothered to check?

He'd gone to Washington, leaving everything and everyone he'd known in St. Louis behind, looking forward to a new life, one that had really never materialized. He had his work, but in D.C., he had no life outside of it.

But had he ever had that, whether he lived in New York, St. Louis, or Washington? A real life?

Eight

KEOUGH FOUND JIMMY PATRICK'S with no problem, right on the corner of Fourteenth Street and Olive. As he entered, it looked and smelled much like most other cop bars he'd been in. It had the prerequisite television screens tuned to sports, and tables and chairs, a jukebox, pool tables, but there the similarity stopped. Patrick's was huge, with high ceilings, windows that went almost from floor to ceiling. It was much larger than any cop bar he'd been in before. Against the far wall was the bar, nothing elaborate, just a rather worn and serviceable bar with about a dozen stools in front of it. There was a divider to separate the bar area from the pool tables.

It was after dinner and the place was about half-full, men and women sitting at the tables, a few guys shooting pool, and three or four men seated at the bar. Sergeant Henry had told Keough he'd be sitting at the bar. As Keough got closer, all four men turned to see who the new arrival was. When he saw their faces, he was able to pick Henry out. He still couldn't remember where they'd met before.

"Sergeant Henry?" he said, approaching.

Henry put his hand out. "Detective Keough. Or is it Agent Keough?"

"I prefer Detective," Keough said, accepting the man's hand. "Kind of makes me feel less like a sellout."

"You feel like you sold out, moving to the FBI?" Henry asked, surprised.

"I feel like it might have been a mistake," Keough admitted, "but one I'll have to live with. And I'm not with the FBI."

"Justice Department," Henry said. "Same difference."

Keough decided not to argue with the man.

Henry studied him for a moment, then nodded to himself, as if he approved. "Drink?"

Keough hesitated, then said, "Beer." He'd been drinking too much lately for his own good—for the diabetes—but he felt he owed it to Jack Roswell to have at least one in his honor.

Henry turned and signaled to the bartender while Keough slipped onto a stool. He'd stopped at his hotel first to pick up the file on the murders. He put the folder on the bar. The barmaid, a pretty young blonde, put a pint glass in front of him, next to the folder.

"Boulevard," Henry said. "I hope you don't mind."

"I like local."

"So," Henry asked, "what's the deal?"

"The deal?"

"Yeah. I talk to you and you decide if the FBI comes in? Or some other federal agency?"

Keough studied Henry. The man appeared to be in his forties, tall, judging from the way he was sitting on his stool. His shoulders were broad, and he looked like he might have played football at one time. His hair was slate gray and cut short; his five o'clock shadow was still black, though. His attitude at the moment was neither resigned nor cocky.

"Are you in charge of this investigation?" Keough asked.

"Right now, I am," Henry said. "If the FBI comes in, though, I guess I won't be."

"How big is your task force?"

"I've got each of the three detectives who caught the original cases," Henry said, "and some civilian help for the office. I can get as many uniforms as I need. Pin me down, I'll say I've got a task force of about twenty-five or so."

"I'm not the FBI, Sergeant," Keough said again, "but if you talk to me and let me help, I might be able to keep them out."

Henry turned in his seat to face Keough.

"Is that on the level?"

"I said I *might*," Keough said. "This unit has only been up and running a year. We're still working out the kinks. There have been times when I worked with locals and FBI, and there have been times when I worked with locals instead of the FBI."

"You got that much pull?"

"No, but my boss might."

"So what do I have to do?"

"Right now, all you have to do is talk to me."

The cop studied Keough for a few moments, then asked, "You eat yet?"

"No. How's the food here?"

"It's good, but I've got a better idea," Henry said. "Follow me."

The better idea was the Eat Rite Diner. There were three in town. One was out in South County, on Lindbergh Boulevard, and one was on Gravois Road. The one Henry and Keough went to was on Chouteau Avenue, near South Broadway. It was the oldest of the three, a St. Louis landmark. Keough just wasn't sure it was a better idea.

They got a table by the window and Henry ordered a slinger. Keough ordered a simple burger and fries. Henry raised his eyebrows as Keough took out two white pills, one slightly larger than the other.

"Diabetes," Keough explained. "Twice a day, with a meal." He still managed to forget his pills sometimes, but finding out about Jack Roswell's death made it easy to remember tonight.

"Okay," Henry said, "what do you want to know?"

"Let's go through the three cases, one at a time."

"You sure you don't want to talk to each of the detectives?"

"I'll want to do that later," Keough said, "and go to each of the crime scenes. First, I wanted to make contact with you and try to come to some . . . arrangement."

"You keep the FBI out of my case," Henry said, "we can come to whatever arrangement you want."

Sergeant Henry took Keough through the three cases step by step, still insisting that Keough would get a clearer picture of each case from the individual detectives who had caught and worked them initially.

"Do you know about the Chicago cases?" Keough asked.

Henry nodded. "Somebody showed me a newspaper story. Cases seem similar?"

"Similar, and close, timewise," Keough said. He went on to tell Henry what he knew about the "Chicagoland Killer."

"Chicagoland?" Henry repeated. "They name him?"

"You haven't named him?"

"I guess we're waiting for the newspapers to do that," Henry said. "They usually do, you know."

"What do you call him in-house?"

"The Killer."

Short and to the point.

Keough pushed away his half-eaten burger but continued to pick at the fries. Henry's slinger was a mountain of potatoes, eggs, and some other stuff smothered in brown gravy. He was almost done with it.

"Can I see your men tomorrow?" Keough asked.

"Whenever you want," the task force leader said. "When will you know if you can keep the Feebs out?" That seemed to be Henry's priority.

"Let me talk to your men and take a look at the crime scenes, and then I'll know better."

"You come by the office tomorrow," Henry said. "You can talk to each detective there, and then I'll have one man take you around to the scenes."

"That sounds fair."

"You working on the assumption ours are being done by the same killer as the Chicago ones?" He pushed his empty and remarkably clean plate away from him.

"It's too early for me to make any assumptions," Keough said. "My partner's in Chicago. I'll have to compare notes with her."

"Whatever you have to do," Henry said. "I've got to get going."

Outside the restaurant, the two men shook hands before going to their cars and each heading his own way. They agreed that Keough would come by the task force's office at 9:00 A.M. the next day.

"Bring doughnuts," Henry said, and then with a shrug, he added, "I know it's a cliché, but what are you going to do? We love the things, right?"

Doughnuts were one of the things Keough had cut out since the diabetes, but he kept that to himself and said, "Right."

"And none of the Krispy Kreme crap," Henry added. "Find a goddamn Dunkin' Donuts."

Nine

WHEN KEOUGH GOT back to his room, there was a phone message from Harriet Connors. It simply said she had called and that she would be in her room. He dialed the Chicago Days Inn. They chatted briefly about whom they had talked to and what they had found out, which wasn't much. They both had pretty much the same kind of day planned for tomorrow, interviewing the detectives originally assigned to the cases and viewing crime scenes. Keough knew they'd be running virtually parallel investigations until circumstances forced them to deviate.

"What's wrong?" she asked just before they hung up.

"What do you mean?"

"We've been partners long enough for me to hear it in your voice, Joe. Something's wrong."

He hesitated. "I went to visit an old friend."

"And?"

"He's dead."

"I'm sorry, Joe. Who was he?"

He told her about Jack Roswell. She listened without comment until he was finished.

"I see why you feel bad," she said, "but people move on. You moved on, and I'm sure he did."

"I let people slip out of my life, Harriet." He thought of the little girl and her mother he'd known in Brooklyn; his newspaperman friend turned true-crime writer, Mike O'Donnell. His friend Mark Drucker, who had been killed awhile back, and while he had managed to find Drucker's killer, he ended up feeling like a bad friend—but apparently that had not taught him a lesson. Now Jack Roswell was gone.

"Joe, who else is there in St. Louis you promised to keep in touch with?"

"No one."

"Then maybe we should just get to work."

"Maybe you're right, Harriet. I'll check in with you tomorrow."

"Give yourself a break, Joe," she said before hanging up. "Nobody stays in touch with all their friends."

He hung up, thought about his partner Al Steinbach, who had died of a heart attack while they were working the Drucker case. He'd lost two friends on that one. But what he'd told her was right: There really wasn't anyone else in town he'd felt close to. The mayor had been his boss, not his friend. The women he'd slept with had probably all moved on and wouldn't want to hear from him. And who knew where Marc Jeter had gone after leaving the East St. Louis Police Department. He'd mentioned something about going into social work, but they hadn't kept in touch. There was a dark secret they were keeping together, and those kinds of secrets usually pushed people apart.

Keough ordered up a pot of coffee from room service. While he was on the phone, he thought about adding a piece of pie, but then Jack Roswell suddenly sprang into his mind. He asked if they had any sugarless pies, and when they apologized and said they didn't, he left the order at just coffee and hung up.

Ten

St. Louis, Missouri
April 29, 2004

SGT. DAN HENRY had explained to Keough that since one murder took place within the city limits and two in the county, the task force was a joint effort. They had been assigned an office in the St. Louis County Police headquarters building at 7900 Forsythe Avenue, in the affluent city of Clayton.

Keough parked in a municipal lot and entered the building. Already informed that the office was on the fourth floor, he grabbed a closing elevator door and squeezed through. When he reached the fourth floor, he had to wander around a bit before he finally located the proper office. All there was on the door was a number, but as he entered, he saw Dan Henry standing across the room in front of a green blackboard. There were five people facing Henry, their backs to the door, four men and a woman. As Keough entered, Henry spotted him and broke off what he was saying.

"Speak of the devil," he said, instead.

The five people turned on their chairs to look at him, every gaze a measured one.

"People," Henry said, "this is Detective Joe Keough of the Federal Serial Killer Task Force."

All five people stood up and turned to face Keough as he approached. Henry ran though the names quickly, but Keough concentrated on the two detectives who had originally picked up their cases.

The detective who caught the case in Clayton was Jim House, fortyish, medium height, and rather benign-looking—until you looked into his eyes. The other detective was one of Henry's own men from the city department, John Berkery. He looked to be fit, in his early fifties, about six two and two hundred pounds, gray hair and mustache.

The other two men were uniformed cops who had been assigned to work plainclothes detail for the task force, Officers George and O'Doul. They were both about thirty and did much of the legwork. The middle-aged woman was a clerical, assigned to do filing and run the computer. Her name was Martha.

"Isn't there a third detective?" Keough asked.

"He's . . . late," Henry said. "Should be here shortly."

"*Detective* Keough?" Detective Berkery asked. "Not Agent? Why is that?"

"Because I'm a detective," Keough replied, "not an agent."

"But you're a fed, right?"

Keough hesitated, then said, "Well, technically."

"So is the FBI coming in to take over?" Detective House asked. He was speaking directly to Sergeant Henry.

"I'm not with the FBI," Keough said.

"Detective Keough is here to look the situation over," Henry said. "We might only have to work with him, and not anyone from the FBI."

The others looked Keough over suspiciously.

"He's an ex–St. Louis cop," Henry added.

"I thought I recognized the name," Martha said. "You worked in the mayor's office, didn't you?"

"That was my last assignment, yes," Keough said.

"Why'd you leave?" House asked.

"I got a better offer."

"Better than the mayor's office?" O'Doul asked.

"Not better money," Keough said, "just an opportunity to do what I'm trained to do."

"Which is?" George asked.

"Catch bad guys," Keough said.

"Like the guy who's killing these kids?" Martha asked.

"Exactly."

She looked around the room at the men. "Works for me."

"That is why we're all here," Henry said. "Can we get on with it now the introductions have been made?"

"Sorry, sir," Berkery said.

"We need to fill Detective Keough in on what's been done so far," Henry said. "I met with him last night and gave him the basics. He wants to speak to each detective who worked on these cases individually before the task force was formed."

"If we could just sit down someplace . . ." Keough said.

"There's a small room at the end of the hall that's empty," Martha said. "Got a desk and some chairs. It was too small for us, but it should be good for you."

"That'll do," Keough said.

"John? You first," Henry said. "Then you, Jim,"

"Yes, sir," House said.

"John?"

"This way, Detective Keough."

"Sir?" Martha said.

"The name is Joe, Martha."

"Joe," she said. "Coffee?"

Keough remembered then that he was supposed to have brought doughnuts.

"If you'll send someone out for doughnuts and coffee," he said to Martha, "I'll buy."

She smiled. "You're on."

Eleven

THE ROOM WAS little more than a closet, but large enough for Keough's purposes. He procured a lined yellow pad from Martha—he already had pens—and then sat down in the small room with Detective Berkery and went over the details of his case with him.

Berkery gave him the *Dragnet* version—just the facts. He did not offer any opinions at all. Keough knew that he wasn't going to get full cooperation out of these cops immediately—if ever—but that was fine. He actually only needed the facts, because he'd be forming his own opinions and conclusions.

"Thanks for your time, Detective," Keough said when they were done. "Would you send Detective House in, please?"

Berkery stood up, started for the door, but then turned around again.

"You think you can solve these cases and we can't?" he demanded.

"I think," Keough said, "that we can solve them if we work together."

"The feds don't work together," Berkery said. "You guys come in and take over. You take all the credit, when the locals do all the work."

"Look, Berkery," Keough said, "I was a New York cop for years, and then here in St. Louis—"

"You're a fed now," Berkery said, cutting him off. "That's all that matters, in my book."

Keough stared at the man and knew he wouldn't get anywhere arguing with him. Hadn't he felt the same way when he was working on the local level? Hadn't he been distrustful of the "feds" when they came in to scoop up a case?

"Would you you send Detective House in, please?" he asked again.

"Yeah, sure," Berkery said, and left. His distain remained behind, hanging in the air like a fart.

House went through his case efficiently, even dropped an opinion or two before he remembered whom he was talking to. While they were working, Martha came in with coffee and a pastry for each of them. The coffee containers were from the St. Louis Bread Company. Keough got an odd feeling of nostalgia at seeing the logo of the local coffeehouse and bakery. She brought cream and sugar, but Keough waved them away. He did not reject the pastry—it had icing, slivers of almonds, and an apple center—even though he didn't intend to eat it.

House drank his coffee, ate his pastry, and spent the rest of the interview giving Keough just the facts. After he left, Keough sipped his coffee, studied his notes, and absently picked up the pastry and took a bite. He had chewed and swallowed before he realized what he'd done. His sugar having already taken a hit, he decided to eat it all.

When he had finished eating, he took the remainder of his coffee and walked back to the task force's office.

"That other detective come in yet?" he asked Martha.

"Not yet," she said, "but he'll be here soon."

"You get what you wanted from them?" Henry asked, coming over to stand in front of Martha's desk with him.

"Just," he said.

"You know what it's like, Keough," Henry said. "Don't hold it against them."

"I won't," Keough replied. "I prefer to draw my own conclusions anyway. Listen, I can catch up with the other detective later. Right now, I'd like to have someone take me to the three scenes."

"Right away," Henry said.

"And when I get back, I'd like to get copies of all the files."

"I'll have Martha run them off for you," Henry said. "John? Jim? Keough needs a ride to the crime scenes."

Both detectives looked down at their desks.

"Maybe Martha would like to—" Keough began, but he was cut off from behind.

"I'll do it."

"Ah, here he is," Dan Henry said. "Better late than never, I guess." Clearly, he was not happy with the third detective.

"This is good," Keough said. "I can interview him at the same time." He turned to meet the man but then stopped short when he saw who was standing in the doorway.

"Keough," Henry said, "this is detective Marc Jeter. Marc didn't catch the case originally, but he took it over when the other detective retired."

Jeter stepped forward, stuck out his hand, and said, "Hello, Joe."

Keough was speechless.

Twelve

"You two know each other?" Sergeant Henry asked.

"We've worked together before," Jeter said, because Keough still seemed unable to form words.

"Well, that's good, then," Henry said. "Maybe you'll make a good liaison, Jeter—if you start getting in on time, that is."

"Sorry, Sarge," Jeter said. "I had a, uh, thing and it took longer than I thought."

"Never mind," the sergeant said. "Take Keough out to all three sites, fill him in on your case, and then come back and we'll take it from there."

"Will do, Sarge."

"That okay with everyone?"

The other two detectives didn't bother to answer, and the two cops had already been dispatched to run some errands, so Martha just said, "Works for me."

Marc Jeter took Keough's arm and hustled him out the door.

"What the hell—" Keough said when they reached the street.

"Let's get in the car first," Jeter suggested. "Might as well take mine, since I know where we're going."

"Fine."

Keough followed the young black detective down the street, his mind confused. The last time he'd seen Marc Jeter, the younger man had been intending to resign from the East St. Louis Police Department. He and Keough were the only two who knew the reason—Jeter had shot and killed Andrew Judson in cold blood because the serial killer had been released on a technicality. Now here was Jeter, more than a year later, carrying a badge again.

"This is mine."

Keough got into the car without even noticing what kind it was. When Jeter got in on the driver's side, he started talking before Keough could ask a question.

"I know you're wondering what I'm doing here wearing a badge again," Jeter said.

"*Wondering* is not the word, Marc," Keough said. "I'm stunned. Last time I saw you, you told me you couldn't be a cop anymore. We agreed you would resign, and that I would keep my mouth shut about what happened."

"Okay, so maybe you're feeling betrayed because I didn't keep my part of the bargain."

"Betrayed?"

"Look," Jeter said, "I better start driving. We don't want anyone from the task force to see us just sitting here and talking."

"Go ahead," Keough said, "start the car, but I need some answers, kid."

They drove for a few moments in silence while each collected his thoughts.

"Okay, Marc," Keough finally said, "tell me what happened."

Jeter took a deep breath. "I resigned, just like I said I would. I—I told them I just couldn't do it anymore. I thought they'd understand, but they didn't really care why I was doing it. They accepted my badge, and that was that. It was over."

"What did you do then?"

"I tried to get into social work, b—but it just wasn't in me, you know? I wasn't . . . I was too jaded by then, Joe. I couldn't go back to doing that. I tried some other jobs for a few months, but it soon became clear to me that I wasn't fit for being anything but a cop. I—I knew I couldn't go back to East St. Louis, so I applied around to some of the smaller departments, figuring I could use my experience to get a job as a detective, again. It was the Sunset Hills department that hired me. They had a couple of men retiring and needed to fill the slots fast."

"What about your morals, kid?" Keough asked. "You told me you couldn't morally justify staying a cop, not after what . . . what happened."

"I know, I know," Jeter said, "and I meant it when I said it, but after a few months I was . . . I just couldn't. . . . Do you know what Mark Twain said about morals?"

Here it comes, Keough thought. The kid had a knack for quoting Twain at the oddest times, and this was no exception.

" 'It is curious that physical courage should be so common in the world, and moral courage so rare.' "

"Oh Jesus . . ."

"And how about this? 'As by the fires of experience, so by commission of crime you learn real morals. Commit all crimes, familiarize yourself with all sins, take them in rotation (there are only two or three thousand of them), stick to it, commit two or three every day, and by and by you will be proof against them. When you are through you will be proof against all sins and morally perfect. You will be vaccinated against every possible commission of them. This is the only way.' "

"First of all," Keough said, "how do you remember all of that?"

"If it means something to me," Jeter said, "I remember it."

"So you're saying that it's okay to commit sins, and crimes, because that makes us immune to them later? It's okay for you to be a cop again because now you're immune to . . . to murder?"

The car swerved at that moment and Jeter jerked it back.

"God," he said, "I never thought . . ."

"All this time, Marc, and you never thought that what you did was murder?"

They were driving along Brentwood Boulevard, and Jeter pulled the car over to the curb and stopped. He gripped the wheel tightly for a few moments, laying his head down on his hands, then turned to face Keough, a tortured look on his face.

"I can do some good as a cop, Joe," he said. "How else can I make up for what I did, other than by doing good? By finding other monsters like Judson and putting them away?"

"Putting them away," Keough asked, "or killing them, Marc?"

"I—that was a onetime thing."

"Can you be sure of that?"

Jeter hesitated only a moment, then said, "Yes."

He turned in his seat and faced front again. Keough did the same. They sat that way for a few minutes before Keough broke the silence.

"Let's go."

"Where?" Fear was plain in Jeter's tone. "Are you turning me in?"

"If I turn you in, I have to turn myself in, too, Marc," Keough said. "Let's go and do what we're supposed to be doing. We can talk about the rest of this when I've had more time to think."

"But what—"

"Just drive, Marc."

Jeter took a deep, shuddering breath and then started the car.

Thirteen

THE FIRST GIRL, Jenny Dobbs, had been found in Clayton, behind a clothing store Dumpster in a strip mall. The school she went to was also in Clayton. Jeter drove Keough to both places, but there was nothing to be seen there—not this late in the game.

"The second girl, Jean Fisher, was found downtown," Jeter said.

"Let's go see the site where the third girl was found first," Keough said. "My hotel's downtown and we can finish up there."

"Suit yourself," Jeter said.

On the way, Keough read the file again on the third girl, Melanie Rudolph, who had been found in Sunset Hills. He hadn't noticed it before, but he knew the detective who had caught the case.

"Knoxx," he said.

"What?"

"Detective Knoxx caught this case."

"That's right. Did know him?"

"I used him on the Judson case, remember?" Keough asked.

"No, I—"

"Wait," Keough said, "it wasn't the Judson case; it was the other thing."

"The guy they thought you killed?"

"Yes," Keough said, "that one."

"The one involving that kid, right? What was his name?"

"Brady," Keough said. "His foster family was involved in a case Knoxx handled. Once I met Knoxx, he wanted in on our case, and I gave him some stuff to do."

"I remember now."

Keough closed the folder.

"He retired?"

"That's what I heard," Jeter said. "I was given the case after he left."

"So you didn't meet him?"

"Oh, we met, when I came on the job," Jeter said. "That was . . . oh, seven months ago, maybe a little more, but I never connected him with our case."

"Friendly?"

"He was friendly enough, but not the type I'd hang out with, you know? Actually, I wasn't the type he'd hang out with, if you know what I mean."

"I think I do."

"You do," he said. "He didn't like black guys."

"Funny. He didn't strike me that way."

"Twain said, 'I have no color prejudices nor caste prejudices nor creed prejudices. All I care to know is that a man is a human being, and that is enough for me . . . '"

Keough ignored the Twain quote. To comment on it would be to invite another.

"Well, he's gone," Jeter said. "Not dead, but retired and gone."

"Did he leave town?"

"I don't know. Why?"

"Since he was the first detective on the scene, I'd like to talk to him."

"I took the case over."

"You didn't see the dead girl."

"I did at the morgue."

"But not where she was found," Keough said, "He might have something to offer that you don't, don't you think?"

"I guess."

"I'll make some calls and check on him," Keough said. "If he's still in town, I'll go talk to him. You won't have to."

"I'll go with you."

"Maybe we'd better let your boss say where you go," Keough said. "We're not partners on this, Marc. You're with the task force; I'm not."

"I imagine the others gave you a hard time for being with the feds?" Jeter asked.

"No more than I expected."

"Well, if they knew you like I do," the other man said, "knew what a good detective you were, they'd be glad to have you around."

"A fed is a fed to those guys," Keough said, "and I can't blame them. I've felt the same way many times."

"And now you're on the other side of the fence."

"So to speak."

"What's it like, being with this special unit?" Jeter asked. "Lots of traveling?"

Keough nodded. "And lots of sick bastards, Marc. Like Judson."

Jeter fell quiet, which had actually been Keough's aim when he mentioned Andrew Judson. The kid was okay—or had been okay when they worked together. He was smart, he listened, and he learned. But that was all before, and this was after murdering Andrew Judson.

Keough still wasn't sure how he felt about Jeter having a badge again, but he wasn't going to discuss it further. Not yet anyway. For now, he was going to concentrate on what he had come to St. Louis to do.

Jeter took Keough to the scene where the third and most recently murdered girl had been found. Both her school and home were in South County; she was also found there.

"He doesn't take them to the same place," Keough observed.

The body was found the second morning after she disappeared, underneath a picnic table in the Jefferson Barracks Park. They were in that picnic area now, Keough looking it over but finding nothing. It was too public a place; too many people had already been there since the girl had been found.

"Why do you say that?" Jeter asked.

"He's dropping their bodies off a morning or two after he snatches them," Keough said. "The Clayton girl in Clayton, the South County girl in South County. I'll have to check the file, but I'll bet the girl who was found downtown lived in the city."

"He could have one place where he takes them to," Jeter reasoned, "to do whatever he does to them before he kills them."

"Too much travel time," Keough said. "He gets a place nearby, so he doesn't have to travel too far once he snatches them. There's less chance of being stopped that way."

"A hotel?"

"Hotel, apartment, whatever," Keough said. "Probably not a hotel. How's he going to get the child into his room? Motel maybe." Keough was talking more to himself now than to Jeter, trying to dope this out.

"So we have to check local motels?"

"No, because he wouldn't be there now," Keough said, "and we don't have a description to go in with."

Jeter remembered something Keough had told him when they first started working on the Judson case.

"Oh God," he said, "we have to wait until he strikes again."

"Probably," Keough said. "Until then, I'll just take a look at the other scene, and then talk to the families."

"What can they tell you?"

"I don't know," Keough said, heading back to the car; "that's why I have to talk to them."

Jeter nodded and hurried after Keough.

Keough had Jeter take him back to Clayton to get his rental car.

"I can take you downtown to see the crime scene and then drop you at your hotel."

"My car's in Clayton."

"I can pick you up in the morning and—"

"Too complicated," Keough said, cutting him off, "and remember, we're not partners."

"We could be," Jeter said. "All you'd have to do is ask."

"And alienate the other members of the task force even more," Keough said. "I think we better stick to the task at hand, Marc. Take me back to my car and give me directions to the other scene. I'll get there myself."

Jeter gripped the steering wheel tightly for a moment, then said, "Fine, if that's what you want."

"I think that's the best course of action right now."

Fourteen

WHEN KEOUGH GOT back to his hotel room, he dropped all the files on the writing desk, the presence of which turned his room into a business suite. He'd driven to the abandoned building that was the downtown crime scene—actually, these were "drop-off scenes," since the girls had not been killed in these places—had his look around, and decided to call it a day.

It was obvious he had come into this investigation too late to be able to derive anything from his visit to the places where the bodies had been dropped off. He had no actual access to physical evidence, and he was going to have to rely on what had been written up in the files. He didn't do his best work that way, relying on what other people—no matter how good or bad a detective was—had decided were the "facts" of the case. He needed to view the scenes when they were fresh. As cold and callous as it was, unless somebody confessed—or one of the task force detectives got lucky—he wasn't going to have anything concrete to work with until another girl was snatched, and then found.

But his gut told him a few things. The killer remained in the general area after he grabbed the girls. This was incredibly ballsy of him, but it gave them an advantage. If and when he snatched the next girl, they would have a general area in which to look. All he had to do was work out what sounded like a logical radius and then get Sergeant Henry to go along with him.

He sat down at the desk and called room service. He ordered a hamburger and french fries, as well as a pot of coffee. There was a vending machine right down the hall, next to the ice machine, and he went out there to get a couple of twenty-ounce bottles of diet Coke. When he got back in the room, he kicked off his shoes, laid his jacket on the back of the chair, and sat on the bed to await his dinner. He grabbed the remote and turned on the TV, then quickly turned it off, knowing he wouldn't be able to concentrate on anything at the moment.

There were no phone messages and he decided to put off checking in with Harriet Connors for a couple of hours. Give them both enough time to eat some sort of dinner.

Finally, he could not keep his thoughts away from Marc Jeter. As much as he had liked the young man when they worked together over a year ago in East St. Louis, he'd found himself increasingly uncomfortable in his presence as the day wore on. That was the reason he'd asked Jeter to take him back to his car.

While deciding to cover up the young cop's killing of Andrew Judson had been a quick decision, it had not been one Keough had made lightly. He understood the young man's frustration at the time, as he had felt it from time to time during his own career as a police officer. He, however—as tempted as he might have been— had never taken the law into his own hands and summarily executed a man he knew to be a killer. Perhaps some might say the young man had showed incredible courage, but at the same time it was a weakness, one that could not be tolerated in a police officer.

With Jeter's decision to leave the department and go on to some other career, Keough had at least been able to make himself comfortable with his decision. Now that Jeter was back on the job— albeit with a different department—he was no longer comfortable.

But what was he supposed to do? If Jeter was convinced that he was doing the right thing, that this was the way he would make up for what he had done, who was Keough to tell him he was wrong? But what if the same frustration built up inside him and he did it again? How would Keough feel then about his cover-up?

Cover-ups were nothing new. They happened every day, both in the police department and in other professions. Perhaps the biggest one in recent history—in his opinion—was the whole 9/11 fund business. He knew somebody had to be lining their pockets with a lot of that money, and somebody else was covering it up. The same went for money raised for cancer research. Surely there was a cure somewhere, in somebody's head, or in a vault someplace, that was being used sparingly because there was too damn much money involved in cancer research. To come out with a cure would be to kill the golden goose. The cure was probably given to certain people who were deemed important, who traded their silence for it.

He knew if he ever voiced these opinions to anyone, he'd be seen as a conspiracy theorist. Once or twice, he'd almost mentioned his theory to Harriet, especially on stakeouts, but he'd stopped himself.

And who was he to judge anyone when he had his own little cover-up going? He'd lied about what happened so that Jeter's murder of Andrew Judson came off as justified. If he was to change his story now, he'd be opening himself up to certain charges, and his own career would definitely be over.

When the knock came at the door, it startled him. He sprang off the bed and admitted the bellman with his dinner tray. As he was tipping the man, his phone rang. He debated leaving it until after dinner but then answered it instead.

"What are you eating?" Harriet asked.

"Just got a hamburger and fries delivered," Keough said.

"How does it look?"

He lifted the metal cover from the plate and looked at his meal. The fries seemed crisp, as did the lettuce and onions for his burger, which looked thick and moist.

"Actually, it looks pretty good."

"Mine looks dry," she said, "but I'm too tired to go out and get something else."

There was a glass of ice water on the tray and he removed the plastic wrap from it so he could take a sip.

"Well, go ahead and eat," she said. "I just—I saw photos of the kids today."

Keough felt guilty. He had the files, but he hadn't opened them yet. He was sure there would be photos inside, though.

"You?" she asked.

"I'm waiting until after I eat."

"Smart man."

"Did you check out the drop-off points?"

"Yes. Didn't find anything."

He popped a fry into his mouth and said, "Me, neither. Sites are too old, been trampled over too many times already."

"What's on your agenda for tomorrow?"

"The families."

"Yeah, me, too," she said. "They're not going to like it."

"Maybe they will," he offered. "It'll show them somebody's still working on their cases."

"I suppose."

He heard her chewing, figured she'd probably popped something into her mouth—knowing the way she'd been eating lately, a carrot or some other vegetable. That was probably the way he should be eating, as well.

"Joe?"

"Hmm?"

"We need a fresh one, don't we?"

"I'm afraid so."

"Makes me feel like such a ghoul."

"I know."

"How they treating you there?"

"Like a fed."

"Me, too."

He thought a moment, then decided to tell her about Jeter. She listened, still chewing, while he told her what a surprise it was to run into him.

"Didn't you tell me he'd left the department?"

"Yep."

"And now he's back?"

"With a new department."

"Couldn't stay away, I guess," she said. "It gets in your blood, you know."

"I know."

"Is it good to see him?" she asked. "A familiar face and all?"

"I suppose."

"What's wrong?"

"What do you mean?"

"Come on," she said, "something's wrong."

"I'm just tired," he said, "and hungry."

"Tell me now or tell me later," she said, doing a bad Arnold impression.

"Later, I guess."

She sighed and said, "Okay, I'm too tired to argue. Why don't we talk in the morning, when we're both rested?"

"Sounds like a plan."

"Eight?"

"Make it nine."

"Nine it is," she said. "Good night, partner."

"Nite, Harriet."

He hung up, picked up his burger, and took a long-awaited bite. He concentrated on his chewing, then put it down and struggled with one of those miniature catsup bottles they give you in hotels. Tell her now or later? Could he ever tell her what he'd done?

Fifteen

April 30, 2004

KEOUGH WAS AWAKE when the phone rang the next morning. He touched base with Harriet again and they agreed to talk after they had each spoken to the parents of the dead children. They still did not have enough facts to decide whether they were dealing with one killer or two. But before hanging up, they exchanged fax numbers—both hotels had fax availability—and agreed to send each other their files so they could both review all the information.

"Are you okay today, Joe?" she asked before hanging up.

"Yeah, I'm fine."

"I mean about that friend from your old neighborhood?"

"I decided to try to find his family—he had a daughter, and grandkids. I'd like to pay my respects to them."

"That sounds like a good idea. By the way, I tried to get an office here at the Federal Building, but no dice."

"What are you going to do? Work out of the local cop shop?"

"I don't think they'd like that," she said. "Remember, I'm still carrying FBI ID. When they saw that, they froze up."

"I'm getting a cold shoulder here, too, no matter how much I claim not to be a fed."

"I got news for you, Keough," she said. "You're a fed."

"There's no need to get nasty. I'm a pseudofed, at best."

"Yeah, okay," she said, "keep telling yourself that."

They said good-bye and wished each other luck for the day.

When Keough entered the task force's office, he went right to Martha's desk and placed a St. Louis Bread Company paper bag there.

"I wasn't sure how you took your coffee," he said. "You struck me as the little bit of milk type, and I put sugar and sweetener on the side."

She didn't touch the bag, just eyed him suspiciously.

"To what do I owe this honor?"

"I need a favor."

"Wait." She opened the bag and looked inside. Next to the coffee was a brownie and a pastry. He'd tried to touch all bases.

"Okay," she said, closing the bag, "what's the favor?"

"I need information on a man who died within the last year."

"Name?"

"Jack Roswell."

"Address?"

He gave her that and all other pertinent information, including how he thought Roswell had died.

"Shouldn't be hard to find this on the Web," she said. "Does this have something to do with the murders?"

"No," he said. "It's personal. He was a friend of mine while I lived here, and we fell out of touch. I went to his house to see him when I got back to town, and was told by a neighbor that he'd died."

"I'm sorry," she said sincerely. "I'll get right on it."

"When you get a chance is fine," he replied. "I just want to pay my respects to the family."

"I'll let you know as soon as I have anything."

She was opening her bag as he walked away from her desk. He had one bag in his hand, with a coffee and pastry for himself. He'd sprung yesterday, and that was enough. Besides, he didn't think he was going to win any points with this group.

"Good morning," Sergeant Henry greeted him.

"Mornin'."

Keough stood there for a moment with the bag in one hand—coffee dripping from the bottom—and the files in his other. He hadn't been in the office enough the day before to have been offered a desk. Now, looking around, he realized he'd have to share a desk with one of the other men who, when they came in, would not appreciate it. Unless . . .

"Set yourself down anywhere," Henry said—which, of course, did not include his desk. "The others have been in and out this morning already."

"I think I need someplace where I won't be . . . disturbed." He realized when he said it that it was the wrong word. It made him sound like a prima donna.

Henry paused in what he was doing and looked up at him.

"The room at the end of the hall is still empty," he commented. "Why don't you take that?"

"I'll need a phone."

"You can come in here and use mine," Henry said. "In the event we decide you'll be with us for a while, I'll have one installed for you."

"All right."

"Speaking of which," the sergeant said, "have you come to any decisions?"

"No conclusion," Keough said.

"But can you keep the FBI out of our hair?" the supervisor asked. Apparently, he was leaning Keough's way on whether he was a true fed or not.

"I won't know that for a couple of days," Keough said.

"All right, then," Henry said. "What about you and Jeter?"

"What about us?"

"When he came back last night, he said you fellas wanted to partner up."

"Are you working in pairs?" Keough asked.

"Well, no, but—"

"That's fine, then," Keough said. "I don't want to change your procedure. I'll just continue to work alone until I do come to some . . . conclusion."

"Well, keep me informed," Henry said. "I got to tell you, though, he's the only one expressing any interest in working with you."

"I understand."

"I hope you do," Henry said. "These are good men."

"No argument from me."

Keough went down the hall to his new "office" and sat at the desk to have his breakfast. He knew that as the other detectives arrived, they'd see this as his way of separating himself from them, assuming he felt he was better than they were. But he was in a no-win situation. If he tried to share their squad room, they'd freeze him out. That wouldn't crush his feelings, but it would not make for a very good working environment. He left his door open as some small concession.

Sixteen

EACH OF GABRIEL'S three kills had made the front page, the coverage longer and more in depth than before. Likewise, the TV coverage was becoming more extensive—and, with the third killing, nationwide. The ex-profilers were appearing on CNN and Fox News to analyze the situation, and Gabriel knew it would not be long before the FBI would get involved officially.

But the killer in Chicago was getting the same kind of coverage, as well. There wasn't a whole lot in the St. Louis newspaper about it, or on local news stations, just some passing coverage, since the case wasn't local. But the cable and network news shows were beginning to ask the burning question: One killer or two?

Gabriel was in the library, reading copies of the *Chicago Tribune* to get the local coverage of the Chicago murders. Thankfully, the local cable channels were getting WGN, Chicago's so-called Superstation, so there was information there, too.

The first thing Gabriel noticed was the similarity in the ages of the victims. After that, the fact that the Chicago murders were committed either the day before or the day after a St. Louis killing. This realization came even before the newspapers and news shows began discussing it. This was too much coincidence for someone who believed in divine intervention to accept.

Also, the proximity of Chicago to St. Louis was too much to overlook. The only question Gabriel didn't ask was whether there was one killer or two, because that was obvious. There were two, but who was the other one?

Gabriel left the library and hurried home, still unsure what to make of this, or of how to proceed.

Seventeen

ABOUT THE ONLY thing Keough liked about his job in Washington was that his desk in the unit office had a window with a view of the Promenade. This office in St. Louis was small and cramped and had no window. It was at the end of the hall, so while he saw people walking back and forth, nobody ever actually passed by. He thought about reconsidering his open-door policy because he kept getting dirty looks tossed down the hall at him. Apparently, word had gotten out that he was from Washington.

An odd thing about being in the new elite FSK unit was that it put him and his fellow members square in the middle between cop and fed. Cops didn't like them because they saw them as Feebs, and FBI, DEA, ATF, and agents of other alphabet law-enforcement units saw them as outsiders, as well. He had never talked with Harriet Connors about whether or not she ever wished she hadn't accepted the position on the Federal Serial Killer Task Force. He knew he did, but that was nothing new. His history showed that he tired of his jobs easily; otherwise, why would he have had so many different ones over the past several years?

He was about to go and ask Sergeant Henry to arrange for a phone so he could make some calls, when he saw Detective Marc Jeter walking purposefully down the hall toward his office.

"Why did you tell the sergeant you don't want to partner with me?" Jeter demanded.

"I didn't say that I didn't want to partner with you," Keough replied, "I said I didn't want to partner with anyone."

That did not appease the younger man.

"Joe, if you're going to hold what happened with Judson against me—"

"Shh!" Keough rose, came around the desk, and abruptly closed the door, stopping just short of slamming it.

"Are you going to turn me in?" Jeter demanded, keeping his voice low, but urgent.

Keough turned and put his face so close to Jeter's, their noses almost touched.

"First of all, that's not something we want to talk about here, is it?"

Jeter backed up a step, and he didn't reply.

"Secondly, to turn you in would mean turning myself in, and I'm not about to do that."

He went back around the desk and sat down.

"Thirdly, I don't need a partner," he said. "I have a partner."

"Where is he?"

"She is in Chicago, working on a similar case."

"The boys being killed there," Jeter said. "We know about that. Is it the same killer?"

"That's what she and I are working on."

"Who's your partner?"

"You met her," Keough said. "Harriet Connors. I asked for her help on the Judson thing, remember?"

"I remember," Jeter said. "She was pretty smart."

"She's the one who offered me the job with the task force," Keough said. "After we were . . . finished with Judson, I took it."

"I knew you'd left St. Louis," Jeter said. "I didn't know where you'd gone, though."

"Washington."

"Do you like it there?"

"No."

"Then why stay?"

"That's my business," Keough said.

Jeter looked properly chastised. He turned and opened the door.

"I'll do whatever you want me to do in this case, Joe," he said. "Whatever I have to do to get back your trust."

"Your CO is Sergeant Henry," Keough said. "Do what he tells you, and everything will go fine."

"But they're not going to solve these murders," Jeter said. "You are."

"We don't know that."

"I do," the younger man said. "I've worked with you before, remember? You're going to be the one to break this."

Keough sat back in his chair and stared at Detective Marc Jeter.

"If I do," he said finally, "there's something I'm going to need."

Jeter nodded and said, "Fresh blood."

The last time they had worked together, Keough had come to the case late, and it took a fresh murder to give him direction, a fresh crime scene to give him something to work with.

He was afraid the same was going to hold true here.

Eighteen

KEOUGH DID IT by the numbers. He talked to all three families that day, driving himself around, getting reacquainted with the city. All of the families seemed to appreciate the fact that he was investigating in addition to the locals, and they spoke with him very freely. Two of them had additional children, older than the ones who had been killed. Keough told them he thought their other children were safe, that it wasn't likely the killer would try to hit the same family again.

When he returned to the office in Clayton, he found two pink phone-message slips on his desk. They both told him to see Martha.

He walked down the hall and found her at her desk.

"Welcome back," she said. "I got that address you wanted."

"Really?"

She nodded and handed him a slip of white paper.

"It's his daughter."

"That was quick work," he said. "Thank you, Martha. I owe you breakfast again."

"I'll collect. Oh, and there was a phone call for you from your partner. Agent Connors?"

"What'd she say?"

"She wants you to call her on her cell. Do you have the number?"

"I have it," he said. "Thanks." He looked around the room, which was deserted except for them. "Which phone can I use?"

"Any one," she said. "Dial nine for an outside line."

He chose a desk and made the call. He had a cell phone as well, but it was in his hotel room. He never carried it unless they were deep into a case and it became essential. He punched her cell number in and waited.

"Joe?"

"It's me."

"Wait." There was some movement and then she came back. "I wanted to get off by myself."

"What's up?"

"You got a profiler coming your way."

"Damn. He gets here and starts flashing his FBI credentials and we're going to lose these people's cooperation."

"I know, but these murders have become national news, and the director wants somebody on it."

"Can't you do anything about it?"

"Me? What am I gonna do?"

"Call Wallace, see if he can help."

"I already spoke with him," she said. "He got them to keep it down to one profiler, since we're both on the scenes."

"Has he been there already?"

"She has, yes," Connors said. "Her name's Nicole Busby. I didn't get to spend much time with her, but I was told she's kind of young but that she's supposed to be really good. I didn't get much of a chance to talk to her myself."

"Yeah, yeah," he said. She knew what he thought about profiling. He felt it was a more inexact science than anyone else let on. He thought that serial killers were not created—they were born. That from the day they were born, there was something wrong in their heads, and sooner or later that something was going to snap. Profilers usually came up with environmental reasons: a broken home, being the victim of abuse—well, there were plenty of abused kids who didn't grow up to be serial killers.

"Anyway," she said, "she'll be on a flight tomorrow, so look for her in the afternoon."

"Maybe that'll give me some time to smooth over her arrival here," Keough said. "She could take me right out of the pseudofed category as soon as she gets here."

"Tell me about it," she agreed. "I barely had time to prepare them here."

"How'd they take it?"

"Badly, but I've been able to establish a rapport here with the head of their task force, so I think I'm okay."

"A rapport?"

"He kind of likes me."

"I knew that new body of yours would come in handy one day."

"Bite me," she said, and hung up. It was so abrupt, he wasn't sure if she was really mad or not. He was tempted to call her back and find out, but he decided against it.

By the time he hung up, none of the other task force members had returned yet. He needed to talk to Sergeant Henry as soon as possible, though, about this profiler, Nicole Busby.

"Martha, where's the sergeant?"

"Out."

"Do you know exactly where? I need to speak to him."

"He just said he was going to be out for a while," she said.

"Does he have a cell phone?"

She hesitated, then said, "Y—yes, but he doesn't like me to call him unless it's an emergency."

Was it an emergency? Probably not. He could talk to the man later in the day, but it had to be before Agent Busby arrived.

"All right," he said, "when he comes in, would you tell him I need to talk to him tonight? It's important."

"I'll tell him," she said. "And where are you going to be?"

Where indeed? He felt in his pocket for the slip of paper she'd given him with Jack Roswell's daughter's name and address on it. He'd already interviewed the families of the dead girls; now he needed to sit at his desk and review his notes, but he could do that later, maybe even at the hotel.

He took out the address and checked it. He knew roughly where it was. He waved it as he headed for the door.

"I'm going to be out."

Nineteen

JACK'S DAUGHTER LIVED with her husband—George Wilkens—
and children in a house in the Kirkwood section of St. Louis.
Keough was unaccountably nervous as he mounted the front steps
and rang the doorbell. It was still early in the day, so he wasn't surprised when a woman answered the door. Kids would be at school,
and, in a traditional household, a husband would be at work. From
everything he could remember that Jack had ever told him, his
daughter had a traditional marriage.

"It's all she ever would have," the old man had told him one
night over a chessboard. "She has no imagination."

It had not been a criticism, just an observation.

"Yes?" she asked him through the screen of the storm door.

"Mrs. Wilkens . . ." he said, and then got stuck.

"Yes, can I help you with something?" She sounded more
annoyed than nervous, having a strange man at her door.

"I was a friend of your father's," he said lamely.

"I see. What's your name?"

"Joe Keough," he said. "I, uh, lived—"

"You lived across the street from him, I know," she said. "Well,
it certainly has taken you long enough to show up." Now she was
definitely annoyed.

"I'm sorry. . . . I just got back in town—I've been living in Washington, and I just heard—"

"I guess if you'd stayed in touch with him like you said you would, you'd have known sooner."

"You're right. I'm so—"

"Wait there," she said abruptly. She turned and went into the house, then returned with a small box and a chessboard. She opened the door and thrust them into his hands.

"He told me to give you this when you showed up." She backed up and let the storm door slam shut, putting the screen between them again. He'd only had a moment to see a woman who looked older, worn-out, possibly from a long period of time caring for her father as well as her husband and children.

"Look," he began, "I know I should have been a better friend. . . ." But he had no defense for the fact that he hadn't.

"My father liked you," she said, as if trying to make his guilt worse. "He said you helped him while you lived here. He told me about that thing with his doctor, how you helped. . . . I thank you for that. He always said you were his friend, and that you didn't call or write because you were busy. My father was like that—he made excuses for people he liked."

"There was no excuse—"

"No, Mr. Keough," she said, "there wasn't. Good day!"

She stepped back and slammed the front door in his face. He stood there with the box and board in his hands, then went back to his car. Seated behind the wheel, he looked at the board. It was one made of inlaid wood, and he recognized it as the board they'd usually played on. He set it aside on the passenger seat and opened the box. Inside were the black-and-white onyx chess pieces, regular Staunton-style. It had been Jack's favorite set. They'd usually played with plastic pieces, but once in awhile he'd pull this one out for a special occasion. Keough felt tears sting his eyes and he swallowed a lump. Why was he always casting his friends aside, and then realizing it when it was too late? It had happened with Mark Drucker, the man who had gotten him his first job in St. Louis, and the place where he lived. He'd fallen out of touch with Drucker, and he'd never had a chance to remedy that, because the man had been killed. All he'd been able to do was solve the murder, but that had done little to appease his guilt. And still he had not learned from that, because in all the time he'd been away from St. Louis, he had never once called or even written Jack Roswell—and now it was too late, for he was dead, as well.

He set the box aside on the seat with the board, started the motor, and drove off. He had no destination in mind at first, but driving aimlessly only afforded him more time to berate himself. He finally decided to drive back to the task force's office. Even the disdain of those local detectives would be more bearable than his own.

When he got to the office, he was surprised at the activity. Detectives and cops were shrugging into their jackets and jamming their holsters onto their belts. Sergeant Henry was behind his desk, the phone snugged between his shoulder and ear. Jeter was standing in front of the sergeant's desk. Keough approached Martha's desk, as she was the only one sitting still.

"What's up?"

She looked up at him and said, "We've got another one, Joe."

"Another body?" he asked.

"No," she said, shaking her head, "a missing child."

"Boy or girl?"

"Girl."

"How old?"

"Nine."

"You know that for a fact?"

"I took the call."

"When?"

"It just came in," she said. "The sarge is still on the phone with—"

"No, I mean how long has the child been missing?"

"Oh," she said, "um, two hours, I think."

Keough checked his watch.

"What was she doing out of school?"

"I don't know. Maybe the sarge—"

He left her desk before she finished and hurried to Sergeant Henry's desk as the man was hanging up.

"Oh, there you are," Henry said. "We're rolling on a missing kid."

"I heard," Keough said. "It might not be the same guy, Sarge."

Henry shoved his holster into his belt and looked at Keough. The room grew quiet as the others there paused to listen.

"What?"

"It may not be the same guy."

"How can you tell that already?" Henry demanded.

"It's too early."

"What are you talking about?" John Berkery demanded from across the room. "We have a missing nine-year-old girl. That's all we know—"

"It's not all we know," Keough said, looking at Berkery. "The first three girls were taken after school, somewhere between school and home." He looked back at Dan Henry. "That's what I meant by 'It's too early.' His pattern is to take them after school."

"Maybe he hasn't set his pattern yet," Jim House offered.

"Three is a pattern," Keough said. "These guys don't usually deviate—"

"Why don't we wait until we get out there to call it?" Henry said.

Keough opened his mouth to argue but then clamped it shut. The man was right. They should at least respond to the call before they discounted it.

"You're right," Keough said.

"Then let's roll."

Keough turned to Jeter and said, "You mind if I ride with you?"

"Suit yourself," Jeter said, and headed for the door.

Twenty

THE MISSING CHILD was a nine-year-old girl named Denise Proctor. She lived with her parents in a modest home on Musick Avenue in the city of Green Park, in St. Louis County. As Jeter pulled his car to a stop in front of the house, they could see that the street was blocked by county police cars. They hadn't spoken during the drive, and Keough knew that Jeter was still feeling the sting of what he considered rejection.

When Keough and Jeter got out of their car, they were met by Sergeant Henry.

"Keough, you're an observer here. Remember that. I'll do the talking."

"That's fine with me," Keough said, "but I'd like to make one suggestion."

"Make it."

"In the past, he's dropped the . . . bodies off in the same general area," Keough said. "He must still be in the area."

"So what?" Jim House said, coming up next to them. "We don't have a description to broadcast."

"Yes, we do," Keough said. "The girl's."

"I'll talk to the county commander," Henry said. "He can have his men on the lookout."

"Tell them to stop any man with a girl who fits this one's description."

"Gonna piss off a lot of fathers walking with their daughters," House said.

"You can apologize later," Keough said. "Make the men show ID and prove that the girls are theirs."

Henry nodded and said, "All right. Jim, I'm going to put you together with the county cops. You relay everything Keough just said."

"Yes, sir."

It took a few moments to arrange this, and then Henry, Jeter, Berkery, and Keough went inside to speak to the parents.

"And why was the girl home, Mrs. Proctor?"

"Not Proctor," she said. "My name is Nancy Keith. My first husband was named Proctor. He was Denise's father. He . . . died when Denise was very young."

Nancy Keith was in her thirties, extremely attractive from the neck down. She was wearing shorts and a T-shirt that showed her body off. It was as if nature had compensated her for making her face so . . . homely. Or maybe time just hadn't beaten down her body as much as it had her face.

Her husband's name was Larry Keith, and he wasn't home at the moment. She said he was out looking for Denise.

"I . . . I didn't expect this much of a response when I called the police." Her hair was the color of wheat, pulled back in a ponytail. Her pale, freckled face displayed her confusion.

"Well, in light of the . . . other disappearances," Dan Henry said, "we're responding in force to any reports of missing children."

"You mean . . . missing girls, don't you?"

"Yes, ma'am," Henry said, "missing girls. You didn't answer my question, ma'am. Why was she home and not in school?"

"She . . . wasn't feeling well when she woke up. She felt a bit warm to me, so I kept her home."

Keough had the impression that the girl often got over on her mother that way.

"Then . . . how did she get outside?" the sergeant asked.

"She was feeling better and wanted to go out and play. I . . . I told her to stay in the yard."

"And your husband? Was he home?"

"No," she said. "When I realized Denise was . . . was missing, I called my husband at work. He was . . . very angry."

"At Denise?"

She rubbed the back of her neck and said, "At me, I'm afraid, for letting Denise stay home. You see, he thinks . . ."

"Thinks what?"

She dropped her hand from her neck and said, "He thinks I should have made Denise go to school. I—I guess he's right."

Henry looked at Keough. They both knew that wasn't what she'd been going to say at first.

They heard a man's angry voice call, "What the hell—"

"Who's that?" Henry asked, looking toward the front door.

"This is my house, damn it!"

"That's my husband," Nancy said; she looked frightened.

"John," Henry said to Berkery, "go and let him in."

"Yes, sir."

"He's . . . uh, mad that he had to leave work."

She'd been hugging her arms most of the time they'd been there, but when she'd had her hand up behind her neck, Keough had noticed marks on her upper arm—bruises, made by the fingers of a strong hand. Now she was back to hugging herself, also hiding the marks. Keough studied her face for evidence of abuse. There was some shading under one eye that might or might not have been a healing bruise. Perhaps, because she was so pale, it was something else, but . . .

"What the hell is going on here?" Larry Keith came into the room, roaring. "You stupid bitch, you called the goddamn National Guard?"

"She called the police, Mr. Keith," Henry said, holding one hand up. "I assume you're Mr. Keith?"

"That's right, I'm Keith, and this is my house. I'd like you to leave."

Keough guessed that Keith weighed about 210, maybe 215.

That meant he outweighed his wife by a good hundred pounds. He also towered about a foot over her, which made him a few inches taller than the tallest man in the room, Dan Henry. He radiated strength, but something else also came off of him in waves—meanness. He was wearing a work shirt with his name on the breast pocket, and a pair of jeans with a grease stain across one shin.

"Why would you want us to do that, Mr. Keith?" Sergeant Henry asked. "We're here to help you."

"We don't need no help." Keith's deep-set eyes were angry. The muscles of his shoulders and chest bulged beneath his shirt. There was black grease under his fingernails, so he was a man used to working with his hands. He was big and powerful, apparently used to getting his way.

"Your daughter is missing, sir," Jeter said.

Keith looked at Jeter as if he was noticing for the first time that he was black. He glared at the young detective for a few moments before speaking.

"That's none of your business—and she ain't my kid; she's hers. Little bitch is more trouble than she's worth."

Nancy Keith looked away and squeezed out a tear. Keough didn't know if it was for herself or for her daughter, but he felt embarrassed for her.

Twenty-one

BEFORE ANYONE COULD say anther word, Keough grabbed Larry Keith's arm and said to Dan Henry, "Why don't I take Mr. Keith someplace where I can talk to him? You can continue to interview Mrs. Keith."

Henry hesitated a moment, then said, "Good idea."

"Come on, Mr. Keith," Keough said, "let's go talk."

"Least you coulda done was put on some clothes," Keith yelled at his wife. "You look like a goddamned whore!"

Keough released the man's arm but grabbed his thumb and exerted pressure. From that point on, Keith had to shut up and "come on," or leave his thumb behind.

Keough found his way to the kitchen, then released the man's thumb and pushed him toward a chair.

"Sit down!"

"Goddamn! That hurt!" Keith complained, cradling his hand.

"You're lucky I didn't tear it off."

"What the hell—"

"I said, Sit down, Keith!"

The big man wanted to stand up to Keough, but his thumb was still throbbing, reminding him of how easily Keough had walked him into the kitchen. He sat down.

"You got no call to treat a man like that in his own house."

Keough wanted to berate the man for abusing his wife—and he was damn sure he had not read those signs wrong—but he knew that would only cause the man to abuse her even more after he and the other cops had gone.

"Why the hell did she call this many cops?" Keith demanded. "She's wasting your time, man. That kid is probably out there playing somewhere. When I was her age, I had a damn job already. She woke up this morning feelin' a little warm and Nancy keeps her home. What's that about?"

"Mr. Keith," Keough said, "if that's the way you feel, then why were you out there looking for the girl yourself?"

"To keep her quiet," the man said disgustedly. "She'd be bitchin' at me all day and I wouldn't get nothin' done, so I left work and started lookin'."

"Where?"

"Just around the neighborhood. Little cunt ain't nowhere to be found. I think she's hidin'."

"Hiding? From what?" Or maybe "From whom?" was the question.

Suddenly, Larry Keith couldn't look directly at Keough. His eyes were flicking all around the room.

"Who knows," he said. "Little bitch's afraid of her own shadow."

"Mr. Keith," Keough said, and now the distaste was his, "you beat your wife—that much is obvious. Do you beat the girl, too? Is she hiding from you?"

"You got some nerve," the man said, still unable to look at Keough. "I don't gotta talk to you."

"Yeah, you do," Keough said. "I'm investigating the disappearance of a child. If you impede me in that investigation, I'll arrest your ass."

" 'Impede'? What's that?"

"Interfere," Keough said. "If you don't answer my questions, I'll arrest you."

Keith started to get to his feet. "I wanna see your boss!"

Keough put his hand on the man's shoulder and pushed him

back down. He had to use all his strength. Keith was stronger than he was, but his thumb was still throbbing.

"My boss is in Washington," Keough said, "and you don't want to talk to him. He's not a pleasant man."

"What about that cop?" Keith asked. "He ain't your boss?"

"I don't have a boss here," Keough said. He leaned closer to Keith, who grabbed his thumb and leaned away. "I can do what I want."

Keith stared at him, and then a crafty glint crept into his eyes. He was going to try a new tactic.

"Aw, c'mon, man," he said, "why are you doin' this to me? We got a missin' kid here. Lemme get back in there with my wife. She needs me."

"She needs you to stop beating on her, Larry," Keough said.

"Shit," Keith said, "she likes it, man. They all do. Don't you know that? Ain't you got a woman of your own?"

"No," Keough said, "and if I did, I wouldn't beat her. Only a coward does that."

"I ain't no coward!" Keith snapped.

"No? Then stand up, Larry," Keough said. "Come on, you're bigger than me. Get by me. Come on."

Keith braced his feet on the floor, but he made no move to get up. His muscles rolled beneath his shirt, but he made no attempt to use them.

Keough stuck his finger in the man's face and said, "Stay right here until I come back."

He turned and left the kitchen to rejoin Dan Henry and Nancy Keith. The woman was handing the sergeant a photo of her daughter. Keough tapped Henry on the shoulder and drew him away from Mrs. Keith so that she couldn't hear them.

"The woman's battered," he said. "The girl may be, too."

A muscle jumped in Henry's jaw. He turned and walked back to the woman.

"Mrs. Keith," he said, "do you think your daughter is hiding from your husband?"

"Hidin'—what? No. Why would she hide from Larry?"

"Ma'am, we know your husband beats you."

"What? No—"

Keough stepped forward and removed the woman's hand from her arm so she couldn't cover the bruises.

"He—he just grabbed me," she said immediately. "He didn't mean it. He was just . . . mad."

"Does he get mad at Denise?" Keough asked.

"No." She pulled her hand away from him and covered the bruises again. "No, he only gets mad at me. He knows if he touches Denise, I'll . . . I'll leave him."

"You should leave him anyway, Mrs. Keith," Keough said. "Nobody deserves to be battered."

"That's enough, Keough," Henry said. "Ma'am, if you say he doesn't beat the girl, that's good enough for me. We'll be in touch as soon as we know something."

"Thank you, Sergeant." She turned to Keough. "Is my husband under arrest?"

"No," Keough said. "He's in the kitchen. He might need some ice for his thumb."

Keough walked away from her and stepped outside, with Henry right behind him. There were still a couple of police cars outside, but most of them—and the other detectives—had left, no doubt scouring the area.

"What was that about?" Keough asked suddenly. "Why'd you warn me off?"

"We're not here to mediate a domestic dispute," Henry said; "we're here to find a missing child."

"Henry," Keough said, "this is most likely not our guy. This girl is probably hiding from the step—"

"Then she'll come back when she gets hungry."

"We can't leave that woman in—"

"She doesn't want our help, Keough," Henry said, "except to find her child. Anything more than that and we mind our own business. Husbands and wives have a way of working things out."

"Henry—"

"We're done here," the sergeant said. "I'm going to go out and find this girl. You coming?"

"No," Keough said. "I'll leave the legwork to you and the locals."

"Suit yourself."

"I'll need Jeter to drive me back to—"

"You can have him. I'll send him by."

"Thanks."

The sergeant started to leave, then turned back and stuck his finger in Keough's face much the way Keough had done to Keith earlier.

"Don't go back in there," he said. "We aren't getting involved in some domestic squabble. Let the man handle his own wife."

"'Let the man—'" Keough began, but Henry turned and walked away.

Keough couldn't believe what he'd heard. Was Sergeant Henry condoning domestic violence? He turned and looked at the house, debating whether to go back in or not. He was still trying to decide when something caught his eye. There was a woman in the doorway of the house next door, waving at him frantically.

Twenty-two

"WOULD YOU LIKE tea?" Mrs. Amanda Dale asked.

"I'd love some."

She went to the kitchen and he looked out the front window. The last of the police cars was leaving. Marc Jeter had not yet returned.

He looked around the house, which was tastefully and inexpensively furnished. Amanda Dale was in her seventies, living alone. The house did not have the musty smell some homes of older folks gave off. She obviously kept it clean and fresh.

She returned with a tray bearing two cups of tea and a dish of cookies. She set them down on the coffee table in front of the sofa and invited him to sit. He joined her on the sofa.

"Sugar?"

"No thank you." He accepted the cup and saucer from her. "Ma'am, I'd really like to know why you called me over here."

"I know things."

"What things?"

"About that man next door."

"Larry Keith?"

She made a face. "He's a terrible, horrible man."

"In what way, ma'am?"

She leaned toward him and lowered her voice. "He beats his wife."

"I know that, ma'am."

Mrs. Dale looked surprised.

"She told you?"

"No," he said, "she didn't, not in so many words. I saw the bruises on her arm."

"You're an observant young man."

"I try to be."

"But she didn't admit it?"

"She . . . didn't deny it. More importantly, though, have you ever known Larry Keith to beat the girl?"

"No," she said, "but that lovely young girl . . . something's bothering her."

"Why do you say that?"

"Because she was the happiest little girl you'd ever want to know until that man moved in with them."

"And when was that?"

"About two years ago."

"And the girl has changed since then?"

"Very much. She comes over here a lot. I give her cookies and milk."

"And does she talk to you?"

"Not really, but I think she comes here to get away from him."

"Amanda . . . do you know where the girl is? Is she hiding here?"

"Oh no," Amanda Dale said, her eyes sad. "I wish she was, Detective. I truly wish she was."

When Keough left the Dale house, Jeter was outside, leaning against the passenger door of his car.

"What were you doing in there?" he asked.

"Having tea with a nice old lady."

"Does she know anything?" He pushed away from the door so Keough could get in, then went around to get behind the wheel.

Keough explained to Jeter what the woman'd had to say.

"Do you think she was telling the truth?"

"Yes. I think she has the girl's best interests in mind. If Denise had been there, she would have told me."

"So if the girl's not hiding from the stepfather, our guy's got her."

"Maybe," Keough said. "Let's get back to the office."

"What happened?" Martha asked as Keough and Jeter entered the office. "Did you find the girl? Was she taken by the same guy?"

"We don't know, Martha," Keough said. "The others are still looking."

"Why'd you come back?"

Keough grabbed a piece of message paper from a pad on her desk and wrote down "Lawrence Keith" on it.

"Put him in the computer and tell me what you come up with."

"In the way of what?"

"Priors."

"Where will you be?"

"We're going back out."

"Marc is going with you?"

"Yes." He looked at Jeter. "You carrying your cell?"

"Yes."

"Call us on his cell with the results."

"What do I tell Sergeant Henry when he gets back?" she asked. "Is Marc your driver?"

Keough stopped at the door; both Jeter and Martha were looking at him.

"No," he said, "he's my partner."

Twenty-three

ONCE THEY REACHED the street, Keough put his hand on Jeter's arm to stop him.

"Where are we going?" the younger man asked.

"Across the street for a cup of coffee."

"To drink to our partnership?"

"Sure."

They crossed over and went into a nearby St. Louis Bread Company. These coffee shop/bakeries were to St. Louis what Starbucks was to Seattle. Keough looked around to make sure there was nobody he knew or recognized present.

When they were seated with coffee and a bagel each, Jeter asked, "What made you change your mind? About being partners, I mean."

"Two things," Keough said. "Once I decided I needed somebody to work with, you were the obvious choice."

"Because we've worked together before?"

"Because nobody else in your squad would have me."

Jeter smiled, but he seemed unsure if Keough was kidding or not. "And second?"

"What happened with us in East St. Louis? What you did? It was easily something I might have done."

"You saying that if I hadn't . . . done it, you would have?"

"I'm saying I could have," Keough said, "if I'd been in your position."

"That means a lot to me, Joe."

"Okay, but here's something else," Keough said. "This is the last time we speak of it. Got it? It's over and done with."

"Okay," Jeter said, "I won't bring it up again." But they each knew it was not something they'd ever forget.

"So what's our first move, partner?"

"Tell me what you know about Dan Henry."

"Not much," Jeter said. "I only met him when I joined the task force. Never worked with him before."

"He's married, right?"

"I guess so."

"Well, he wears a ring," Keough said. "He's either married or divorced and can't let go."

"No, he's married," Jeter said. "Now that you mention it, I've heard him talk about his wife once or twice."

"In what way?"

"How do you mean?"

"Well, lovingly? Complaining?"

"I don't know," Jeter said. "The way men talk about their wives, I guess. Why?"

Keough hesitated, wondering how much he actually wanted to tell Jeter.

"Okay, this missing kid, Denise Proctor? I think it's a separate case."

"She fits the profile."

"Never mind profiles," Keough said. "The kid's nine. There are a lot of nine-year-olds. You want to talk profiles? The first three girls taken were eight, nine, and ten. Logically, he'd take an eleven-year-old next."

Jeter frowned.

"I hadn't noticed that. You really think that's a pattern he's going to follow?"

"I'm not sure yet," Keough said. "I think we're going to have to wait for another girl to be taken before we know. I just don't think this is the one."

"So then where's this girl?"

"Probably hiding from the stepfather," Keough said, "but this is something Missing Persons should be working on, not us."

"Have you told Sergeant Henry?"

"I've mentioned it," Keough said, "but he'll make up his own mind."

"And you think he'll commit the efforts of this unit to looking for the wrong child?"

"Yes."

Jeter waited, then asked, "And what else? Why were you asking me about his wife?"

"He wasn't concerned with the fact that Keith beats his wife," Keough said. "It made me wonder about his own . . . domestic situation."

"You think Henry beats his wife?" Jeter asked. "Isn't that a leap of logic, even for you?"

"He indicated that if Keith was beating his wife, he was simply taking care of his own business," Keough said.

"So what are you worried about?" Jeter asked. "That we're wasting our time looking for the wrong child, or that Larry Keith beats his wife?"

"Both."

"Well . . . you're not really part of this unit, Joe. You can do whatever you like."

"You're part of the unit," Keough said.

"Not really."

"What?"

Jeter looked at him.

"The others, they don't really accept me."

"And why is that?"

Jeter shrugged. "Maybe because I came in late, replacing someone else," Jeter said. "Maybe it's . . . something else."

Unspoken between them was the fact that Jeter was black, and maybe someone in the unit had a problem with that.

"Besides," the younger man said, "they all know I've worked with you before. I think that separates me from them, as well."

"All right, then," Keough said, "it'll be you and me again. If

Henry is going to insist on looking at Denise Proctor as the next missing child, we'll just let him. I'm not going to argue. But there's something else you should know."

He told Jeter about the FBI profiler who would be showing up the next day.

"Is she going to listen to you, or Sergeant Henry?" he asked.

"She'll make up her own mind, I guess."

"What's your partner's found out so far in Chicago?"

"Not much."

"Nothing that suggests these murders might be the work of the same person?"

"No," Keough said, "but the more I think about it, the more convinced I am that it's not the same killer."

"Why not?"

"They have a definite preference as to boys and girls," Keough said. "I think that's enough to differentiate them. I really can't see why a killer would go back and forth between the two cities, killing boys in one and girls in the other."

Jeter shrugged and said, "I can't see why anyone would kill children, period."

"Crazy people do crazy things, but the fact that it's all boys in Chicago and all girls here . . . I just think that separates the two."

"I wonder if the profiler will agree with you."

"I really don't care if she agrees or not."

"This should be interesting, then," Jeter said.

Keough finished his coffee and asked Jeter, "You done?"

"Yes.

They stepped outside. Keough hadn't decided whether he wanted to go to his own car or to Jeter's.

"Have you decided on our next move?" Jeter asked, as if he could read Keough's mind.

At that moment, the young detective's phone rang. Keough said, "Maybe our decision's about to be made for us."

Twenty-four

JETER HANDED KEOUGH the phone so Martha could relay to him the information on Lawrence Keith.

"What'd she say?" Jeter asked as he accepted the phone back.

"Keith's got a sheet peppered with violence toward kids, from when he was a kid. But lately—the last five years or so—his violence has been directed against women."

"Other women, besides his wife?"

"Girlfriends, and other wives," Keough said. "Two of them. Martha's got names and addresses written down for me."

"Jesus."

"That's not the worst of it."

"What is?"

"He's got sex offenses on his sheet, too."

"Rape?"

"No," Keough said, looking at him, "kiddie porn."

"Owning or making?"

"Both."

Keough and Jeter went back up to the office. They collected from Martha the addresses of one ex-wife and one ex-girlfriend of

Keith's who had filed battery charges against him. They also got the address of his place of business.

"What have you heard from Sergeant Henry?" Keough asked her.

"He called in to say that the search was continuing," she replied.

Keough looked at Jeter. "It's going to start getting dark soon. They'll have to call it off."

"What do you want to do?"

Keough started to answer, then stopped and took Jeter out into the hall.

"I'm going to go and check in where Keith works, see if I can talk to his boss," he said once they were out of Martha's hearing. "You go and talk to these two women."

"What are we looking for?"

"A reason to take Nancy Keith and her daughter out of that house."

"But this isn't what we're supposed to be working on," Jeter complained. "You yourself said—"

"I know what I said, but if we can prove that Denise Proctor ran away from her stepfather, we can keep this squad from wasting precious time."

"But I thought you—"

"I changed my mind!" Keough snapped, then relented and softened his tone. "Look, we can afford to give this a few more hours if it'll help that woman and little girl, and save the unit some time, right?"

"Okay," Jeter said. "So we'll work on it this evening, and then get back to business tomorrow."

"Right," Keough said. "I'll be here bright and early to greet the profiler and introduce her to the sergeant."

"Should we meet up again later tonight?"

"No need," Keough said. "Call me at my hotel."

"Don't you have a cell phone?"

"It's in my room, and I don't remember the number. I know it's a little old-fashioned, but just call the hotel."

"All right," Jeter agreed. "I'll talk to you later."

They left the building together, then split up and went to their respective cars. It occurred to Keough as he drove away that he probably should have left Dan Henry a message about the profiler coming to town, but then he decided what the hell. Let it come as a surprise.

Twenty-five

KEOUGH DROVE TO the garage where Larry Keith worked as a mechanic, on Reavis Barracks Road in South County. It had a couple of gas pumps, but its main business was repairs. Somehow, gas and auto repair had become separated over the years and been replaced by gas, eat, and wash. There were many repair shops in the area that had no gas pumps at all. This one appeared somewhat run-down, and it probably relied heavily on a regular clientele.

Keith's boss was named Harry Zelnor. He stopped working and wiped his hands on a dirty rag after Keough flashed his ID.

"Whataya need?" he asked.

"Just some background on one of your mechanics, Larry Keith."

Zelnor tucked the rag into his back pocket and placed his hands on his ample hips. His face was covered with black, a combination of grease and stubble. Mentally figuring it, Keough made him out to be in his early fifties.

"What'd he do now?"

"Nothing, really," Keough said. "His daughter is missing, and we're just covering all bases."

"He ran outta here earlier today," Zelnor said. "I was gonna fire his ass, but if his kid is missin', I guess I can understand."

"That's nice of you. Can you tell me something about him?"

"Like what?"

"What kind of guy is he?"

Zelnor screwed up his face and said, "Kind of an asshole, I guess. Doesn't really get along with anyone, but he's a good mechanic."

"What about at home?"

"What about it?"

"How's his home life?"

"Damned if I know," Zelnor said. "I don't pry into my employees' personal business."

"Well, what's his attitude toward female customers?"

Zelnor pursed his lips and raised his eyebrows.

"I did have to call him on the carpet once or twice about comin' on to female customers. They bring their cars here to be fixed, not to be fixed up themselves." Zelnor seemed pleased with himself for his turn of phrase.

"Have you ever seen him be violent with a woman?"

"Not here," Zelnor said. "Why . . . did somebody complain? Is that what this is about? I'll fire his ass—I don't care if his kid is missin'. Ain't even his kid; it's his wife's."

"No one complained," Keough said hastily. He didn't like Keith, but he didn't want to get the guy fired. "Does he talk about that? I mean, that the child isn't his?"

"I told you—I don't talk to my people about their home life."

"Do you mind if I interview some of your other employees?"

"Go ahead, as long as you don't disrupt my schedule. I don't want to get too far behind. But all they're gonna tell you is how much they don't like him."

"Okay, thanks."

Zelnor nodded, turned, and stuck his head back under the hood of the car he'd been working on when Keough arrived.

Keough hesitated a moment, then decided to leave rather than question the other employees. Zelnor was probably right. Nothing would be gained except to let Keith know he'd been there asking questions. He knew that abusers needed little or no reason to take their anger out on their loved ones. He decided to give Nancy Keith a break.

He got in his car and drove to his hotel.

Twenty-six

THE MESSAGE LIGHT on his phone was flashing when he entered, and he got an odd impression of urgency from it. He checked it immediately and found a recorded message from Harriet Connors.

"Joe, call me on my cell as soon as you can. We got another one here. Oh, it's . . . four-thirty here. Shit, it's the same there, isn't it? . . . Just call me!"

He dialed her cell phone immediately.

"There you are. Good. Another boy's gone missing."

"How old?"

"Eleven. Our killer is following a pattern. The next one should be twelve. Shit, we have to catch this bastard before the next one, don't we? God, listen to me. I've given up on this one already."

"It's still April, Harriet," he said. "Your kid is still alive. Remember the pattern so far has been one a month."

"The pattern also has the bodies being dropped off, or found, one to two days later."

"So I'm saying May first, then," Keough commented. "That's when yours will be found."

"Mine?"

"We had another one here, too. A girl gone missing."

"On the same day?"

"That's the point," Keough said. "This one can't be part of the pattern."

"And mine?"

"We can't discount yours yet. He's the same age group. There are too many discrepancies here in St. Louis though." He went on to outline them to her.

"And on the same day," she reiterated, "although that could be a coincidence. Seems to point out two killers, though."

"I'm convinced this little girl was taken by a third party."

"Like who?"

"Like maybe her father. He's an abuser, but so far I've only determined that he beats his wife, not the child—who, by the way, is his stepdaughter."

"Okay, then if your girl is not part of this, you're probably going to have another victim within the next couple of days. That would fit the pattern."

"I wonder if these bastards know each other and are working together. One hits and the other follows."

"Could be. Do you think you should come here and work on this for a couple of days?"

"I think I should stay here, Harriet. For one thing, your profiler will be here tomorrow. She might be able to help me convince the task force that they're working on a simple missing person case."

"Is this Joe Keough who's going to ask a profiler for help?"

"Never mind," he said. "Fill me in on your case."

He listened for fifteen minutes while she told him where the body had been found, in what condition, and where the child had likely been taken from. It all fit with the other killings.

"So he was taken on the way home from school?" Keough repeated. "I'm surprised parents aren't picking their kids up."

"I'm surprised they're letting the kids go to school at all. Listen, I'm on the street. We're interviewing the parents, and other family and friends, to see if someone saw anyone hanging around, blah, blah, blah. You know the drill. I just wanted to warn you. If the pattern follows with these sickos, you're going to have another one."

"I'll talk to the sergeant in command of the task force tomorrow, see if I can convince him. Also, I think I'll try to have him call the head of the task force there in Chicago. Who would that be?"

"Commander Fowler," she said, and gave him a direct phone number. "Listen . . . you're not going to get involved in this other case, are you? I mean, I know how you get caught up sometimes."

"I'm going to try to get Sergeant Henry to pass it along to Missing Persons, but meanwhile I'm going to keep working on our serial case. I'm working with Detective Marc Jeter to—"

"Oh, right, the kid you worked with on that East St. Louis case."

He'd forgotten that he'd told her about Jeter the night before. She knew nothing about what had happened with Andrew Judson in East St. Louis, though, only that he and Jeter had worked together. In fact, she had met him briefly.

"Well," she commented, "at least you're working with someone you know, who doesn't despise you for being a fe—uh, pseudofed."

"Yeah, it works out okay." Keough said. "Look, I'll touch base with you tomorrow, after I talk with the profiler. What is she like?"

"Oh, I think you'll find her . . . interesting. Take care."

She hung up before he could ask, "Interesting in what way?"

After a long shower, he wrapped himself in a terry robe, sat on the bed, and stared at the phone. He was thinking about children and how he often got involved in cases involving them. Harriet had been right: He did get caught up in some cases, usually the ones involving kids—like Denise Proctor. He couldn't tell her how far he'd already gone with the case of the missing nine-year-old girl. Maybe he should just follow his own advice and pass what he knew on to Missing Persons.

But thinking about Denise Proctor and children like her made him think about Brady Sanders—the young boy he'd met on practically his first day in St. Louis—and thinking about Brady made him think about Valerie Speck. He'd left St. Louis abruptly, without ever contacting her again, without seeing if Brady had been placed with another family after his foster father had been murdered. Keough had caught the killer, even though he'd been knee-deep in the East St. Louis case at the same time. He wondered now where Brady was and how he was doing, but the only way to find out was to call Valerie, and he wasn't sure if he wanted to do that.

So instead of making a call, he sat down at the writing desk in his room, intending to make a few case notes. It was three hours later when he looked up at the clock because he felt hungry and light-headed. He needed food, and he had to take his pills, which he'd forgotten to take all day.

He tore himself away from his notes, because it seemed most of them concerned the Keiths. He ordered food from room service, spent the rest of the evening surfing the cable channels, and finally turned in early.

Twenty-seven

May 1, 2004

GABRIEL WOKE WITH a start, drenched in perspiration. It was the dream again, only this time it was so vivid, it almost wasn't a dream. He'd always felt there was something missing from his life. That was why the dreams were so important to him. In them, he didn't feel alone. No, *alone* wasn't the word. *Incomplete*—that was what he'd felt most of his life, but in the dreams he was whole.

He sat up in bed, swung his feet to the floor and checked the clock. It was almost 8:00 A.M. Time to get up. He went to the front door, opened it, and picked up his delivered copy of the *St. Louis Post-Dispatch*. He placed it on the kitchen table, then went and took a shower. He came back to the kitchen naked, wet, and prepared his breakfast of grapefruit, cereal, and coffee. Only when he was ready to eat did he open the paper and see the headline. EIGHT-YEAR-OLD GIRL MISSING. KILLER STRIKES AGAIN?

He dropped his spoon into his cereal bowl, splashing milk onto the table and the newspaper, which was already wet from his hands. He hadn't gone out yesterday, and he certainly had not "snatched" another little girl "off the street in broad daylight." It wasn't time yet. He read the story and realized that someone else had kidnapped a little girl and he was going to get the blame.

He put the paper down and drank some of his coffee. He was almost dry now, but for his hair. It was all right. The girl's body hadn't been found yet, and when it was, they'd know it wasn't him, because there wouldn't be an angel pin. Or maybe she'd even resurface, alive and well. Sometimes they did.

Poor little girl, he thought, digging his spoon into the grapefruit. He wondered what she had done to get herself snatched.

Sariel read the piece in the *Chicago Tribune* about the little girl who had been taken off the street yesterday in St. Louis. Another one? Or a coincidence?

All of the disappearances to this date in both Chicago and St. Louis had remarkable similarities—most notably the timing. But the timing on this one was all wrong.

This little girl could not be one of the chosen, because the time was just not right yet.

Twenty-eight

WHEN KEOUGH ARRIVED in Clayton the next morning, FBI pro-filer Nicole Busby was waiting for him in his office.

"Agent Keough?" she asked as he entered the tiny room.

She had been sitting in a chair with her legs crossed, wearing a suit that consisted of a cream-colored jacket and a short skirt. The jacket was open, revealing a sweater underneath of mixed paisley colors. The V-cut neck showed the merest hint of cleavage. She uncrossed her excellent legs, a movement he found himself paying full attention to, and stood up. She was possibly the most beautiful black woman he'd ever seen. She had short hair and smooth choco-late skin. She resembled Halle Berry, except that he thought she was even better-looking, more exotic.

"Detective Keough," he said, correcting her. "I prefer being called that."

She was about five five, so she had to look up at him when she frowned.

"I thought you were FBI," she said.

"A common misconception, Miss Busby. It is Miss Busby, isn't it?"

"Agent Busby."

"Yes, well, in my unit, we've been able to keep the rank we're most comfortable with. I like being called 'Detective' because it's what I am, and what I do." He paused. "If you don't mind."

"I don't mind what you want to call yourself, Detective Keough."

"Well . . . good."

The next moment was awkward, so he used it to sit behind the desk. She turned and sat back down in her chair, crossing her legs again. Harriett was right: She was young, probably not yet thirty.

"Have you talked to the commander of the task force yet?" Keough asked.

"No," Busby said, "I wanted to report to you first."

"I appreciate that," he said. "I'll introduce you when we're through here."

"I understand you had another child snatched yesterday."

"Yes, but I don't think it's part of the same case."

"Why not?"

"There are too many discrepancies."

"Do the locals agree with you?"

"No."

"Well, they will."

"Will they?"

"Yes," she said, "as soon as the body is found."

"And if she's found alive?"

"Well, that will also be proof, won't it?"

"Why are you sure they'll agree with me when she is found . . . dead?"

"The angels."

He frowned. "What angels?"

"The angel pins that have been found on all the victims."

He sat forward in his chair, heat rising in his face.

"You didn't know?"

"No," he said tightly, "nobody told me."

"It's here in my report," she said, opening a folder in her lap. "The three bodies found here in St. Louis were found with small angel pins on their clothes. Also," she said, opening another folder, "angel pins were found on the three bodies in Chicago."

"What? The same pins?"

"No," she said, closing the folders. "These were slightly different, but the fact that all six victims had angel pins affixed to their clothes is enough of a similarity, don't you think?"

"Yes, I do think. Do you have photos of these pins?"

"I do, but I also have samples. She dug into her purse and brought out a plastic angel pin. It was colorful, and cheap. She put it on the desk between them.

"This is the one they found on the Chicago victims," she said. "I found it in a gift shop in the Water Tower Mall. It's inexpensive, and it doesn't represent any particular angel."

Keough leaned forward and reached out with his forefinger, but he did not touch the pin. Without moving it, he could see the pin glued to the back of the plastic.

"Have you seen the pin that was found on the St. Louis victims?" he asked, sitting back.

"No," she said, "I only just got here, and I haven't spoken to anyone. Apparently, the police in both cities held back the information about the pins so it wouldn't appear in the papers."

Keough stood up and said, "The newspapers aren't the only ones they held it back from. Give me a minute."

"Where are you going?"

Moving past her to the door, he said, "I want to have a chat with Sergeant Henry before I introduce the two of you."

"I could come and sit in," she said, starting to rise.

"No," he said. "Having you there might inhibit the language I use, and I wouldn't want that. I might need it to get my point across."

Twenty-nine

W HEN K EOUGH ENTERED the task force's office, only Sergeant Henry and Martha were present. He walked directly to Henry's desk and faced the seated man.

"Morn—" Henry began, but Keough cut him off.

"You might want to send Martha for some coffee," Keough said.

"I think she drinks tea."

Keough leaned on the man's desk and loomed over him. "Just do it!"

There was something in his eyes that kept the sergeant from arguing.

"Martha," he called out, "why don't you go and get some tea?"

"I already have some," she said, holding up her cup.

"Then would you go and get me one?"

She frowned. "But you don't drink—"

"Martha!"

She could tell by looking at him that she should keep quiet, and she left the room, muttering to herself.

"What's on your mind, Keough?" Henry asked.

"Angels."

"What?"

"You heard me. Angel pins, found on the clothing of the victims."

Henry sat back in his chair and made a face.

"Yeah," Keough said.

"We kept that to ourselves so it wouldn't appear in the newspapers."

"That's fine," Keough said. "The question is, Why didn't you tell me about them?"

"How did you find out?"

"Never mind that," Keough said. "I want to see them. Where are they?"

"They're in evidence," Henry said.

"That's bullshit!" said Keough. "If you wanted to keep it out of the papers, you wouldn't stick them in an evidence locker. You've got them here, probably in your desk."

Henry stared at Keough for a few more moments, then opened the left-hand drawer of his desk. He brought out a clear plastic bag and dropped it on the desk. Inside were three metal angel pins, either made of gold or gold-plated. They looked more expensive than the Chicago pins. Keough touched the bag with his forefinger, then withdrew it.

"You son of a bitch," he said softly. "When were you going to tell me about these? Or were you even going to?"

"I would have told you . . . eventually."

"Like when Denise Proctor was found dead, without an angel pinned to her clothes?"

"Or with one."

"No, it'll be without." Keough stood up straight, his disgust evident. "How do you expect me to be of any help if you don't share everything you have with me?"

"I never asked for your help, remember?"

"But you agreed to accept it, and to cooperate."

"Come on, Keough," Henry said, "how did *you* react when feds came in to horn in on one of *your* cases?"

"I'm not a fed," Keough said, "and I'm not trying to horn in; I'm trying to find a killer."

"Because you don't think we can?" Henry demanded.

In frustration, Keough said, "I don't care who finds him, as long as he's found. Take the credit, I don't care."

"The FBI will care," Henry said. "They'll want credit."

"Is that what this is about, then?" Keough asked.

"You may claim not to be a fed," Henry said, "but you think like one. What does it matter who gets credit as long as your name gets mentioned, right?"

"Jesus Christ, man—" Keough cut himself off. He heard someone entering the room behind him and turned, to see the two detectives, Berkery and House.

"What's going on?" Berkery asked.

"Nothing," Henry said. "I'm just keeping Detective Keough informed about our progress."

The two detectives approached their boss's desk and saw the angels in the plastic bag.

"I thought we were keeping those to ourselves," Berkery said.

"We are," Henry said. "Keough's a member of this team."

"Is that a fact?" Berkery asked, giving Keough an unfriendly look.

"You might want to call the head of the Chicago task force, Sergeant."

"Why would I want to do that?" Henry asked.

"Because there are more similarities between your murders and theirs than you think."

"Like what?" Berkery asked.

"Angels," Keough said, looking at Henry and not the two detectives.

Henry looked stricken.

"You mean—"

"I mean angel pins were affixed to their clothing, as well," Keough explained. "Different pins, but still angels."

"Jesus!" House said.

"You'd have known this if you'd checked with them," Keough said.

"And how do you know about it?" Berkery asked.

Still addressing himself to the sergeant, Keough said, "I've got somebody I want you to meet—and she *is* FBI."

He brought Agent Busby into the room and introduced her

around. By this time, the plainclothes members of the team had also arrived, so there were five pairs of eyes giving her hostile looks.

"Agent Busby is an FBI profiler," Keough said.

"I thought you said you could keep the FBI out of this?"

"Like I said, she's a profiler. She's not here to . . . to try to take over," Keough said. "She's here to help."

"Like you?" Berkery asked.

"That's right, Berkery," Keough said, the man beginning to get under his skin even more than the others, "like me."

"Sarge," Berkery said, "first Keough, now this one—"

"Agent Busby," Keough said. "She's got a name, Berkery—and she's a lady."

"That's hardly releve—" Busby started to say, but all the men ignored her.

"How long before we're overrun by FBI agents?" Berkery asked Henry.

"I don't know, John," Henry said. "For now, let's just deal with the two that we have."

Thirty

"So what's the point of the angels?" Sergeant Henry asked Nicole Busby.

He had called Commander Robert Raymond Fowler—that was the way the man had identified himself during the call—of the Chicago Police Department and they had exchanged all pertinent information. They agreed to have a direct phone line set up between the two task force offices to facilitate further communication.

Now they were sitting around the office, all armed with coffee or tea.

"Obviously," Berkery said before Busby could respond, "it's his signature, so we know that all the murders are his."

"Berkery—" Keough began.

"No, he's right," Busby said, "it is his signature. This serial killer is unusual, in that rather than taking a momento, he's leaving something behind."

"To tell us what?" Henry asked.

"That these children have been chosen."

"For what?"

She shrugged. "Sacrifice, maybe."

"What kind of sacrifice?" Henry asked.

"I don't know."

Henry looked at Keough, who shrugged.

"So are these signature killers, or serial killers?" Jeter asked.

"There are elements of both," Busby said.

"Did you share this knowledge with Commander Fowler in Chicago?" Keough asked.

"We . . . talked," she said. "He wasn't very . . . appreciative of my input."

"What about my partner?" Keough asked. "Agent Connors?"

"What about her?"

"What did she say when you informed her of the angels?" Keough asked. "Or did Commander Fowler share that with her?"

Busby frowned. "I didn't really get a chance to talk with your partner," she admitted, "and my impression was that she wasn't getting much more from the police there than I was."

Jesus, Keough thought, Harriet doesn't know about the angels. He was going to have to call and tell her. She wasn't going to be happy.

"What can you tell us about those angel pins?" Keough asked Henry.

The sergeant picked up the bag and said, "They're on sale in many gift shops around town. We've seen them in Union Station, some other malls, as well as the gift shop on the *Casino Queen*."

Keough leaned forward and noticed that the pins had stones on them, different-colored stones.

"What do the stones mean?" he asked.

"Well, ostensibly they are birthstones," Henry said. "We checked, though, and the stones don't match the birthdays of the dead girls."

"Maybe the killer got them mixed up," Jeter said. "Maybe they were supposed to match."

"No, we don't want to start assuming that," Keough warned.

"Why not?" Berkery asked.

"Because it may send us off in a wrong direction," Keough said. "We'd have to start looking for someone with intimate knowledge of each child, someone who knew their birthdays. That could take us in an entirely wrong direction."

"Someone who works at their school?" Busby suggested.

"They all came from different schools, remember?" Keough said. "That's in your files, I'm sure."

"Yes, of course."

"Well," Henry said, "this has been . . . fun, but we have a child to find."

"Are you still assuming she's been taken by the same person?" Keough asked.

"Until it's proven otherwise, yes," Henry said.

"And it won't be proven until she shows up dead," Jeter said, "with or without an angel pin."

"Or until she shows up alive," Keough said.

"Not much chance of that," said Berkery.

"What about the stepfather?" Keough asked. "He's an abuser; we know that much."

"If and when she shows up dead, and there's no angel pin," Sergeant Henry said, "we'll turn this case over to the Major Case Squad and let them work on it."

"You could turn it over to Missing Persons now and save some time," Keough pointed out.

"I'm not ready to give up on this child being part of a string—"

"From what I can see in the files," Busby said, breaking in, "both in Chicago and here, the next child should be eleven, and although they might have been grabbed in April, they won't be found dead until sometime in May."

Henry frowned at her and instructed his men to get to work. Keough thought that at least he and Nicole Busby agreed on something.

Thirty-one

KEOUGH'S ANGER AT being left out of the loop and kept in the dark about the angel pins was less than appeased. And he knew that Harriet was going to go through the roof. He walked to his small office to call her before he realized that a phone had not yet been installed for him.

"Need this?"

He looked up and saw Agent Busby standing in the door, holding a cell phone.

"Thanks," he said. "Mine's, uh, in my hotel room."

"Calling your partner to tell her about the pins?" she asked as he accepted the phone.

"Yes." He sat behind the desk and dialed Harriet's cell number.

"Do you mind if I wait?" Agent Busby asked. "I'd still like to talk to you."

"Sure," he said. "I have to give you back your phone anyway."

She remained in the doorway.

"Why don't you go into the other room?" he asked.

"They're not very friendly out there."

"Talk to Jeter," he said. "He'll be friendly."

Keough noticed that from the moment Jeter had seen Agent

Busby, he had not been able to keep his eyes off her—not that Keough blamed him.

"All right," she said, and walked down the hall.

"Motherfuckers!"

Keough moved the phone away from his ear while Harriet finished venting her anger and frustration.

"Are you done?" he asked when she had run out of breath.

"Doesn't this piss you off?" she asked.

"Yes, it does, but you're regular FBI, Harriet. You've been through this before, haven't you?"

"Damn right," she said, as if he'd reminded her. "You and I have always been on the opposite side of this question. How does it feel to be on my side of the fence?"

"Not good," Keough said, 'but I kind of feel like I'm straddling the fence."

"Well, if that's the case, you're going to have to pick a side eventually. You usually have to make some kind of a choice."

"I realize that, but that's for another time."

She sighed heavily and said, "I guess I'm going to have to go into this Commander Fowler now and fight with him."

"Maybe it'll be easier now that the heads of the two task forces have agreed to cooperate."

"You think the spirit of cooperation will extend to us?"

"I hope so."

"How you doing with the profiler?"

"Fine," he said, "I'm using her cell phone. You didn't tell me she was gorgeous."

"I thought that would be a nice surprise for you," she said. "I wonder why she didn't tell me about the angel pins?"

"She told me that you and she didn't get a chance to talk."

"She's right," Harriet said. "Fowler just about threw her out of his office. Her credentials didn't impress him."

"Maybe it was her youth."

She sighed again. "Well, I'm afraid he doesn't have that excuse when it comes to me."

"Use your charm," Keough said; "use that new body you're so proud of."

"Just because I have a new body doesn't mean I know how to use it," she said. "Besides, he's sixty and married, and he smokes the most god-awful cigars."

"Do the best you can, then," Keough said. "I'll check in with you tonight or in the morning."

"Enjoy yourself with Agent Busby."

He broke the connection, then walked down the hall and found Martha, Jeter, and Agent Busby in the office, having a three-way chat. From the look on Jeter's face, he was wishing Martha would go out for more tea.

"Thanks for the use of the phone," Keough said, handing it back to Agent Busby.

"No problem."

"Agent Busby's been giving us a lecture on profiling," Jeter said.

Keough checked his watch. They'd spent the morning inside, and now all the others were gone and his stomach was growling.

"Why don't we buy her lunch and let her continue it in the restaurant?" he suggested.

Martha gave him a sad look and said, "I have to stay and man the phones."

In a gesture that surprised Keough, Nicole Busby leaned over, touched Martha on the arm, and said, "I'll come back and fill you in." Her smile lighted up the room.

Thirty-two

ASIDE FROM HOUSING the municipal buildings—including the new jail—Clayton was all office buildings, galleries, and restaurants. They went to Crazy Fish for lunch, and when Keough realized he had chosen the place to try and impress Agent Busby, he became annoyed with himself. The atmosphere was funky, the menu eclectic, and Keough had not found anyplace in Washington to rival it.

During lunch, she continued to fascinate Jeter, whether with her knowledge of profiling or her exotic looks, Keough wasn't sure—maybe both.

When she began to discuss how many serial killers were able to keep that side of them private from the world because they were sociopaths, Jeter hauled out one of his Mark Twain quotes: "Every one is a moon, and has a dark side which he never shows to anybody."

"Well," she commented, "with the serial killer, or the sociopath, that side of them does eventually come out. It's very difficult to hide that total lack of morals for very long."

Jeter then quoted his hero again. "Twain said, 'A man should not be without morals; it is better to have bad morals than none at all.'"

"I don't know that I agree with that," she said. They were seated at a table, with Jeter on one side and Keough and Busby sitting side by side on the other. She turned her head, looked at Keough, and asked, "Do you?"

Keough, who was picking at his food, said, "When he starts quoting Mark Twain, I don't argue. The man was supposed to be a genius."

"Well," she said, "I'm not a very big Twain fan."

Jeter looked so stricken, Keough felt sorry for him, yet he had to keep himself from laughing.

"His comments are so cynical," she went on, "that I can never figure out if he was kidding or not."

"For instance?" Jeter asked, rushing to his hero's defense.

"Well, I know he had a terrible life, and he was a very sad man," she said. "His brother died on the river and he blamed himself, and his daughter died, as well. He used humor to hide his bitterness, but his humor . . . it had a bite to it. I don't remember quote after quote like you do, but I remember one from college."

"Which one?" Jeter asked. Keough noticed that the young detective had to wet his lips before he spoke. He suspected the man was very close to being in love.

" 'I have no color prejudices nor caste prejudices nor creed prejudices. All I care to know is that a man is a human being, and that is enough for me; he can't be any worse.' That's the only one I remember. Man can't be any worse than being man? Why would anyone want to live among men if that were the case? Why wouldn't he just commit suicide?"

Jeter was speechless.

"Maybe," Keough said, "he thought it was a worse punishment to stay alive."

She looked at him and said, "I never thought of it like that."

"H—how do you know as much as you do about Twain?" Jeter asked.

"I told you," she said, "I studied him in college. That's how I know enough not to like him."

"B—but," Jeter stammered, caught between his desire to defend

Twain and his desire to impress Agent Busby. Keough saved him from both.

"Why don't we try discussing business over dessert?" he suggested.

"Sounds good to me," Busby said. The prospect of dessert seemed to loosen her up a bit. She was even smiling, dazzling both men. "First, I have to visit the little-girls' room."

Keough pushed his chair out a bit to give her room to get up and move around him. They both watched as she walked to the back of the restaurant.

"Man, she's gorgeous!" Jeter said. He looked at Keough, his eyes shining. "And you work with her?"

"I don't work with her," Keough responded; "she's FBI."

"But you're—oh."

"I only met her today, like you did, Marc."

"Do you think she likes me?" the younger man asked.

"I don't know," Keough said. "She sure doesn't like Mark Twain, though. Isn't that a turnoff for you?"

"I think I could learn to live with it, for her," Jeter said.

"Well, you know what?" Keough said. "I'll give you your chance." He took out some money and dropped it on the table.

"What are you doing?"

"I'm going to give you time alone with her."

"Really?"

"Yes, and lunch is on me."

As Keough stood up, Jeter said, "B—but what should I tell her?"

"Tell her I got a call and had to leave."

"B—but then what do I do?"

Keough smiled at him and said, "Make your move, kid . . . but talk about business, too. See what you can find out from her about the Chicago killings, and how they match up to ours. You know . . . pump her for information first, then ask her out later."

"Ask her out?"

"Isn't that what you want to do?"

"Well, yeah, but . . . this soon?"

"No time like the present, kid," Keough said. "I'll see you back at the office later."

"Okay, but—"

Keough got out before Jeter could ask him another question.

When Agent Busby returned, she predictably asked what had happened to Keough. When Jeter told her he'd gotten a call and had to leave, she said, "I thought he told me his cell phone was in his hotel room?"

To which Jeter, still mesmerized by her beauty—even if she wasn't smiling—replied, "Uh . . ."

Thirty-three

KEOUGH HAD OPTIONS, but one he didn't want to consider at the moment was returning to the task force's office. Nobody there but Martha was friendly, and he already hated the closet he was using as an office. His files were there, though, so he couldn't go somewhere and study them. In any case, he was still convinced they were going to need fresh blood to be able to move with any effectiveness on this killer—either that or they had to wait for the killer to contact them. Leaving the angel pins behind indicated to Keough that there was an ego at work. He was used to tracking both kinds of killers, the ones with low self-esteem, who hid behind their crimes, and the ones with superegos, who eventually had to step out from behind their victims and show themselves in order to initiate a battle of wits.

He walked to his car and got behind the wheel. As he started to drive, he thought about the angel pins. He came up with some questions and listed them in his mind.

Was there significance behind the fact that the St. Louis pins were of a more expensive variety than the Chicago ones?

Did this mean the two killers were operating on different budgets?

Was the St. Louis killer more affluent?

He decided to check and see what kind of school districts the three dead girls had been taken from, lower-, middle-, or upper-class. He'd also check with Harriet and get the same information about the Chicago boys. This might, at least, give them some idea of the lifestyle being led by the two killers.

When he almost rear-ended a car that had slowed for no apparent reason, he realized he was letting his mind wander too much to be behind the wheel. Besides, he'd forgotten the one thing he'd never been able to figure out about Missouri—its drivers. Apparently, they thought that merge, yield, and stop signs were all the same.

He decided he needed a definite destination to drive to, and since he didn't have his files with him, he decided to drive to the Keith home and see if he could get some alone time with Nancy Keith while her husband was—hopefully—at work.

Nancy Keith was surprised to see Keough at her front door, and she did not look happy, which was either because of him or her black eye.

"That's a new one," he said, and she immediately knew what he meant. Her hand went to her eye before she could think, then dropped back to her side.

"What do you want?"

"I'd like to talk to you about your daughter," he said. "May I come in?"

"My husband isn't here."

"Good," he said, "because I want to talk to you alone. May I come in?" This time he asked the question while opening the screen door and taking a step forward. She had no choice but to back up and allow him to enter.

She turned and walked away from him, slightly hunched over, hugging herself again. He assumed this had become a normal posture for her.

"Nancy, don't you think you've taken enough abuse from your husband?"

"He—he doesn't abuse me."

"Oh no? I suppose you got that black eye from walking into a door?"

"N—no," she said. "He . . . he said I made a mistake calling you. He . . . he just . . . punished me for not checking with him first."

"Punished you?" Keough asked. "By punching you around?"

"He says he's the man, so he makes the decisions," she said. "He—he's right."

Keough moved toward her and reached out to touch her, but she flinched and backed away.

"Nancy, look what he's done to you," Keough said. "You're as jumpy as a cat. That's no way to live."

"No, no," she said, "my momma told me that the man is the boss. I shoulda listened."

Now he realized he was bucking years of upbringing—or downbringing.

"Okay," he said, "never mind that." She didn't need a cop digging into her life; she needed a team of marriage counselors and psychiatrists. "Have you heard anything about your daughter?"

She turned so her back was to him and said, "N—no. Nothing."

"Nothing yet, but we're still looking."

"Then why are you here, mister?"

"I thought there might be something you wanted to tell me."

She hunched even more and asked, "Like what?"

"Nancy . . . if something happened to your daughter . . . if your husband . . . did anything—"

She turned on him abruptly. That surprised him, but the look on her face stunned him. It was fierce, the look a woman who's about to defend or protect her child, not her abusive husband.

"He didn't do anything to her!" she insisted vehemently. "He didn't touch her."

"If you're protecting him out of fear—"

Just when he thought he couldn't be any more surprised, she began pounding on his chest with her fists, shouting, "Get out! Get out of here! Out of my house!"

He backed away, unable to escape the blows that rained down on him. When he reached the door, he opened it and stumbled out. She didn't follow him, just slammed the door in his face and locked it.

He stood on her front steps, still stunned. He knew he could arrest her if he wanted to, but what would be the point? But why was she so vehement—to the point of violence—that her husband hadn't touched little Denise, when it was obvious that he did beat the mother? Why not the stepdaughter—especially when the man already had a rap sheet involving children?

And what was even more puzzling, why hadn't she once asked about her daughter?

Thirty-four

KEOUGH WANTED TO buy one of the angel pins for himself. Since he was staying in the Drury Inn downtown, he went to the closest mall, the one in the old Union Station—coincidentally, one of the places Sergeant Henry had mentioned finding the pin. He stopped at the mall, checked several stores before he found what he wanted. He grabbed a pin, not paying attention to what the stone was, since that didn't matter to him. After paying for it, he briefly considered visiting the food court, then decided to get out of there instead of fighting the crowds of kids and before-dinner moms. He went back to his car and drove back to his hotel.

When he entered the Drury Inn, he was surprised to find Agent Nicole Busby waiting in the lobby.

"Why are you here?" he asked.

"They wouldn't let me into your room," she replied with a straight face.

"No, I mean why are you here at all? Why aren't you with Detective Jeter?"

"He's a nice young man, but you can only talk about Mark Twain for so long," she said.

"I'm sure you just made him nervous, Agent Busby," he replied. "After all, you are a very pretty—"

"I'm aware that I'm attractive, Detective Keough," she said, cutting him off, "and as an attractive woman, I'm not usually in need of being fixed up. I'm sure your partner is very nice, and he's quite good-looking, but I didn't come to St. Louis looking for a good time. I came to do a job, and to do it, I must have some of your time."

"My time," he said. "Why not talk to the cops on the task force?"

"I didn't get a chance to speak to Agent Connors," Busby said. "I don't know if she was avoiding me or not."

"Not, I'm sure." He didn't want to tell her that of the two of them, he was the one more likely to avoid a profiler than Harriet Connors.

"Well, whatever the case, I really would like some of your time. That is, unless you prefer I recommend to my director that he send in a team of agents?"

"Don't do that," Keough replied. "You'll only end up alienating everyone."

"Not my intent, Detective, I assure you."

"All right, then," he said. "Are you hungry? I need some dinner."

"We had lunch not long ago."

"I wasn't so hungry then."

"Very well," she said, "but this will be my treat. You paid last time."

He'd left the money for Jeter to pay the check, but he hadn't expected him to tell Busby that. He was going to have to talk to his young partner about his technique for impressing women.

"Pick out someplace nice and expensive," she said, "I'll put it on my expense account."

Every time he started to think of her as regular FBI, she said something to change his mind."

"You're on."

There were three Drury Inns in St. Louis. The one Keough had chosen was right near the America's Center, which was St. Louis's convention center. And across the street from the center was the Mayfair Hotel, a historic hotel, which had recently been taken over by the Wyndham Hotel chain. It had an excellent, and expensive, restaurant. Keough and Busby walked there and had to wait only a short time for a table, as it wasn't quite dinnertime.

"This is lovely," she said. "Have you been here before?"

"No," he replied, "but I've heard it's very good."

The weather was mild, so he was wearing only a lightweight suit jacket. She wore a similar outfit. As they were seated at a table, neither removed their jacket, which was just as well, as far as he was concerned. She was an inordinately attractive woman. The V-necked sweater was quite enough to have to deal with. He realized his logic would be considered chauvinistic by most modern women, but what the hell. As far as he knew, none of them was a mind reader—yet.

They ordered drinks and looked at the menu. Busby ordered duck and Keough beef Wellington, since she was using her expense account.

When their drinks came, they each took a healthy sip. She had ordered a gin and tonic, while he had an imported beer called Warsteiner.

"What's on your mind, Agent Busby?" he asked.

"I have a confession to make."

He waited.

"I need this assignment to go right for me. I need to contribute to this investigation."

"And why's that?'

She hesitated, then said, "I probably should wait until after dinner for this, but . . . do you remember the I-Eighty killer?"

He hesitated also, but only for a moment.

"Yes, I do."

"Well . . . I was the profiler on that case." She suddenly looked a lot younger, and less confident. "I screwed that one up. I profiled that killer as a momma's boy who was headed home, and I got it all wrong."

"Yeah, you did."

"I—I know that you were the one who had to kill him at that . . . that hotel, Little America. I'm the reason you had to go in without backup."

"You're not the reason I had to kill him, though," Keough said. "That was his choice."

"I'm the reason you got in trouble over that."

"Just with the newspapers," he said, "and the girl's family."

"B—but she was already dead when you took that shot," she said. "You knew that."

"No, I didn't, Nicole," he said, suddenly able to call her by her first name. "I took the shot not knowing whether she was dead or alive, but knowing she'd be dead if I didn't. And no matter what happened in that room, the sick bastard who had her was going to be dead. Her family just didn't want to believe that she was dead."

"So they sued you?"

"They tried to get compensation, any way they could," Keough said.

"What is that going to do to you the next time you have to take a shot like that?"

"I don't know," he said, "but I hope I never have to find out."

Their food came and they suspended the conversation until after the waiter asked all his annoying questions—"More water?" "Pepper for your salad?" "Can I get you anything else?"—and had left them alone again.

"Tell me about yourself," he said as they began eating. "Why did you become a profiler?"

"Truthfully?"

"Yes," he said. "I'm a cop; I like just the facts. . . ma'am."

She smiled and said, "You'll laugh at me."

"Why do all the women I know think I'm going to laugh at them?"

"I'm psychic," she said, "and I thought becoming a profiler was the only way I'd be able to use my abilities to help people and not be . . . scoffed at. You see, I've never had the courage to just come out and say, 'I'm a psychic.' People laughed at Jeane Dixon and

Sylvia Browne and John Edward before they took them seriously. I don't know if I ever could have taken being laughed at."

"You should talk to my partner."

"Jeter?"

"No, Harriet Connors. She's taking a course in—what did she call it?—remote viewing?"

"I've heard of that!" she said excitedly. "Yes, I should talk to her. I'm sorry we didn't have time in Chicago."

"So you believe that being psychic helps you to be a better profiler?"

"I hope it does," she said. "It didn't work very well with the I-Eighty killer, did it?"

"Put that behind you, Nicole," Keough advised. "I have."

"Anyway," she said, taking a sheet of paper from her purse, "I'm going here tomorrow. You should come."

He took the sheet from her. She had obviously printed it out from her computer. It was an announcement of a psychic fair in St. Louis over the next few days at a local Best Western. He handed it back.

"I think we'll be kind of busy tomorrow," he said.

"You don't believe your serial killer has struck again with Denise Proctor, do you?"

"No, I don't."

"And there's not much you can do but go over old ground until . . . until he strikes again, right?"

He nodded. Unfortunately, she was right—although many cases were solved by going over old ground.

"So come with me," she said. "Take a couple of hours off, clear your mind. It'll be good for you."

"I don't know—"

"And you'll find out if you're psychic," she added. "Maybe you can learn remote viewing."

He flicked the paper in her hand with his finger and asked, "What goes on at these things?"

"Sometimes they're just like a big flea market, venders selling tarot cards and crystals, people doing readings—and sometimes there are demonstrations and seminars."

"We might be able to use a psychic—sorry, I meant a real psychic—oh, sorry again—"

"No, that's okay," she said. "I'm not a true psychic, like them. I haven't developed my abilities yet. That's why I go to the fairs."

He wavered, and she sealed the deal.

"We could also spend the time talking about these cases," she said. "The ones in Chicago and St. Louis. I don't know how you feel about profiling, Detective—"

"Joe," he said.

"All right, Joe. . . . I don't know what you think of what I do, but I might have some fresh thoughts."

He didn't want to tell her that he put about as much credence in profiling as he did in psychic ability.

"All right, Nicole," he said. "I'll go with you."

"Good," she said, pushing her plate away. "And now I want a rich, sweet dessert."

"I'm sure they have them," he said, "or are you just sensing that they do?"

After dessert, they walked outside. "Where are you parked?" he asked. "I'll walk you to your car."

"Actually," she said, "I'm staying at the same hotel you are."

"Really?" He raised his eyebrows.

"Nothing psychic about that," she said. "It's the one thing I was able to learn from your partner before I left Chicago. She told me where you were staying, and I figured, 'Why not?'"

"All right, then," he said, "I'll walk you back to our hotel."

He extended his arm and she took it in the spirit in which it was given—lightly.

Thirty-five

May 2, 2004

KEOUGH WOKE EARLY the next morning, his stomach growling. He decided to stop at the Eat Rite for breakfast before driving to Clayton. He briefly considered calling Nicole Busby's room to invite her along, then decided against it. Last night had been very pleasant, but he wasn't looking for any personal involvement with the woman For one thing, she was too young, and for another—well, he just wasn't looking for a relationship. In any case, he was going to see her later in the day, as she had convinced him to accompany her to the psychic fair. Before parting company in the lobby of the hotel, he'd told her he wanted to go into the office in the morning and that he would meet her there.

Before going to breakfast, he called Harriet Connors and touched base with her, as he had done every morning since his arrival in St. Louis.

"Today's going to be the day," she said sadly. "We'll find the little boy's body today."

"Maybe not."

"You know as well as I do that if we don't, it'll be a break in the pattern, and if there's a break in the pattern, then all conventional investigative techniques go out the window. These killers are not supposed to deviate from their established patterns."

"So say the profilers," he responded. "Tell the killers that, though. Look, there's one more thing that has to happen for us, Harriet."

"What's that?"

"The killers have to contact somebody," he said, "a cop, a newspaperman, someone, in order to brag. I mean, they're leaving the pins, which means they want it known that they are serial killers. Both of them. If that doesn't happen, then we really are going to be up the creek."

"They don't always contact someone, though."

"The organized ones do," he said. He had been contacted by the Lover in New York, and by Andrew Judson in East St. Louis, although Judson's way of making contact had been to come to the police station in disguise. The Mall Rat had been disorganized, as had the Kopykat. He heard himself sharing his thoughts with her and knew what was coming.

"You're using the terminology, Joe," she said. "Does that mean you're coming over to the profiler's way of thinking?"

"It means I accept all contributions, even psychic ones."

"What?"

He explained about his conversation with Nicole Busby the night before.

"Over dinner?"

"A business dinner," he said tersely. "I'm not here looking for a girlfriend."

"Okay, I get it," she said. "Don't bite my head off. She does sound interesting, though. I'll have to get together with her and talk. Is she coming back to Chicago, returning to Washington, or staying there?"

"I don't know," he said. "I'll find out."

They agreed that she would call him as soon as the body was found, which they both estimated *should* be within the next twenty-four to thirty-six hours. That meant he had to carry his cell phone.

"I'll put it in my pocket as soon as we hang up," he promised.

"If I call you and the maid answers, you're in trouble," she warned.

He was about to leave the room, when he spotted the chess set Jack Roswell's daughter had given him. It reminded him of how she'd slammed the door in his face. He supposed he deserved it for not contacting the old man at some point after leaving St. Louis. Time goes by so fast, though. You mean to call, you mean to write . . . lame excuses.

He walked over, opened the set, and arranged the pieces on the board. It wasn't much, but maybe seeing it there would make him feel like Jack had forgiven him.

After a full breakfast of toast, bacon, eggs, and potatoes, he drove to the office in Clayton, where he planned to go over his files again.

When he entered his office, he found a phone had been installed. Next to the phone were new file folders—thicker folders this time. Apparently, these were the complete files, which he had not been given before—or at least more complete than the ones he'd had before. They'd either decided to cooperate with him or to give him a little more to keep him happy. He was sure of one thing: There was no way he could trust these people to share everything with him. He felt he could trust Jeter, but he probably did not have all the facts, either.

As for Agent Busby being trustworthy—well, the jury was still out on that. There was almost as much rivalry between federal agencies as there was between locals and federals. The spirit of cooperation was just that, a spirit, a ghost, something that wasn't there because it couldn't be touched.

Thirty-six

Roseland Community Hospital, Chicago
May 25, 1974

EDDIE SHUR PACED *the hospital waiting room nervously. There were other expectant fathers pacing as well, but they weren't nervous for the same reasons.*

"What do you hope it'll be?" *one of the other men asked him.*

"Hmm?"

"Boy or a girl?"

Eddie ran his hand through his prematurely thinning hair.

"It better be a boy," *he said hoarsely.*

Several of the other men laughed, and the one who had spoken before asked. "Whataya got, a pool going or something?"

"Something," *Eddie said. These men had no idea that his life depended on the baby being a boy. In that respect, he did have a pool going all right—for his life.*

To make matters worse, it was a long labor, and he was the last father in the waiting room, still pacing. He chain-smoked, and a nurse had to tell him not to grind the butts out on the floor, but to put them out in an ash-

tray. She frowned at his stained T-shirt and shied away from his foul breath while telling him that.

He went to the window over and over again, looking down at the parking lot. Even if the baby was a boy, if the people didn't show up, he was still in deep shit.

"Mr. Shur?"

He turned and looked at the nurse, the same battle-ax who'd snapped at him about his cigarette butts.

"Yeah?"

"You're a father."

"Boy or girl?" he asked convulsively.

"What?" she asked, taken aback.

"The baby, what is it?" Spittle covered his chin.

"My God," she said, "what difference does it make?"

"I'll tell you what difference," he said, wiping his hand over his mouth. "About ten thousand fucking dollars—and my life!"

As Eddie entered his wife's room, she turned her head and looked at him. Her face was streaked with tears, some shed during the delivery and some after.

"Eddie?" she said, reaching her hand out to him. "Please."

"Sally," he replied, "you know we have to do it."

"B—but Eddie . . . I want to see—"

He shook his head and said, "That's not a good idea, Sally. It'll only hurt you to see him."

The tears started again, and her lower lip began to quiver. He'd never seen her look so ugly before. After he paid off his bookie to keep his legs from being broken, he'd still have some money left over. Maybe it was time to leave Chicago . . . alone.

"Oh, Eddie—"

"We need this money, Sally," he said. "We needs it!"

Sally wiped away the tears with the palms of her hand. Her red hair was stringy, her face pale and shiny. There was no sign of the vivacious, pretty girl he'd married three years before. What Eddie Shur didn't know was that the disappearance of that girl was his fault. He'd squeezed the life out of her, and what was left was staring at him from a hospital bed.

"Eddie—"

"I have to go, Sally," he said. "The buyers will be here soon."

"B—but . . . did they tell you—"

"Yeah, they told me. It's a boy."

"No, but—"

"I'll—I'll see you Sally."

He opened the door and slipped out into the hall. When he reached the waiting room, the man and woman were there.

"Mr. Shur?" the woman said. Her tone was tremulous, her face luminous. Now here was a pretty woman! And the man standing next to her, he looked like a statue of one of those Greek gods. Eddie suddenly felt self-conscious in his torn and stained T-shirt, his ripped jeans, his tattered jacket.

"Mr. and Mrs. Delacorte. Did you bring the money?"

"Half of it," the man said.

"Half? Who said—"

"We can't take the baby today, can we, Mr. Shur?" the man asked.

"Well . . . no. It'd look . . . suspicious."

"Okay, then," Delacorte said, "half now and half when we get the baby."

Eddie was going to argue, but the woman looked at him with those big blue moist eyes and whispered, "Please."

"Okay," Eddie, "okay, fine. Half now." He looked around to make sure no one was watching. "Hand it over."

Delacorte took a white envelope from his pocket and held it out. Eddie grabbed it, took a quick look. He was satisfied with the flash of green and the thickness. He stuffed it into his jacket pocket.

"What about the doctor?" Eddie asked.

"I'll take care of him," Delacorte said.

"Can we see him?" Mrs. Delacorte pleaded. "Can we see our baby?"

"Sure, why not?" Eddie said, shrugging. "Follow me."

He took them from the waiting room into the maternity ward, where the same nurse stopped them.

"Are these people family?" she demanded.

"Yeah," Eddie said, enjoying the irony of the question, "yeah, they're family. They wanna see the baby."

"Well, all right. This way."

She took them to the ward where the infants were kept, so they could look through the window.

"Which one?" Mrs. Delacorte asked anxiously, her eyes scanning all the newborns behind the glass. "Which one is he?"

The nurse looked at Eddie, who said, "She's the godmother. Which one is mine?"

The nurse pointed and said, "Those."

"Those . . . what?"

"Those two, right in front," the nurse said. "Your wife had twins, Mr. Shur."

Eddie stared at the two babies, saw his last name on both beds.

"Two?"

"That's right," the nurse said, and walked away.

Eddie looked at the Delacortes. "There are two babies."

Mr. Delacorte looked at his wife, but she was ignoring him. She was staring adoringly at the baby in the bed on the right.

"We only want one, Mr. Shur," he said.

Eddie was going to argue that two was better than one to a childless couple, maybe even offer them a two-for-one price, but then he backed off and kept quiet, beaming proudly through the glass at his two children. He could find another childless couple, maybe one who would even pay more. . . .

Gabriel woke that morning with the absolute realization that he had not always been alone. Once, he'd had someone else, his other half, and now was the time to find that person. He knew how to do it, too, because he was a man who did not believe in coincidence. But first there were some other things that needed to be done. He couldn't let one thing interfere with the other. He was going to have to find a way to accomplish both.

Luckily, he had the one thing that made all other things possible. Money!

Sariel stared down at the boy who—if it was possible—was even more beautiful in death than he had been in life. It was time to leave him, to leave his body behind, for his soul had been delivered, had been sacrificed, and there was no more need for the earthly shell. There remained only the choice of places to leave it, so that it would be easily found, for if it went undiscovered, the sacrifice would be in vain.

As the trunk door started to close, sunlight reflected sharply off the surface of the plastic angel pin affixed to the child's shirt.

Thirty-seven

KEOUGH WAS SURPRISED at the turnout for a psychic fair. He knew about gatherings for comic books, and *Star Trek* and baseball cards, but this was a new one on him, and he was impressed.

Not that it was huge, but the two meeting rooms that it took up at the Best Western at I-70 and Page were full. People were rubbing shoulders to get a look at the books, crystals, tarot cards, and whatever other paraphernalia was on sale. And, of course, they were standing in line to get readings from attending psychics.

He had spent the morning in the office, going over the files once again on the three dead girls. He'd also gone to Martha to ask her to find out the class of schools they had been attending, and the income bracket of each family.

"I'll also need the names and addresses of all the adults employed at the schools, or sitting on school boards," he'd told her.

"We did all that," she said. She got up, went to a file cabinet, and came back with a sheaf of printouts several inches thick.

"Good," he said, and he meant it. Henry and his men were on the ball. He'd never doubted they were good at their jobs; he just thought their focus was a little narrow. This broadened it somewhat.

"We cross-referenced the lists, trying to match names, but came up empty."

"What about the family income brackets?"

"I can get that, but my recollection is that they're all pretty well-off."

"Maybe you can find out just how well-off," Keough suggested.

"I'll do that, Detective."

"Leave the results on my desk, if you would. I'd appreciate it."

"Okay. The sergeant was wondering why there was never a ransom demand."

"That's because this isn't about money."

"That's what he finally decided."

"I'm going to take these down the hall and go through them," he said, hefting the printouts.

"Go ahead," she replied. "We have copies."

He was leafing through the printouts when Nicole Busby entered.

"Are you ready?'

He looked up at her, frowning slightly as he tried to remember what he was supposed to be ready for.

"The psychic fair," she reminded him, leaning against the doorjamb.

"Oh," he said. "Nicole, I really can't—"

"You promised," she said. "It might open you up to many possibilities."

"But I—"

"I'm not taking no for an answer," she told him, pushing away from the door. "I'm coming to get you in half an hour."

As she turned to walk away, she almost slammed into Marc Jeter.

"Whoa, sorry!" he said, raising both hands.

"Good morning," she said, and kept walking.

"Why doesn't she like me?" Jeter asked.

"Beats me."

"Is it the Mark Twain thing?"

"I don't know, Marc. Maybe you're not her type."

"I'm young, handsome, and black," he said. "What's not to like?"

Keough looked up at him to see if he was serious. Apparently, he was.

"Why is she coming back in half an hour? And where is she taking you?" the younger man asked.

"To a psychic fair."

"A what?"

"We talked about it at dinner last—"

"Wait, wait," Jeter said, "hold on. You had dinner with her last night?"

"Yes."

"How did that happen?"

Keough closed the printouts and gave Jeter his full attention.

"We happen to be staying in the same hotel."

"Man, this gets better and better, doesn't it . . . for you?"

Keough stood up.

"Marc, I have only a professional interest in Agent Busby."

"Yeah, sure. That's why you're going with her to a psychic fair." My God, Keough thought, he's pouting.

"We were discussing a possible correlation between profiling and psychic ability. She told me she was going to this fair and invited me to come along and see for myself. Now, if you're worried that I'm trying to cut in on your action, you're willing to come along."

"Great!" Jeter said. "I'll do that."

"Fine," Keough said. "Just don't quote any Mark Twain today. Can you keep from doing that?"

"I'll try."

"And you better check in with your boss and be back here in twenty-five minutes."

"Oh," Jeter said, "where do I tell Sergeant Henry I'm going?"

"You're going with me and Agent Busby," Keough said. "Just tell him that."

"Okay." He turned to leave, then stopped and turned back.

"You're really not interested in her?"

"She's beautiful, Marc," Keough said, "but I'm afraid she's a little young for me."

"Well," Jeter said, "luckily, I don't have that same problem. I'll see you in twenty-five—no, make that twenty-four minutes."

Thirty-eight

WHEN THE THREE of them arrived at the psychic fair, Keough went one way and Jeter followed Agent Busby the other way.

In Jeter's car—Keough and Busby had left their rentals behind—Jeter tried to talk to Busby about a variety of subjects, all of which she replied to rather coolly. Keough gave the young man credit for staying away from Mark Twain, but it didn't seem to help. Busby was in St. Louis for the same reason Keough was—business. He hoped Jeter was not going to take her lack of interest to heart.

Keough walked around, paying little or no attention to the wares—stones, tarot decks, statues of dragons and unicorns, books—being hawked. He decided to go to the area where the psychics were sitting, selling their own items, as well as their talents. They all looked like normal people: men and women wearing T-shirts and jeans, some women with flowery tops, earrings, and headbands, and even men with earrings and, in one case—right out of the seventies—a dashiki.

The psychics were seated at tables surrounding the room, their backs to the walls. He saw that some of them had hung signs on the walls behind them; others simply had their names on the tables. He wondered if this was an indication of how well known they were. He also noticed all the different kinds of readings that were being done. The most common were tarot and palm readings, but one table advertised something called a "cold reading." And he saw one man doing a reading just using a regular—albeit worn—deck of playing cards.

He spotted Busby and Jeter standing in line in front of one of the tables, waiting their turn. As he reached them, the person ahead of them moved and Busby stepped up to the table.

"Nicole, my love," the man behind the table said.

"Maurice," she said, "how lovely to see you."

The man took her hand. He wore a sweater and trousers, and his white hair was closely cropped. He had tarot cards spread out in front of him, and a few crystals by his right hand sparkled.

"Have you come for another reading?" Maurice asked.

"I don't know that I've gotten over the last one," she said, laughing.

Keough joined her, so that he was standing on one side and Jeter on the other.

"These are my friends, Maurice," she said. "Joe and Marc."

"Gentlemen," he said, "how do you know our lovely Nicole?"

Before Keough could answer, Jeter said, "You tell us."

Maurice raised his eyebrows in amusement and said to Nicole, "A nonbeliever." He looked at Jeter, then at Keough. "Colleagues, I think—no, I *know* they're colleagues."

Jeter scoffed and said, "Good guess."

Maurice looked past Nicole and saw that no one else was in line at the moment, and no one was within earshot.

"You are local police," he said to Jeter, then looked at Keough and added, "but you're not—but you are. Ah . . . you used to be, but now, like Nicole, you're"—he lowered his voice—"FBI . . . and yet, you're not." Maurice frowned. "You have a very confused aura."

"Well," Keough said, "that sounds accurate at least."

"I'm here for your seminar, Maurice," Nicole said, "and I thought my friends would also be interested."

"He might," Maurice said, indicating Keough, "but not him."

"I'll skip it," Jeter said, "and look around some more."

Maurice checked his watch and said to Nicole, "You're right on time, my love. I have ten minutes to get myself ready. I'm in suite B."

Nicole turned to Keough as Maurice stood up. He was about five six and barrel-chested.

"Will you come, Joe?"

"Sure," Keough said, "why not? I'm always anxious to learn new things."

Maurice came around from behind the table, got between Keough and Busby, and took their arms. "An open mind. Very important in both our businesses, wouldn't you say . . . Detective?"

Keough had seen psychics work on TV before, but never in person. He'd always felt there were some shills in the audience, some key phrases that were used, some baseline questions and answers that could establish a pattern. Watching Maurice work in person, though, he couldn't help but be impressed. There were people in the audience he felt certain were strangers to the man, and yet the psychic seemed able to tell them things that were very personal to them. He stayed away from stock pronouncements like "You're going to meet a tall dark stranger," or "You're going on a long trip," or "You're going to come into a great deal of money." At one point, he even reduced an older couple to tears by telling them he was communicating with their deceased daughter.

"Isn't he wonderful?" Nicole said, pressing her shoulder against Keough's.

"He's impressive," he had to admit. "Why isn't he on TV?"

"He won't do television," she said. "He's turned down many lucrative offers."

"Is he wealthy?"

"No," she said. "He gets by, and lives simply. He does this for the love of it."

"Uh-oh," Keough said, "he's coming this way."

"I told him not to read you," she said. "I said we didn't want to give away who we were."

"Thank you for that."

He came down the aisle toward them but only nodded benignly

as he went by. He did, however, let his hand rest on Keough's shoulder for a moment—and then suddenly he clamped down on it almost painfully. He backed up a step and looked into Keough's face.

"You've lost someone recently."

Keough frowned.

"No. I think I'd know—"

"Yes, you have," Maurice said, looking off into the distance at something only he could see. "A friend, an older man."

Jack Roswell! How could he have known that?

"He wants you to know he doesn't forgive you, because there is nothing to forgive." Maurice patted Keough's shoulder and looked into his eyes. "Do you understand this?"

"Uh . . . yes."

"Very good." He started to walk away, then stopped again and looked at him. "Are you a Gemini?" he asked.

"Uh, no," Keough said, "Virgo, I think."

Maurice stared at Keough for a few more moments, then shook his head and said, "No, I see Gemini—are you a twin, by any chance?"

Keough laughed and said, "No, I think one of me is enough."

Maurice patted him on the shoulder and said, "See me after the seminar is over, please," and moved on.

"What was that about?" Keough asked Nicole.

"I don't know," she said. "I guess we'll find out later."

Thirty-nine

THERE WAS NO applause when Maurice announced he was finished. People filed out of the room in a hushed, somewhat stunned silence. One man snickered nervously, as if trying to prove he hadn't been impressed with the demonstration.

Finally, only Keough and Busby were left, and they joined Maurice in the front of the room.

"What was that about, Maurice?" Keough asked. "Were you trying to use me to—"

"Would you like a drink?" the psychic asked. "I can always use a drink after a session. We can talk in the bar."

"I'd really like to know—"

Someone walked in, presumably a staff member, and called out, "Are you finished with this room? There's another seminar scheduled."

Maurice looked at Keough and raised his eyebrows.

"Okay," Keough said, "let's go to the bar."

Maurice knew the way through the maze of corridors and led the way. They did not encounter Jeter, but Keough decided the younger man was off sulking somewhere. He was going to have to have a talk with him about Nicole Busby, but that was for later.

The hotel bar was not doing a brisk business at midday, so they had their pick of tables. An attractive middle-aged waitress came over and greeted Maurice familiarly.

"Back again, honey?" she asked. "You must have been reading my mind. I was thinking I needed a big tipper."

"Ah, the lovely Julianna," Maurice said, obviously recalling the woman's name, as she was not wearing a name tag. "I am in dire need of sustenance, my dear."

"Gin and tonic, right?"

"How sweet of you to remember. And please bring my friends what they'd like."

"Diet Coke," Keough said.

"I'll have the same," Busby echoed.

"Comin' up," Julianna said, executing a neat turn and heading for the bar. Maurice admired her sturdy derriere all the way.

Maurice sat back and began to massage his temples with both hands.

"Headache?" Busby asked.

"I usually have one after a demonstration," he said. "Especially if I see something . . . disturbing."

"And when was that?" Keough asked. "When you looked at me?"

Maurice brought his hands down as the waitress returned with their drinks. He flirted with her some more, and when she withdrew, he turned his attention to Keough.

"So you are not a twin?" the older man asked.

"No," Keough said, "and I don't know any."

"And not a Gemini?"

"Virgo," Keough said. "August twenty-fourth. That's Virgo, right?"

"Just barely," Busby said.

Maurice sipped his drink with obvious enjoyment and then said, "I don't know why I'm seeing Gemini when I look at you, and . . . danger. You need to be very careful in the coming weeks."

"Careful of what?"

"You're working on something—both of you are—that will bring you into harm's way."

That was the kind of statement Keough expected from a self-proclaimed psychic. Knowing they were both in law enforcement, it was a pretty safe bet.

"That's not one of your most impressive observations, Maurice."

"Perhaps not," the man said, "but I'm speaking about more danger than usual."

"From where?"

Maurice sipped his drink again, then leaned back and said, "Gemini."

"That's not telling me much."

"I'm sorry," Maurice said, "I can only tell you what I see."

"And that is?"

"Darkness . . . danger . . ." The man shrugged helplessly, finished his drink, and signaled the waitress for another. "But I was right about your friend, wasn't I?"

"I did have a friend die recently."

"Diabetes."

Surprised, Keough said, "Yes, he had—"

"No," Maurice said, "you have diabetes. You need to take better care of yourself."

Keough sipped his Coke, then said to Busby, "I better go and find Marc."

"Time to get back to work?" she asked.

"That's up to you," he said. "This is your afternoon."

"I'll be here talking to Maurice," she said. "When you find your partner, come and get me."

Keough nodded, then looked at Maurice. He was slightly shaken by the fact that the man knew about his diabetes. Busby didn't know, so there was no way she could have told him.

"Thanks for an interesting afternoon."

"My pleasure, Detective," Maurice said. "I'm only sorry I couldn't tell you more about that danger."

"Yeah," Keough said, "so am I."

The three of them were walking across the parking lot to the car when both Jeter and Keough's cell phones rang.

"Not me," Busby said.

Keough groaned, took his phone from his pocket, and answered it.

"Keough."

"It's me," Harriet Connors said. "We found him."

"Shit," he said, and then added, "Well, we expected it."

"Yeah," she said, "I'll tell that to the family."

"Angel pin?"

"Yup," she said. "That makes it official. Expect yours pretty soon . . . unless you can stop him first."

"This can't be coincidence, can it?" he asked. "I mean, they've got to be working together, don't they? Coordinating their efforts?"

"Don't ask me," she replied, "ask your friend the profiler."

"Damn," he said.

"I've got to go. Stay in touch."

"Yeah."

He ended the call and tucked the phone back into his jacket pocket. He had stopped walking when he answered it. Jeter had continued on and was now standing by his car, engrossed in conversation. Agent Busby had remained at Keough's side.

"Chicago?" she asked.

"Yes, they found their fourth victim, angel pin and all."

"Too bad."

"You heard my end," he said to her. "What do you think? Two serial killers with roughly the same MO operating this close to each other?"

"Anything's possible," she said. "Could still be one, driving back and forth."

"Killing boys there and girls here?"

"That is puzzling," she said. "They'll usually stick to one or the other."

"Unless somebody's writing a new chapter in your profiling book."

She looked glum and said, "That's also possible."

He was watching Jeter while he talked to Busby. The young

detective terminated his call and pocketed his phone, then turned and waved to them. They walked over to join him by his car.

"They found her," he said.

"What?" Keough said.

"Who?" Busby asked. "Another one?"

"No," Jeter said. "Well, maybe."

"Denise Proctor?" Keough asked.

"Yeah."

"Where?"

"On her block, apparently."

"Dead?" Busby asked.

Jeter nodded.

"Angel pin?"

"I don't know," he told her, then looked at Keough. "The sergeant wants us on the scene."

"Fine. Let's go."

Jeter looked at Busby.

"Well, we can't leave her here," Keough said.

"No," Jeter said, "of course not."

"Then let's go, Marc," Keough said. "This is our chance to find out if this is victim number four, or an isolated incident."

And if it wasn't victim four, he wondered, then what? The task force would back off? Who would hunt for Denise's killer, then?

Forty

WHEN THEY ARRIVED at Musick Avenue, the street was once again clogged with police cars, but this time they were several houses down. There was also a medical examiner's van and a forensics unit, which was never a good sign. In addition, the neighbors had crowded around to find out what was going on.

Keough told Jeter to pull up in front of the Keith house and they walked the rest of the way. As they approached the other house, Sgt. Dan Henry came out of the front door and spotted them.

"Oh good," he said, "all three of you."

Keough ignored the sarcasm.

"Where is she?"

"Out back," Henry said. "Come on through and I'll show you."

They entered the house and walked through. It was almost identical to the Keith house, except it had a garage in the back. This was where all of the activity was centered.

Keough followed Henry across the yard to the garage, where Detective Berkery was standing talking to both the ME's men and the forensic unit's. Keough assumed the other members of the task force were canvassing. All of the men he saw were wearing white latex gloves.

He entered the garage behind Henry, pulling on his own gloves, which he produced from his pocket, and looked around. Since the ME's men were leisurely talking to John Berkery, he assumed they hadn't removed the body.

"Where is she?" he asked.

"In there." Henry pointed to an old white refrigerator.

"Christ," he said, and approached. It was an outdated model, almost an antique, with a big silver handle. There was powder residue on the handle, which meant that the forensics team had already gone over it.

On the floor just in front of the refrigerator was a stripe of grease or oil. He opened the door and saw Denise was inside, curled up in an unnatural-looking fetal position. He squatted rather than knelt, in order to avoid getting oil on his pants. Hearing a sharp intake of breath behind him, he turned and saw Nicole Busby with her hands over her mouth.

"Get her out of here, Marc."

Jeter took her by the shoulders, turned her around, and walked her out.

"Some FBI agent," Berkery scoffed.

"She's a profiler," Keough snapped at him. "She's not used to seeing bodies."

Berkery grew quiet.

"She must have opened it and crawled inside to play," Henry said, "and it closed behind her, locking her in."

Keough crouched down to inspect the body without touching it. There were bruises on her upper arms, and ligature marks on her wrists. He could see only one side of her face, but it was damaged. He could feel by the coldness that the old refrigerator still worked.

"She was dead when they put her in there."

"What?" Henry asked.

Keough stood up and faced the sergeant.

"The ME will tell you she was dead before somebody put her in there. Tried to pose her, make it look as if she'd curled up and died after being locked in."

"How can you tell that?" Berkery asked.

"Read the ME's report."

"What do you mean?"

"Shut up!" Henry snapped at Berkery. "So you're saying she was murdered?" he asked Keough.

"That's what I'm saying."

"By our guy?"

"No."

"Why not?"

"He strangles," Keough said; "he doesn't bludgeon or beat. This girl was beaten to death."

"Shit! What if there's a pin?"

"When the ME's men take her out, you won't find an angel pin on her. I'm sure of that."

"He could be wrong, Sarge," Berkery said.

"Yeah," Henry said, "he could be."

But they all knew he wasn't.

Keough stepped outside the garage, followed by Henry. He walked over to where Agent Busby was standing, trying to catch her breath.

"You okay?"

"That poor girl," she said by way of answer. "She must have been terrified, being locked in there."

"I'm pretty sure she was already dead," Keough said.

"You mean . . . someone killed her and put her in there?"

"That's exactly what I mean."

"B—but . . . that's not the pattern."

"Don't worry," he said, "your profiling is not in danger. This isn't our doer."

"So you say," Henry said from behind him.

Keough turned. "I don't want to argue the point, Sergeant. If the ME says I'm wrong, I'll admit it."

"That's big of you."

Keough realized the man was speaking from frustration, so he cut him some slack.

"Who found her?" he asked.

"The lady of the house," Henry said. "She's inside. Came out to put some meat in the fridge and got the shock of her life."

"I'll bet," Busby said.

"The locals got the call, had the girl's description on their clip-boards. They called us."

"We canvassing?"

"As we speak. Look, Keough, if you're right, we got two ways to go."

"And they are?"

"Turn it over, or pick up the stepfather. If it's not our guy, it's got to be him."

"Why?"

"You saw his sheet."

"He's a wife beater," Keough said. "That doesn't mean he killed the girl."

"So you're saying he didn't do it, and our guy didn't do it?" Berkery asked.

Keough hadn't seen him come out of the garage; he turned to face him.

"I'm saying let's see what the ME has to say before we jump to any conclusions." He turned back to Sergeant Henry. "You mind if I talk to the woman who found her?"

"Be my guest, if you can get more than two words out of her."

Keough looked at Nicole. "Will you come with me?"

"I—I'm not at my best interviewing witnesses," she admitted.

"I just want to have a woman with me," he said. "It might put her at ease."

She shrugged. "Whatever I can do to help."

Keough said to Henry, "I'd like to know when the ME gets here."

"Fine," Henry said, and turned to go back into the garage, taking Berkery with him.

"What about me?" Jeter asked.

"Stay with them," Keough said, jerking his head toward the garage.

"They may not want me."

"You're one of them."

Jeter held his hand out and waggled it. "That's open for debate."

"Stick with them unless they chase you away," Keough said, removing his gloves and tucking them away in his pocket. "I'd like to know what they talk about when I'm not there."

"Okay, Joe."

"Agent Busby?"

She took a deep breath and followed him.

Forty-one

HAVING BUSBY ALONG just barely helped. The woman who had found Denise Proctor's body in her refrigerator was still near hysterics when Keough and Nicole approached her. Her name was Gerda Hoffs, and she was a sixtyish, sturdily built German woman with a hint of an accent.

She told Keough she had heard about Denise being missing and was sorry, because she was such a nice little girl. Quieter, she said, since her mother had married "rhat" Larry Keith, but, oh my, still such a sweet girl.

"I wish I didn't haf this extra meat," she said to him.

"Why is that, Mrs. Hoffs?"

"Then I would not haf gone out to the garage and maybe somebody else would haf found her."

"Like your husband?"

"Mr. Hoffs has been dead many years," she said. "I lif alone."

Then who else, Keough wondered, would have found her out there?

"Joe?"

He turned and saw Jeter sticking his head into the kitchen from the back door.

"Yep?"

"ME's here. He's going to examine the body."

"I'm on my way."

Keough saw Nicole Busby swallow as she stood to follow him.

"Nicole, why don't you stay with Mrs. Hoffs and have some tea."

"Ach, I am a bad host," Mrs. Hoffs said, preparing to heave her bulk from her chair.

"No, ma'am," Keough said, "Agent Busby can make the tea."

"Yes," Busby said. "All right."

Keough figured that would keep her out of the garage and take her mind off the body of the little girl. She'd be seeing it enough in her dreams as it was.

"Mrs. Hoffs, why do you have such an old refrigerator in the garage?"

"It was our first," she said, "Mr. Hoffs and me. And it still works. I could never bear to part with it."

He nodded, turned, and followed Jeter back to the garage.

"Setting's high on this refrigerator," the ME said. "It's gonna make time of death kind of difficult."

"We know when she went missing, Doc," Henry said. "Guessing a time of death ain't going to be hard."

"Fine," the ME replied, "just so you know."

Keough knew the man who had his head stuck in the fridge. The perpetually cheerful "Smiley" Donaldson was apparently still the ME in St. Louis. And, as usual, he was thorough—got into the refrigerator as much as he could to examine the girl.

"Somebody pounded on her pretty good," he said almost to himself. "Tied her hands, too."

"But they weren't tied when she was found," Henry said.

He slid out of the fridge and turned to face them. "She was dead when she went in there. Wouldn't be any reason for her to be tied anymore."

"So somebody killed her and hid her in there," Henry said.

"That's my guess," the ME said, pulling off his rubber gloves. It was then he noticed Keough. "That you, Keough?"

"It's me, Doc."

Donaldson tucked the gloves away and shook hands.

"I heard you went to a better place."

"Makes me sound dead, Doc."

"You workin' on this?"

It was Dan Henry who answered the question.

"He's with the FB—um, a national serial killer task force, Dr. Donaldson. He's . . . assisting us with the investigation."

"Was the beating she received the cause of death?" Keough asked.

"I can't say for sure what killed her, but the amount of damage to her face and head looks bad enough to have done it. I don't see any obvious fatal wounds."

"Does she have, um, anything on her clothes?" Keough asked.

"Like what?"

Keough looked at Henry, who shook his head.

"You mean the pin?" the doctor asked, surprising everyone.

"How do you know about any pins, Dr. Donaldson?" Sergeant Henry asked.

"Please, Sergeant," Donaldson said, "I'm not stupid. I examined two of the other three girls. I saw the angel pins."

"But you haven't said anything to anyone?"

"As I said," Donaldson repeated, "I'm not stupid. I didn't see anything about them in the newspaper, so I assumed you held that information back."

"I'm sorry," Henry said, "it was stupid of me to think you hadn't noticed. Um, did she have an angel on her clothes?"

"I didn't notice," the doctor said, not bothering to comment on the sergeant's stupidity quotient.

Keough looked at the man to see if he was making a joke. Apparently not. The usually jovial doctor did not seem to like Sergeant Henry.

"We can examine her clothing when we get her out of there. Can we have her now?"

"Yes," Henry said, "you can have her."

The ME nodded to his men, who had been idly standing around for quite a while. They ground out their cigarettes on the heels of their shoes, stowed the butts in their pockets, then snapped on their gloves and moved toward the refrigerator.

Keough, Henry, and the others backed away to allow the men to do their job. Outside the garage, Keough noticed quite a few people in the yard—both in and out of uniform—many of whom looked to have nothing to do. He would have shooed most of them away, but it wasn't his crime scene; it was Henry's.

The ME's men got Denise out of the refrigerator, placed the body on a gurney, and wheeled it out of the garage. The coolness of the refrigerator had delayed rigor, so they had no trouble placing her on her back.

"Hold up," Henry said.

He and Keough moved forward to examine the girl's clothing. There was no sign of an angel pin.

"John," Henry said to Detective Berkery, "check the fridge."

Berkery went back inside, then reappeared almost instantly.

"Nothing, Sarge."

"Dr. Donaldson, was she strangled?" Henry asked.

Donaldson looked as if he was about to object, having made his initial examination, but instead he stepped forward to have a look without touching her.

"She doesn't appear to have been," he said. "I'll know better when I get her to the morgue."

"Okay, then," Henry said. "Take her."

"Thank you." Donaldson nodded to Keough, then followed the gurney from the backyard.

Henry looked at Keough, as if waiting for him to say something. Keough remained silent, also waiting.

"Not our guy," the sergeant finally said.

"I guess not."

Forty-two

ONCE THE BODY had been removed, people started to drift out of the backyard. The crowd in front of the house also began to disperse.

Keough went back into the garage, and that's where Jeter and Busby found him, crouched down near the still-open refrigerator, staring at it.

"Here you are," Jeter said. "We were wondering where you were. We waited by the car for a while."

"What are you doing?" Busby asked.

"Thinking," Keough said, "just thinking." He looked at Jeter. "Did you hear where Denise's mother is? Does she know she's been found?"

"Henry sent Jim House over to tell her."

"Why him?"

"He said House was better at breaking that kind of news than either he or Berkery."

Keough turned his head and stared at the refrigerator again for a few moments. He leaned over and ran his fingers underneath the front of it. Certainly enough room for something to have rolled underneath. He wondered if the forensics team had moved it.

Probably not, with Denise still in it, and certainly not since. Some-body's oversight. He stood up and looked at them.

"What else did you hear?"

Jeter hesitated, casting a sidelong look at Agent Busby.

"Go ahead, Marc. You can talk in front of Nicole."

"Sergeant Henry thinks if he can nail the stepfather for this, maybe he can close out the other cases, too."

"And what happens when the real killer hits again?" Busby asked.

Jeter shrugged, still not comfortable talking in front of her, and said, "He said that, uh, maybe he could pass it off as a copycat."

"And how did Berkery react to that?"

"I think he's willing to go along."

"Maybe House wouldn't go along, and that's why he was sent to talk to the mother," Keough suggested.

"Could be."

"But why would they discuss it in front of you?" he asked.

Jeter cast his eyes downward and said, "Well, I wasn't really in the garage. I was just outside."

"They didn't know you were there?"

"Not at all."

Keough smiled and said, "Good move, kid."

Jeter seemed pleased by the praise. Keough knew the young man wanted to repair the rift that was obviously between them because of what had happened in East St. Louis. Keough just wasn't sure it was completely repairable, but this was a start.

"Should we get out of here?" Jeter asked.

"I want you to help me with something first."

"What?"

"I want to get a look underneath and behind this refrigerator."

"Sure?"

"Let's get it away from the wall first."

Together, they managed to ease it away from the wall. The marks left on the dirty floor indicated it certainly had not been moved recently. Keough crouched down again, not only looking but running his hand over the floor. Then he stood up and slapped his empty hands together to get the dirt and dust off.

Next, they tilted the appliance to one side and then the other.

They could see that the floor beneath it was clean, except for some dust, a couple of coins, and gum and candy wrappers.

"Okay," Keough said as they settled the refrigerator back against the wall, "now we can go."

As the refrigerator touched the floor, the door popped open. Keough closed it, then tried to open it without touching the handle. He did it.

"Son of a bitch," he said, slamming it shut. "If she'd been alive when the door closed, she could have gotten out easily."

As they walked across the yard and back to the car, Busby asked, "What were you looking for?"

"Nothing in particular," Keough said. "Just wanted to be thorough."

As they reached the front of the house, Keough paused before they reached Jeter's car.

"What's wrong?"

Keough rubbed his face with both hands. "If Henry's going to try to pin this on the stepfather, along with the other three murders, he's going to have to find the guy first."

"That shouldn't be hard," Jeter said. "He'll either be home or at work. He doesn't know that he might be arrested."

"Henry can't arrest him, not yet," Keough said. "He doesn't have enough hard evidence, but he might take him in to sweat him a bit."

"May I ask a question?" Agent Busby asked.

"Sure."

"What happens if there's another girl taken while he's sweating the stepfather?"

"That'd put a crimp in his plan," Keough said.

"What if it is him?" Jeter asked.

"It's not."

"What if—"

"I'm not even convinced he did Denise."

"Then who did?"

"That's what I'm thinking about."

"You want to talk to the mother?" Jeter asked.

"Chicago found their fourth victim today," Keough said. "That means we should be finding one within the next couple of days. Right, Nicole?"

"That's the profile."

"In all the excitement here, I didn't get a chance to apprise him of that fact," Keough said. "I think I'll go and do that now."

Jeter looked at Busby and said, "I guess we're heading back to Clayton."

Busby shrugged and started for the car.

Forty-three

IN THE CAR, Busby said, "I don't understand why Sergeant Henry would want to try to close this case out falsely."

"He may not be thinking of it that way," Keough said. "He may be trying to buy time."

Jeter cleared his throat, kept his eyes on the road.

"You don't think so?" Keough asked.

"Joe, it sounded to me like he and Berkery just wanted to be rid of this thing and get back to their routine."

"Could they do that?" Busby asked.

Keough said, "I suppose they could close this out, using Larry Keith as a scapegoat. If the killer starts up again, they can pass him off as a copycat, and if another task force needs to be formed, Henry's already done his bit. They'll hand it off to someone else."

"So he goes back to his regular squad," Busby said.

"Exactly."

"With a clear conscience?" She looked at him over her shoulder, turning toward the backseat.

He smiled and said, "I never said that, Nicole."

* * *

When they got back to Clayton, Keough found Henry at his desk, talking on the phone. The sergeant looked at him when he hung up.

"Keith's on the lam."

"What?"

"Not at work, not at home, according to his wife," Henry said. "I've got men out looking for him."

"I thought you were going to hand this off to Major Case if it wasn't our boy?"

"Keith may be our boy, Keough," Henry said. "In fact, until I'm proven wrong and you're proven right, I'm going to go on that assumption."

"You're making a big mistake, Sarge."

"Am I?"

"Call your counterpart in Chicago," he suggested. "They got another one."

"And so do we," Henry said.

"You'll have another missing girl within the next two days," Keough said. "What are you going to do when she shows up dead?"

"Hopefully, by then it'll be somebody else's problem," the man said.

Up to that point, Keough had considered the possibility that Marc Jeter might have misinterpreted something he heard the sergeant say. Now he knew that the young man had understood correctly.

"What are you looking at?" Henry demanded abruptly.

"Nothing, I, uh—"

"I'm getting pressure, Keough," Henry said. "The mayor and the chief want this thing solved. No, that's not right. They want a solution, and that's what I'm going to give them." He slammed some folders down on his desk. "I never asked for this damn assignment!"

Keough had nothing to say to Sgt. Dan Henry. The man was obviously in a position that did not suit him. Whoever had assigned it to him should have known that. He was probably a good cop; he was just out of his element.

"Why don't you ask them to replace you?" he asked, even before he realized he was going to. If he could have, he would have caught the words in his hands and put them right back where they'd come from.

"With who?" Henry asked. "You?"

"No, not me," Keough said. "I'm not after your job. Maybe they should have put someone higher up in charge. That's all I—"

"Look," Henry said, suddenly backpedaling, "I don't know what you think you heard, or who you heard it from, but I'm going to solve this thing, understand? Me and my men, with or without your help. Got it?"

"I've got it, Sergeant," Keough said. "I understand perfectly."

"Good," Henry said. "Now that we've got that out of the way, why don't we both get back to work."

"Are you handing this over to Major Case?" Keough asked.

"I'll decide that after I get the ME's report," Henry said. "And after I've talked with Larry Keith."

"You have to find him first," Keough reminded him.

"We will."

"Okay," Keough said, "I'll leave you to it, then."

On his way out, he heard Henry open a desk drawer and then slam it viciously.

Keough went down the hall to sit alone and use his cell phone. He dialed Harriet's number, but when she didn't answer on the eighth ring, he hung up. Why hadn't she had her message on? He'd try her again later. He wanted to compare his experience here in St. Louis with what she was experiencing in Chicago. Hopefully, their task force up north was being run by a stronger, more confident man.

He walked down the hall to wash garage dirt from his hands, then returned to the office. Both Jeter and Nicole Busby were sitting in chairs in front of the desk, their faces somber.

"You talk to Sergeant Henry?" Jeter asked.

"Yes," Keough said, seating himself behind the desk. "He said he and his team—you included, I suppose—are going to solve this case."

"Yeah," Jeter said, "by pinning it on Larry Keith."

"Maybe he's guilty," Busby said.

Both men looked at her.

"He's violent, has a history with children—I don't know about his own childhood, but I'd be willing to bet on what I'd find."

"It doesn't matter," Keough said. "It's all conjecture until the ME's report comes in."

"When will that be?" Busby asked.

"Not until tomorrow morning, I'm sure," Keough said. "Why don't you two young people go . . . go home." He'd been about to say, "Go get something to eat together," but he did not want to put either of them on the spot.

"What are you going to do?" Jeter asked.

"Try to get hold of my partner in Chicago and see how her case is going," he said. "They got a new one today."

"I remember," Jeter said.

As they started to leave, Keough was suddenly struck by an idea. He said, "Wait a minute," causing both of them to halt.

"What's up?" Jeter asked.

"Close the door."

Jeter closed the door and then sat back down.

"Nicole, how much do you know about the three Chicago cases—up to now, that is?"

"Everything, I suppose."

"Your files appeared complete?" he asked, remembering the sketchy files he'd received at first from the task force.

"I believe so," she said. "Do you think the Chicago PD might have withheld valuable information, like they did here?"

"I don't know," Keough said. "My partner is not receiving all the cooperation she would like, but maybe you got more than she did."

"My director contacted both departments and asked for all the information they had for the benefit of profiling," she said. "I believe they complied."

"Okay," Keough said, "maybe both departments were impressed by that communication, and then the individual task force commanders decided to give us a hard time on the spot. Whatever . . . What have you ascertained so far about both killers?"

"I haven't written up my report yet."

"Surely you must have made some observations on both?"

"Well, yes, but—"

"One killer or two?" he asked. "Your expert opinion."

She hesitated a moment, then said, "Two."

"Why?"

"Several reasons," she replied. "Girls and boys, for one, and the Chicago children come from a different economic class than these."

"Poorer?"

"Those families are well below the income of these," she said. "There are reasons for both choices, and those reasons have to come from two different minds, two different backgrounds."

"What else?"

"Well, logistically, it just doesn't make sense to me that a killer would drive back and forth. He'd want to establish a home base, someplace he could be comfortable between killings."

"And there couldn't be two home bases?"

"Two home bases," she said, "two killers . . . in my expert opinion."

"Okay," Keough said, "then we're in agreement."

"You and a profiler?" Jeter was skeptical.

"Maybe just this once," Keough said. He looked at Busby. "I'm going to go through this same sequence with my partner tonight. Thanks for your help. When do you go back to Washington?"

"When I'm ready to finish my report."

"And you're not yet?"

She hesitated, then looked at Jeter and put her hand on his arm.

"Marc, may I talk to Detective Keough alone?"

Her use of Jeter's first name while addressing Keough by his rank was perfect—and the touch on the arm didn't hurt, either. The young detective melted.

"Uh, sure," he said, standing up.

"Wait for me outside and we'll go for a drink."

The reward. Do women learn this stuff, or does it come naturally? Keough wondered.

It had the desired effect. Jeter's face brightened and he was bouncing on the balls of his feet as he left the room, closing the door behind him.

"What's on your mind?' Keough asked.

"You know that I'm here to redeem myself," she said. "I don't have a lot of fans in the Bureau. Frankly, I think they're looking to cut me loose."

"Why are you telling me this?"

"Because you know what happened with the I-Eighty killer," she said. "You know I fucked that up. Why would you listen to me now?"

"You're smart, Nicole," he said.

"That's it?"

"Honestly?"

"Please."

"There's no one else here whose opinion I put any credence in."

"Marc?"

Keough still had doubts about Jeter, but he couldn't tell Busby why.

"Not in this instance."

"Why not?"

"Because he's smitten with you," he said. "It's clouding his judgment."

She was taken aback. "I'm sorry. I didn't mean—"

"Forget it," he said. "It's not your fault. He can't help himself."

"I haven't encouraged him."

"Maybe not, but you just played him, didn't you? To get him to leave the room?"

"Well . . . yes . . ." She was embarrassed.

"What's going to happen when you go for that drink?"

"I don't know," she said. "I didn't think—"

"Didn't think past getting him out of the room," he said. "Look, just let him down easy, will you? He's no good to me crushed."

"So . . . I was just the lesser evil here?"

"You wanted me to be honest," he said. "But . . . if I didn't think you knew what you were doing, I wouldn't have asked for your opinion at all."

"Well," she said, "thanks for that." She stood up. "You don't mind if I stay for a few more days?"

"A few more days is what it's going to take to stand this entire thing on its head," he said. "I can't really count on anyone out there, except Marc . . . so stay. I can use the extra brain."

"Thanks," she said. "I'll see you in the morning."

"Bright and early," Keough said. "Hopefully, the autopsy report will be here—if I get to see it."

"Good night, then."

"Night."

As the door closed, he picked up his cell phone to try Harriet again, but then he got an idea. He opened one of the new files Henry'd had somebody drop on his desk. Sure enough, there was a sheet of contact numbers inside. He found the number he wanted and dialed.

"Dr. Donaldson, please," he said.

Forty-four

GABRIEL FINISHED HIS dinner and arranged the plates and utensils in the dishwasher. There was a time when he'd enjoyed eating alone, but that was no longer the case. In fact, he no longer wished to be alone at all. He yearned for someone to complete him. It was the dreams, he knew, and perhaps the reason for killing the little girls. Maybe if he found his other half, the dreams would stop, and there'd be no reason for any more girls to die.

He went to his parents' bedroom, which he had not touched since their death two years before. To him, it was like entering a mausoleum. It was hushed and still, smelling ever so faintly of his mother's perfume, his father's cologne.

He went to the closet, opened it, and took out the metal box. As a child, he was told never to touch it. His father would only tell him that it contained "important papers." He took the box with him and left the room, for he did not like being there.

His parents were liars. He knew that, felt it. He'd had suspicions for most of his life that he had been adopted. He never asked them, but discrepancies popped up from time to time, like eye color, hair color, and, more specifically, blood type. He'd been injured in his early teens and had needed a transfusion. Neither of his parents had been able to provide blood. That was when he really knew they were liars—but still, he did not ask. He was the only child of a wealthy couple, who doted on him, gave him everything he could ever want. What was there to complain about?

Emptiness.

He took the metal box to the dining room table and set it down. He had no idea what was in it. His parents' lawyer had been the last person to open it, and that was to remove the will. When he asked Gabriel if he wanted to see what else was in it, the young man had said no. He told the lawyer just to return the box to the closet in his parents' room.

Now his hands shook as he reached to open it. Would it contain the answers to all his questions?

He got himself a drink—the good scotch—sat down, and opened the box. He was not surprised to see some money in there, but he put it aside without even counting it. His parents had left him a lot of money.

There were some old photos, which seemed to be of him when he was younger. In most of them, he was with his mother; in some, he was with his father; and in some others, he was alone. In a good many, he was smiling—the perfect picture of a happy child. Even then he'd been able to fool his parents, as well as everyone around him.

He set the photos aside, intending to dispose of them later. He found some stocks, and paperwork that looked legal, having to do with his father's ball-bearing business. He had inherited the company—one of the largest medical-supply companies in the country—and had promptly sold it, to the utter amazement of the members of the board. He understood that the new owner had come in and cleaned house, causing most of those shocked men and women to lose their jobs. He didn't care.

He set the paperwork aside and kept digging. He found a waxed envelope with some stamps inside. He assumed they were of value. He put them with the money, since he'd probably sell them at his earliest convenience. He found a few military medals. He knew his father had been in Vietnam, but he'd rarely listened when the old man started telling stories. He'd get rid of them, too.

He was almost to the bottom of the box. Most of the items were either of sentimental value—he'd throw those away—or monetary value—he'd cash those in. There was nothing in the box that he was sentimental about, hardly anything he was even interested in— until he got to the very bottom.

He found an old brown envelope, slightly stained, stuck to the metal bottom. He pried it loose and removed it. It was the last item, leaving the box empty. He set the box aside and put the envelope on the table. This, he felt certain, contained the answer to a question always gnawing away deep inside him. The question he hadn't dared ask himself until a few months ago, when the dreams started.

The front of the envelope was blank. He turned it over and looked at the back. It had either never been sealed or had come open over the years. Suddenly, his heart calmed and his hands stopped trembling.

He opened the envelope and slid out a piece of paper. He unfolded it, smoothed it out, and read the contents. It was a birth certificate for a male child born in Chicago at Roseland Hospital on May 25, 1974. The child was named Michael, and the parents were listed as Edward and Sally Shur. The name Delacorte did not appear at all.

Forty-five

May 3, 2004

WHEN KEOUGH ROSE the next morning, he turned on the TV just to have some noise while he showered and dressed. He had it tuned to a local station, so when he got out of the shower, he heard them talking about the arrest of a suspect, who had been charged with four "area" murders. He came charging out of the bathroom and stood there dripping on the rug while he listened to the story.

"A local man has been arrested and charged with the murder of four area girls ranging in age from eight to ten. We go live to Mandy Moon in Clayton."

"Thank you, Kathryn." Mandy Moon went on explain that early that morning a man named Lawrence Keith had been taken from his home in Green Park, arrested, and charged with the murder of the four girls, the latest of which was his own stepdaughter. She said they did not have any further information but that they'd be following the story throughout the day.

"Now back to the studio."

Keough switched to other channels and found two more of them covering the story, although not offering any more information. He wondered if Fox or CNN had picked it up. When he switched to them, he found it on Fox—not being covered live as yet, but in text beneath the picture, as many of the news stations were now doing with breaking stories.

He grabbed his cell and dialed Harriet in Chicago. She had not heard anything about it.

"I'll turn on my TV now," she said, "We got plenty of coverage here yesterday on our case, but an arrest in yours is going to blow us off the screen."

"I've got to get dressed and get down there," Keough said. "I don't know how they can make this arrest without finding an angel pin on Denise. Obviously, Sergeant Henry is trying to give the mayor what he wants."

"Maybe it's a ploy," she said, "to throw the real killer off."

"If it is, and they release the info about the angel pins, somebody might start to wonder about the Chicago killer."

"You're right," she said. "They're still holding the pin back here. Wait a minute. Here comes something . . . Jesus Christ, Joe! Do you get WGN?"

"Yeah," he said, grabbing the remote, "wait a minute."

"Police here in Chicago say they have been coordinating their investigation with a task force in St. Louis that has been investigating similar killings there, only of young boys instead of young girls. And since an arrest has been made there, they are exploring the possibility that the killer may be the same man. In fact, we have word about the similarity between the cases, specifically involving the presence of angel pins. . . ."

Keough was heading for the door when his cell phone rang. He took the call on the way to the elevator.

"Joe, have you seen—" Nicole Busby began.

"I'm on my way to the elevator," he said, arriving there. "I'm heading down there now."

The doors opened and Nicole was standing inside, looking back at him.

"Me, too," she said.

They decided to go in one car and took his rental.

"I can't believe this," he said, guiding the car onto Highway 40. "I never thought he'd do it."

"Why not?"

He shook his head. "I just misjudged him, I guess."

"What's the real killer going to do when he hears this?" Nicole asked.

"You're the profiler," he said. "You tell me."

"Well, one of two things. He'll either stop or . . ."

"Or what?" he asked after a moment.

"He'll increase his efforts so that Lawrence Keith doesn't get the credit for his accomplishments."

"That's the part that has me scared," Keough said.

"Well, you'll just have to catch him before that can happen."

"Your confidence in me is overwhelming," Keough said. "I'd love to catch him, but I haven't got a thing to go on. No evidence, no eyewitnesses . . ."

"There's got to be something, Joe," Nicole said.

"Oh, I agree with you, Agent Busby," he replied. "There's got to be something. . . ."

Forty-six

THE JOINT WAS jumping when they arrived at the task force's office. With Busby in his wake, Keough plowed through the crowd of journalists being held back by cops, trying to get to Sergeant Henry, who was standing at his desk, looking frazzled.

"What the hell do you think you're doing?" he demanded.

"My job, Keough," he said. "I'm getting a killer off the streets."

"You just might be getting Denise Proctor's killer off the streets," Keough said, "but not the killer of the other three girls."

Henry paused to glare at Keough, then opened his desk drawer, took out a glassine envelope, and dropped it on the desk. Inside was an angel pin, identical to the ones Keough had already seen.

"What's that?"

"We found it at the scene."

"In the garage?"

"That's right."

Keough hesitated, then asked, "Where?"

"Under the refrigerator."

Keough saw that Busby was about to speak, and he shook her off.

"Now, if you'll excuse me," Henry said, "I have a press conference downstairs with the mayor and the chief." He paused, then looked at both Keough and Busby. "I'll be sure to mention how much help you both were."

Henry headed for the door. The reporters and cops parted to let him through, then trailed after him as if he were some kind of Pied Piper.

Keough turned and rested his butt on Henry's desk.

"They could not have found an angel pin in that garage," Busby said. "I saw you look under the refrigerator myself—and it hadn't been moved until you moved it."

"I know."

"Then why didn't you say something?"

"This arrest is going to shake things up, Nicole."

"Yes, but how?" she asked. "If the real killer goes on a rampage—"

"Tell me something."

"What?"

"Shouldn't we have heard from him by now?" he asked. "I mean, if we were going to at all?"

"Possibly."

"Probably, right?"

Grudgingly, she said, "Yes."

"And the fact that we haven't may mean we're not dealing with a huge ego here. He doesn't want to challenge us; he just wants to kill."

"That might be true."

"And will that kind of man go on a rampage because somebody's stealing his thunder?"

"Well, no," she said, "he wouldn't care. . . . But what if he's not that type? What if he is planning to contact the police after his fourth victim but just hasn't taken her yet? This might urge him on to take a fourth, fifth, and maybe a sixth."

"The Chicago killer took his fourth already. Ours will probably take one in the next day or so. I can't find him until he does."

"Joe—"

"I can't, Nicole," he said honestly. "We have to wait for him to hit, and when he does, all hell will break loose, and maybe that will be the encouragement he needs to contact the police."

"Yes," she said, "but which police? Will this task force even be here after the press conference?"

Keough rubbed both his hands over his face.

"Okay, maybe I should have told Henry we knew he was lying," he said. "We know he went out and bought an angel pin and planted it, or he just used one from his drawer."

He walked around the desk and looked inside. All the pins were gone, including the one the sergeant had just shown Keough and Nicole.

"He took them with him." He closed the drawer. "Maybe I should have stopped the press conference, but it's too late now. We just have to let this play out and see what happens."

After a moment, she asked, "Was that what you did in Wyoming that time? Let the situation play itself out?"

"No," he said without hesitation, "I forced the issue there. If I hadn't, the girl would have—" He stopped, because the girl had died, after all. "My partner or I might have died."

She looked around the quiet room. Even the civilian, Martha, was gone. Jeter must have been down at the press conference, too, since he was a member of the team.

"Shall we go down and listen?" she asked.

He looked over at a TV stand in the corner. "No," he said. "Let's just watch it here."

Gabriel rose that morning, showered, ate breakfast, and then turned on the TV. His intention today was to make arrangements to fly to Chicago. He thought he'd watch the Weather Channel to see what the conditions were like, but when he got to CNN and saw what they were broadcasting, he stopped, watched, and listened. . . . And when he'd heard enough, he picked up the phone and dialed 911.

The phone on Sergeant Henry's desk rang as the mayor was taking the podium to congratulate the chief, the sergeant, and the other members of the task force.

Keough looked over at the phone, let it ring five or six times, and then—for no reason he could think of—picked it up.

"Task force."

"This is the nine-one-one operator," a woman's voice said. "I have a call for the Serial Killer Task Force?"

"Well, this is the office, but they're all down at the press conference."

"Um, are you a detective?"

"Yes," he said, "I'm Detective Keough, but I'm not—"

"I have a call from a man who says he must speak to someone on the task force."

Keough sat up straight. Nicole noticed and came over to stand by him.

"Did he give you his name?"

"Well . . . sir, he says his name is . . . he says he's not a crank but that his name is . . . the Angel Gabriel."

Forty-seven

KEOUGH THOUGHT FAST.

"Operator, wait three minutes and then put the caller through."

"Yes, sir. Who shall I say—"

"Just put it through."

"Yes, sir."

"And what's your operator number?"

"I'm operator two forty-six, sir."

"Thanks."

Keough hung up the phone, then turned to Nicole.

"When the phone rings, you answer it."

"Who is it going to be?'

"The Angel Gabriel."

"What?"

"That's who he says he is."

"A crank?" she asked. "Or . . . You don't think it's . . . him?"

"It could be."

"W—what am I supposed to say?"

"Feel him out," he said. "You decide if it's him or not."

"And then what?"

"See what you can find out."

"He's not going to tell me anything."

"Of course not," he said. "Use your talents, Nicole. Figure out whatever you can."

"And what do I do if he gets . . . antsy?"

"Then you tell him I just walked in, and you hand the phone to me."

"I—I've never—" She stopped, then lowered her voice, as if she were imparting some great secret. "I've never actually spoken to a serial killer before. Have you?"

"Yes," he said, "one or two."

She shivered, rubbed her arms, then smiled and said, "Actually, it's kind of exciting."

"Just make sure you stay calm and do your job."

"I can't believe—" she began, but the phone rang at that moment, causing her to jump.

Forty-eight

Special Agent Nicole Busby's voice quivered just a bit when she said, "Hello?"

"Who am I speaking to?" a man asked in a nonthreatening tone.

"Agent Nicole Busby, FBI."

"Agent Busby, are you a member of the task force?"

"No. They're all down at the press conference."

"I'm watching that on television now," he said. "They have it all wrong, you know."

"Do they?"

"You know they do," he said. "If you don't know, then you're not a very good FBI agent, are you?"

"Can you prove—"

"I know about the angel pins."

"Yes, but now everyone knows, since it's been broadcast on the news." Her tone had become steady.

"Yes," he said, "but I know about the birthstones on the pins."

Nicole caught her breath, looked at Keough, and nodded. "It's him," she mouthed.

"Agent Busby," the man said, "you sound very young. Tell me, are you a real FBI agent, or just a profiler?"

"What does that matt—"

"I need to speak to someone who is actually a member of the task force," he said, cutting her off. "They're making a huge mistake. If you can't help me, I'll have to try something else to—"

Busby waved at Keough and said, "Wait, wait. Don't hang up. Someone just walked in."

"Well then, put them on, by all means."

She handed the phone to Keough, who propped himself on the edge of the desk, putting his hand on her shoulder to keep her where she was.

"This is Detective Keough," he said. "Who am I speaking to?"

"You know who this is, Detective," the man—Gabriel—said. "Are you a member of the task force?"

"Yes."

"You're lying," Gabriel said. "If you were a member, you would be down at the press conference."

"I am working with the task force," Keough said, "but I'm a member of the Federal Serial Killer Task Force."

"That sounds very important," Gabriel said. "A nationwide task force to search for serial killers?"

"Yes."

"And that makes you an expert?"

"Of sorts."

Gabriel sounded amused. "Tell me: Do you believe I am who I say I am?"

"And who is that?'

"I am Gabriel, the man who killed those three girls."

"Three?"

"Yes," Gabriel said. "I am not responsible for the fourth. Do you believe me?"

"I do."

"Completely?"

"Yes."

"Then you have to tell them," he said. "I did not kill that fourth girl."

"But you are going to kill another one, aren't you?"

"Yes," Gabriel said without hesitation, "of course I am."

"Why?"

"Because it's what I do."

"I'll stop you."

"You'll try," Gabriel said, "because that's what you do."

"Look—"

"Make them believe you, Detective Keough," Gabriel said. "I don't like being blamed for something I didn't do."

Amazingly, Keough had been through something like this once before, in New York. When the Kopykat started to emulate a killer called the Lover, the original turned himself in so that people would believe there was a copycat.

"Gabriel, come on in, turn yourself over to me," Keough said, "and we'll make them believe you."

Gabriel laughed in Keough's ear, a honest, heartfelt laugh. "Detective Keough, you're a funny man. Turn myself in and let them put me away, or execute me, just so they'll believe I didn't kill that fourth girl? That's your job, Detective. You catch whoever killed that girl. I'm going to take care of my fourth girl, and then take a little vacation."

"What? A vacation? Where?"

Gabriel laughed again.

"That's for me to know and you to find out, Mr. Expert."

"A cliché, Gabriel?" Keough said. "We've only spoken for a short time, but already I know that's beneath you."

There was silence—no laughter. He could hear the man breathing.

"I have a family matter to take care of, Detective," Gabriel said. "After that, you'll hear from me again."

"Gabriel, wait! Gabriel—"

Forty-nine

GABRIEL BROKE THE connection and put his cell phone down next to him on the bench. It amused him that people walked by him in the park and yet had no idea who he was or what he was doing. To them, he was just another person out enjoying the park and the fresh air.

He'd lied, of course, about watching the press conference. He didn't have to watch it to know that it was going on. The police thought they had their man. Of course they'd be holding a press conference to tell everyone about it. They'd want to put everyone in St. Louis at ease. In fact, the conference was taking place not far from where he was sitting in Shaw Park. Each June since 1993, this park had filled up with 35,000 people, who came to enjoy Taste of Clayton, local restaurants making their wares available for tasting. Today, there were very few people here, because it was a workday and this part of Clayton was all businesses. At lunchtime, some of them would come out of their cement boxes to get some air, have some food before they went back in. Gabriel had never had to do that, never had to punch a time clock or work in a cement box.

He thought about the profiler he'd spoken to, the young woman, Agent Nicole Busby. He could just imagine what her take on him was. Probably had him pegged as some poor abused child who had grown up warped inside. Nothing could be further from the truth. He'd been treated very well by his parents, who had never laid a hand on him in any inappropriate way. The only time they'd touched him was to hug him and love him, and he'd allowed it because he knew it would get him what he wanted. What they never knew—until the end, that is—was that he could never feel for them what they felt for him. He could tell from the very beginning that they were not his people—and now he had the proof.

The birth certificate was at home, in his bureau drawer. It told him all he needed to know to get started. He was born in Chicago in 1974; his parents were Edward and Sally Shur. His father had kept this birth certificate because he was a man who never threw anything away. "What if I need it?" he'd asked, or "What if something happens?" For a rich man, his father had been remarkably pessimistic. Always afraid something was going to happen that he was not prepared for.

Thanks to his father—his adoptive father—he now knew where to start looking for his people.

There was only one thing he had to do first.

Fifty

KEOUGH HUNG UP the phone and walked to the window, where he looked down on Forsythe Avenue.

"What did he say?" Nicole asked.

Keough folded his arms across his chest.

"He's going to kill his fourth victim and then take a vacation," he said. "He's got some family business to attend to."

"What kind of family business?"

"He didn't say."

"Well . . . what are you going to do now?" she asked.

She turned and looked at the TV, where the mayor was holding the chief by one arm and Sergeant Henry by the other, raising their locked fingers over his head.

Keough turned and looked at the screen, as well. This was not the mayor he had worked for—this was a new one—and from what he had seen and heard on the television, he was more of a politician than the other one ever was. Keough had respected his mayor, but he could never have worked for this man.

"What can I do?" he asked. "When they come back up here I'll tell them about the call."

"They're not going to believe you, Joe."

"That's their problem."

"You mean you're giving up?" Nicole asked. "But this is your job."

Keough turned completely around so he could face her. She looked every year of her twenty-five, judging him with big innocent eyes.

"I'll do my job, Nicole, don't worry."

"And what should I do?"

"Did you learn anything from talking to him?"

"We're dealing with an ego," she said. "What we don't know is which way he's going to go."

"Well, he said he was taking one more," Keough replied, "and I believe him."

"What if he comes back from his . . . his vacation and there's nothing in the newspaper about Denise Proctor being killed by someone else?"

"I don't know," Keough said. "We're just going to have to go one day at a time. First, we've got to get through today, a day when everybody in this squad is celebrating."

"And you're going to burst their bubble."

"I'm going to give them a message, Nicole," he said. "What they do with it is their business."

She frowned and said, "We should have traced that call."

He smiled. "Do you know what number to call to start a trace?"

"No, but—"

"Neither do I, not offhand. Besides, he's too smart for that. My guess is he made the call from a blind cell. We're dealing with an intelligent, clever man who is not smart enough to control his ego."

"That's a profile."

"That's just obvious, Nicole," he said.

There was noise in the hall. People were returning from downstairs, being followed by the press. They both looked at the TV, which was no longer broadcasting the press conference, but was now showing a soap opera.

"They're coming back," she said.

"Just relax," he said. "Once I tell Henry, he's going to react one of two ways, and with one of those ways, he's going to want to talk to you."

"And with the other?'

"He's going to throw us out."

Fifty-one

DAN HENRY LED the mob into the task force room and headed straight for his office. The other members of the squad followed him in, laughing and slapping one another on the back, while uniformed cops kept the press corps from entering. Jeter was with the detectives, but he wasn't doing much backslapping. When he saw Keough, he frowned and shook his head. Martha was the last one in, bracketed by two cops, who kept her from being trampled.

The uniforms finally got the press far enough from the door to be able to close it.

"Oh man, it's going to be good to get back to work!" Detective John Berkery shouted.

"You said it," Jim House agreed.

"You men are to report back to your regular squads at oh nine hundred two days from now," Sergeant Henry announced to the room. "Take tomorrow off with pay, compliments of the mayor."

The half dozen men in the room cheered. Henry looked over at Keough, who was still standing by the window.

"And what about our friends from the FBI?" Berkery asked. "Going back to Washington, Miss Busby? I could show you around town tomorrow, if you like." He laughed. "After all, I have the day off."

Nicole gave him a bland look and said, "I think I'll pass, but thanks."

"What's it look like out there, Officer?" Henry asked the uniform on the door.

The cop opened the door and peered out.

"Looks like we got them off the floor, sir."

"You guys can go," Henry said. "Martha and I can clean up the files."

"You got it, boss," Berkery said. "Jim, how about a drink?"

"You're on," House said.

"You're buying," Berkery told him as they headed for the door.

The cop opened the door, let out the task force members, then followed, closing it behind him. That left Henry, Martha, Jeter, Busby, and Keough.

"Well," Henry said, looking at Keough, "it's over."

"Far from it," Keough said. "We need to talk."

"About what?"

Keough looked around the room. All eyes were on him. Busby knew what he was going to say. What did it matter if Jeter and Martha heard?

"There was a phone call while you were . . . gone," Keough said.

"You answered my phone?"

"Yes."

Henry smirked and said, "Did you take a message?" He pretended to be searching his desk for a pink message slip.

"Yeah, I took a message," Keough said. "It was from the Angel Gabriel."

"What?"

"That's what our killer is calling himself."

Henry became serious.

"Our killer is named Lawrence Keith, and he's in a cell."

"The man on the phone knew about the angel pins," Keough said.

"Everybody knows—"

"About the stones, Sergeant. He knew they were birthstone angels. You didn't reveal that to the newspapers, or at the press conference."

Henry clenched his jaw and squinted at everyone in the room. They all cast their eyes down except for Keough.

"When did this call supposedly come in?"

"Just a while ago, while you were on TV," Keough said. "And it didn't 'supposedly' come in. You can check with nine-one-one operator two forty-six."

"A call came in," Henry said, "from somebody identifying themselves as Gabriel. That's all the operator is going to tell me." He looked at his clerical civilian. "Martha, get started on those computer files."

"Sir?"

"Back them up, then delete them from the hard drive."

"But sir—"

"Do as you're told, Martha."

"Yes, sir."

"Don't you want to know what he had to say, Sergeant?" Keough asked.

"I'd only have your word for what, wouldn't I, Detective?"

"I spoke to him, too," Nicole said.

Henry glared at her. Keough gave her credit—she stared right back.

"That figures."

"Sergeant," Keough said, "it's my job, my responsibility, to pass along what he said to me. After that, you can do what you want."

Henry stared at him a moment longer, then abruptly sat down in his chair and leaned back.

"I'm listening."

Fifty-two

HENRY AND THE others listened intently while Keough relayed his conversation with Gabriel. He had Nicole share her brief conversation, as well. Martha listened openmouthed, while Jeter's eyes expressed his reactions. Henry listened with a stony silence until Keough indicated he was finished.

"So he called us to say he was taking a vacation?" Henry asked.

Keough exchanged a glance with Nicole and asked, "Weren't you listening?"

"I heard every word, Detective," Henry said. "The killer, calling himself Gabriel, called you and told you everything you needed to know to support your theory that we have the wrong man."

"That's one way of looking at it."

"That's the only way to look at it, Detective," Henry said, standing up. "Until we have proof that we have the wrong man, I'm not going to the chief or the mayor with your story."

"You're going to keep this to yourself?" Keough demanded. "Allow this task force to be disbanded?"

"My men go back to their units in two days," Henry said.

"That's pretty quick, isn't it?" Keough asked.

"These men were taken from their units, leaving them shorthanded. Anyway, according to you, there'll be another child abducted and killed within that time. If it happens, we can get everyone back here."

"And if it takes a day or two longer than I estimated?"

Henry looked surprised.

"Are you saying you might be wrong, Detective?"

"I'm saying I might be off by a day or two, Sergeant," Keough replied.

"You won't be," Nicole said.

"You have something to say, Agent Busby?" Sergeant Henry demanded.

"Yes, sir, I do," she said, "My profile of this man—of both killers—indicates they take their victims at least two days apart. That's not even my profile; it's a fact."

"Then we don't have a problem keeping this to ourselves for two days, do we?" Henry asked.

"What about them?" Keough asked, indicating Jeter and Martha. "Maybe they will talk to the press."

Henry paused to look at the others in the room. He felt sure Martha wouldn't talk, but he had not known Jeter before he joined the task force, and Keough had.

"Are you saying you'll have Jeter leak information to the press?" he asked.

"What?" Jeter said.

"Marc's not my man; he's yours," Keough replied.

"He's your friend."

"He's not my friend."

"Hey!" Jeter said.

"You know what I mean," Keough said. He looked at Henry. "Jeter's a cop; he's not going to leak anything."

"Then you will?"

"Forget what I said," Keough replied. "Forget everything I said, Sergeant. You run your task force the way you see fit."

Keough walked to the door but paused before opening it. "You want to disband your task force? Be my guest."

He opened the door, walked to the end of the hall, entered his own temporary office, and slammed the door behind him. He walked around the desk and flopped into the chair. Why had he even answered the phone? What business was it of his if they wanted to disband their task force? It wasn't as if they'd been working closely. He could still continue his own investigation without them.

At that point, he noticed an envelope on his desk with his name written on the front. It was an interoffice envelope and had come from some other municipal office. He grabbed it, opened it, and saw that it was from the coroner's office. He pulled out the report on Denise Proctor and read the note attached: "Thought you'd like a copy of your own." It was signed, "Smiley."

Keough wondered if Henry had even taken the time to read the coroner's report. He opened the folder on his desk and leaned forward to read. Before he could start, however, there was a knock on the door. Busby, he thought, or Jeter.

He sat back in his chair. "Come in."

Nicole Busby opened the door just wide enough to slide in, then closed it quickly, as if she was worried someone might follow her.

"Are you all right?" she asked.

"Me? I'm just fine."

"What's that?" she asked, indicating the folder on the desk.

"The coroner's report on Denise Proctor. The doctor was kind enough to send me my own copy. Guess he figured I might not get a look at it otherwise."

"What's it say?"

"I don't know," he said. "I was about to read it when you knocked."

She sat in the chair opposite him. "So read."

"What's going on in the other room?"

"I assume they're in the process of dismantling the task force," she said.

"And Jeter?"

"When I left, he was being torn a new one by Sergeant Henry."

"Ah, that's my fault," he said, rubbing his face with both hands. "I should have left the kid alone."

"It was my impression he wanted to work with you."

"That doesn't mean I should've let him."

A cell phone rang.

"Not me," she said.

"Mine."

He took it out, frowned at it, and then answered it.

"Joe?"

"I'm still here, Harriet," he said sourly.

"Things are crazy here."

"And they're real normal here?"

"No, I mean it," she said. "They saw the press conference here."

"Our press conference?"

"Yeah, CNN ran it, and they watched in the task force squad room."

"Don't tell me; let me guess," he said. "They're wondering if Larry Keith is good for their cases?"

"You got it. What's happening there?"

"They're breaking down the task force."

"What are they going to say when he hits again in the next—oh, what, thirty-six hours?"

"That's their problem."

"You giving in?"

"I'm still going to do my job, Harriet," he said, "but my guess is that after today, I'll have to do it from my hotel room."

"Me, too, I guess. How's Busby working out?"

"Okay," he said. "She's been helpful, and supportive."

"Uh-huh."

"You have a dirty mind."

"What'd I say?"

"It's what you didn't say. Call me and let me know when they decide to piggyback our suspect here."

"Suspect?"

Keough fingered the autopsy report on the desk and said, "Well, he's a suspect for something."

Fifty-three

"I'M GOING TO read this," Keough said to Nicole Busby when he got off the phone.

"I'll wait."

"Wait?"

She smiled. "We came in the same car."

"Oh, right," he said. "Okay, just let me go over it and then I'll drive you back to the hotel."

"Fine."

Keough skimmed over what he already knew and got to the meat of Dr. Donaldson's report. When he'd read it twice, he pulled out the folders on the other three murders, just to be sure.

"What is it?" Nicole asked.

"Denise Proctor's body showed evidence of sexual abuse."

"You mean . . . she was raped and then killed?"

"No," Keough said, "the abuse had taken place over a period of time. It had no bearing on her death."

"And the other girls?"

"They had not been abused," Keough said. "Denise was not a virgin, and, in fact, she showed signs that she'd had sex both vaginally and anally."

"My God," she said. "The stepfather?"

"Probably," he said, closing both folders.

"What are you going to do?"

Her question took a moment to sink in, and then he said, stupidly, "What?"

"I asked what—"

"Oh, I heard you," he said. "I'm, uh . . . I'm not going to do anything."

"What?"

"It's not my case, is it?" he asked. "And they've already arrested the stepfather. There'll be an investigation; somebody else is going to read this file."

He picked up all the folders, straightened them, then stood up and tucked them under his arm.

"We better get out of here before they come and throw us out."

He opened the door and strode out into the hall. She grabbed her purse and hurriedly followed. As they passed the office—or former office—of the task force, Marc Jeter was coming out.

"Where are you off to?" he asked.

"The hotel," Keough said. "You?"

Jeter shrugged. "I'm supposed to go back to my unit day after tomorrow. Until then, I'm on my own time. We can still investigate."

"Investigate what?"

"Joe, I know they've got the wrong guy," Jeter said. "I believe you. Let's go out there and get the right guy." He looked at Nicole. "The three of us."

"I'm game," Nicole said.

Keough looked at both of them.

"Did you not hear what went on in there?" Keough asked. "I told the head of the task force that I talked with the killer? And he didn't care? You know what? If he even told the chief and the mayor what I said, they wouldn't care, either. You saw them at that press conference, with their hands waving in the air in victory? You think they're going to call another press conference to tell the city they were wrong?"

"But when he hits again—" Nicole began.

"Maybe he won't," Keough said. "Maybe when he thinks it over and realizes they've hung his crimes on another guy, he'll give it up."

"You don't really believe that, do you?"

"I don't know what I believe, Nicole," he said. "I just know there's nothing for me to do here."

"So you're just going to give up?" Nicole asked.

"I'm not giving up," he said. "Maybe I'll go to Chicago and help my partner find her serial killer." He started down the hall, then stopped and looked at Nicole. "I'm going back to the hotel. Are you coming?"

She stared at him for a moment and then said, "No. I'll catch a ride with Marc."

"Huh? Oh, sure," Jeter said. "I'll take her."

"Fine," Keough said, "whatever," and he stalked off down the hall.

"What's the matter with him?" Jeter asked after Keough had gone down in the elevator.

"He's mad," Nicole said. "You can't really blame him, I guess." She looked at Jeter. "You think he'd really give up and leave?"

"No."

"What makes you say that?"

"He left here with the files, didn't he?"

Fifty-four

May 4, 2004

AN INSISTENT KNOCKING on his door woke Keough the next morning. He staggered out of bed, stepping on the files he'd been reading the night before. They'd fallen off the bed and were spread out all over the rug.

"Shit," he said as a sheet of paper stuck to the bottom of his bare foot.

The knocking increased in both tempo and volume.

"I'm coming, I'm coming!" he yelled.

Two men in suits were standing in the hall, one of them with his fist poised for yet another knock.

"Yes?"

"Detective Keough?" The knocker asked.

"Yes."

"Could you get dressed and come with us, please?"

"And where would we be going at—what time is it?" Keough asked.

"Nine A.M., sir."

"Where would we be going at nine A.M.?"

"To see the mayor, sir."

"The mayor? He wants to see me?"

"Yes, sir."

"You guys got ID?"

They both showed him ID cards similar to the one he'd carried during the short time he worked in the mayor's office.

"Do you guys know what this is about?"

"No, sir," the knocker said, "we were just sent to . . . invite you."

"Invite me?"

"That's right, sir."

"And drive you," the other man said, speaking for the first time.

"In a limo?"

"If you like, sir," the knocker said. "We can get one, but—"

"That was what passes for humor from me at nine A.M.," Keough assured him.

The man just smiled.

"You're going to have to give me half an hour," he said.

"That's fine, sir," the knocker said. "We'll wait in the lobby."

"Okay."

"Thank you, sir."

"Don't mention it."

He closed the door and went to take a quick shower.

The only thing the current mayor of St. Louis had in common with the former mayor was the location of his office. This man was Caucasian, in his fifties, beefy, and looked uncomfortable in his suit.

"Mr. Mayor," Keough said, as he was ushered into the office by the mayor's secretary.

"Detective Keough," the mayor said, crossing the room with his hand extended. "Or is it Agent Keough?"

"Detective is fine, sir." Keough shook hands and looked around the room. "Just the two of us?"

"Who else were you expecting?"

"Maybe the chief of police?"

"He's here in spirit," the mayor said. "Please, sit down. I hope my invitation wasn't too abrupt?"

"I'll adjust."

"Would you adjust better if you had a cup of coffee?" the mayor asked.

"Yes, sir . . . black, no sugar."

The mayor got on his intercom and asked someone named Barbara to bring in two coffees, "neat."

"How are you finding St. Louis on your return?" the mayor asked, seating himself behind his desk.

"Everything is where I left it, sir."

Barbara came in with the coffee, served it up, and left quickly, before Keough could even thank her. He sipped his coffee.

"Is it all right?"

"It's fine," he said. "In fact, it's very good."

"I have it ground special for me."

"I'm sorry, Mr. Mayor," Keough said, "but I was hoping we could get past the small talk to the point of my . . . invitation?"

The mayor sat back in his leather chair and said, "Of course. Forgive me. I assume you saw me at yesterday's press conference?"

"Yes, I did."

"You watched me make a fool of myself, then."

"Sir?"

"I understand you spoke on the phone yesterday to a man who called himself Gabriel? Said he was the serial killer of these little girls, not the man we arrested?"

"Well, yes, sir," Keough said. "How did you know—"

"Sergeant Henry came forward and told the chief last night," the mayor said. "Also admitted to planting the angel pin at the fourth crime scene. Apparently, his conscience got the better of him."

"Well, I'm glad he saw the light," Keough said. "He's a good-enough cop, sir, just not—"

"Not a cop anymore," the mayor said. "Not on my police force."

Most cities called it a police department. Keough had first become a cop in New York when it was still called a force. Oddly, he liked this man for using the old term.

"I'm sorry to hear that."

"Did it to himself, I'm afraid," the mayor said. "Wasn't fit for command, I guess."

"No," Keough said, "perhaps not."

"Let me get to the real point, Detective," the mayor said. "You are a member of the Federal Serial Killer Task Force."

"Yes, sir."

"And you are very experienced in these investigations?"

"Fairly experienced."

"You're modest," the mayor said. "I know about your investigations in East St. Louis, and I know about the so-called 'Mall Rat' case when you first arrived here. I've even found out about your 'Kopykat' case in New York. I know of your relationship with my predecessor, and your short time on his staff. You see, I've done my research."

"You're very thorough, sir," Keough said. "All right, yes, I'm experienced, but what has my relationship with the former mayor got to do with anything?"

The mayor sat forward. "I'd like you to work for me."

"Doing what, sir?"

"Take over Sergeant Henry's task force and find this maniac."

"He disbanded it. I thought—"

The mayor waved his hand and said, "Put it back together. Choose your own men. We can get them back into that office by tomorrow."

Keough was surprised. After watching the mayor "make a fool" of himself on television, this was the last thing he'd expected. Perhaps the man was not the total politician he'd appeared to be at first glance.

"Sir . . . I have a job."

"I'll talk to your superior," the mayor said. "I'm sure he won't refuse my request. I would really appreciate it if you would take this on."

"Sir," Keough said, "I'm flattered, but—"

"Let me be blunt," the mayor said, "and I apologize for cutting you off, but if you don't do this, I'm afraid the investigation will suffer. And when this monster hits again, he'll get away with murder again. I understand the concept of 'fresh blood,' Detective. When this crazy strikes again, we need to be in position to act and act quickly. This would be your first opportunity to work on one of his . . . victims, cases, whatever you want to call it . . . as soon as it happens."

Keough thought it over a few moments, finishing his coffee at the same time. When he'd returned to his hotel room the evening before, he'd been thinking about leaving St. Louis, but it took only a few moments for him to realize he couldn't do it. He'd ordered something from room service and started going through the cases again, even taking them to bed with him. He did want to catch this self-proclaimed "Gabriel," but he realized he wanted one more thing.

"I'll do it."

"Excellent," the mayor said, beaming. "As I said, pick your own crew—"

"I'll keep the same men."

The mayor frowned.

"Why would you do that?" he asked. "Won't they resent you—"

It was his turn to cut the mayor off.

"They're good cops, Mr. Mayor, and they've been in on this longer than I have. I don't want to have to brief new men. As for being Sergeant Henry's men . . . well, they'll come around. They want to catch this guy, too."

"All right, then," the mayor said. "Anything else you need? Would you like an office in this building, or something downtown?"

"We can stay where we were," Keough said. "And I'll need the same clerical woman."

"No problem."

"A few other things, though."

"Name them."

"First, you'll have to call my director, make it official," Keough said. He dug one of his business cards out of his wallet and wrote Wallace's name on the back.

"I'll do that right away," the mayor said, accepting the card. "What else?"

"There's an FBI profiler in town, Special Agent Nicole Busby," Keough said. "I'd like you to make the same request to her director so she can stay and work with me."

"Done. What else?"

"The fourth girl who was killed, Denise Proctor?"

"Not by the serial killer, though. We still have her stepfather in custody, although he's not being charged with the first three murders."

"Is he being charged with his stepdaughter's murder?" Keough asked.

"That'll be up to the DA."

"I want that case, too."

"Why? It'll just distract you."

"Nevertheless, I want that case assigned to the task force. I'll work on it myself, though. I won't commit any of the task force's energies to it. And I'll speak with the DA."

"All right," the mayor said. "You've got it, whatever you want. Is that it?"

"For now," Keough replied. "I may have some more requests along the way. For instance, I may need you to talk to someone in Chicago."

"Ah, yes," the mayor said, "they're having a similar problem, aren't they?"

"Very similar."

"Well, we'll deal with each of your requests when they arise, then." The mayor handed Keough his card. "Call any time; I'll make sure you get through." He then opened his desk drawer and took out two items. As he set them on the desk, Keough saw that they were his old ID card and a parking pass from the mayor's office.

"These were in a file," the mayor said. "I thought you could put them to some use."

Keough picked up the parking pass. "I have my own ID, Mr. Mayor, but I'll take this." It would allow him to park without being ticketed, and without charge in municipal parking lots.

The mayor stood up and extended his hand across the desk. "You've got my appreciation, Detective, and the appreciation of the people of St. Louis—especially the parents."

Keough stood up and shook the mayor's hand. "I'll accept that after the job's done, sir."

Fifty-five

THE PREVIOUS NIGHT, before falling asleep Keough'd had his nightly conversation with Harriet Connor. Things were not going well for her in Chicago. She did not have a Jeter to work with, and she had never really gotten to talk with Busby. He had suggested that he go to Chicago and work with her. Now, in his car on a street alongside City Hall, he dialed her cell phone from his. When she answered, he explained what had happened.

"So you're not coming?" she asked.

"Harriet, they asked me to run this task force."

"Do you think Director Wallace is going to go for this?"

"Are you kidding? This is what he's been waiting for—especially with possible extinction hanging over our heads—an official request for our involvement in a case."

"You're right," she said. "I wish I could get something like that here. I'm just not being included in the loop."

"Have they found out that Keith is not being charged here?"

"How do I know? Nobody tells me anything."

"Well then, maybe I'll make one more request of the mayor here."

"And that would be?"

"That he call the mayor of Chicago."

"And force the task force here to include me?"

"Maybe even put you in charge," he said, "or, better yet, you and I jointly in charge of a bicity task force."

"That second part could work," she said. "We could keep in touch and exchange info by computer." She was getting excited.

"Slow down," he said. "Do you think you could get any men there to work for you if that happens?"

"If they want to solve these murders, they will," she said. "Or we could bring more of our men in."

"Let's take baby steps here," Keough said. "I'll see if the mayor will go along."

"You know," Harriet said, "we could solve both murders and save our jobs while we're at it."

"I'd settle for solving all of these murders, right now."

"What about the other little girl?" Harriet asked. "The stepfather look good for it?"

"Probably," he said. "I'll find out soon enough."

"How?"

"I got the mayor to give me that case, as well."

"Is that wise? Why do you want that one, too?"

"I have some ideas," Keough said. "I'd like to see it through."

"Well, don't get too distracted."

"I'll be in touch."

His next call was to the mayor, and, true to the politician's word, he was put right through. That alone was encouraging.

He explained to the mayor what he wanted, and was surprised to find that not only did the man not resist the idea, he thought it was a good one.

"Cooperation between our two cities, and our two police departments, sounds like a good idea," he said. "By the way, I spoke to your director and he was very helpful. I assume he'll be calling you."

"That's fine." Keough figured he'd make the call first.

"I'll call my opposite number and get back to you."

Keough thanked him and hung up. While the mayor seemed

very cooperative and supportive at this early stage in their relationship, he couldn't help being suspicious. There was probably a political reason for it.

He turned his attention back to his cell phone.

"This is fantastic!" Director Gregory Wallace exclaimed. "I don't know how you managed it, but this is exactly what we needed."

"I know," Keough said. "Harriet and I discussed it."

"I can send more men as soon as you need them," Wallace said.

"Let's hold off on that for a while," Keough said. "They wouldn't know their way around and we'd have to waste time giving them directions."

"Well, luckily you don't have that problem," Wallace said. "What about the locals? Will they work for you?"

"I think so," Keough answered. "I think they'll put aside any resistance in order to solve the murders."

"I hope you're right," Wallace said. "Goddamn, this is exciting. Get back to the mayor right away and find out if he talked to Chicago. If we set up a joint task force, I'll have ample ammunition to keep us active."

"I'll do my best, sir," Keough said, "but my first concern is to catch these killers."

"Of course, of course," Wallace said, "that's the whole point of our unit, Joe. You're doing great work there. Keep me informed."

"I will, sir."

Keough broke the connection and dropped the cell phone onto the passenger seat.

Fifty-six

SINCE THE TASK force would not be re-formed until the next day, Keough decided to spend this one on the murder of Denise Proctor. Hopefully, by the end of the day he'd hear something from the mayor about the possibility of a joint task force.

As he drove to the Keith house to talk to Denise's mother, he picked up his cell phone again and, dialing with a clumsy one-handed system he had not yet perfected—but probably would by the end of this case—he called his hotel and asked for Nicole's room. When she answered, he explained the situation to her and suggested she call her director.

"So you want me to stay?" she asked.

"Yes," he said. "I want us to work together on this."

"Why?"

He thought a moment, then said, "Maybe because we both came out of that I-Eighty case the worse for wear. Maybe we both need this to be a success."

"Maybe," she agreed. "Okay, I'll stay. What's next?"

"Just be at the task force's office tomorrow," he said. "Bright and early."

"Same place?"

"Same bat time, same bat station?"

"What?"

"You're so young," he said, and broke the connection.

He knocked on the door of the Keith home on Musick Avenue. When Nancy Keith came to the door, it was plain she was not happy to see him.

"What do you want?"

"I need to speak to you, Mrs. Keith. How are you doing?"

"My daughter is dead and my husband is in jail," she said. "How do you think I am?"

"I'm sorry," he said, "I know this is a difficult time. May I come in?"

"I don't care," she said, and walked away from the door.

He reached out for the screen door, found it unlocked, and entered the house. He went looking for her and found her sitting in the kitchen, which looked as if it had been hit by a hurricane. There were cups and plates on the table, crusted with food. Against one wall were the remnants of a plate or plates that someone had thrown on the floor.

Keough looked around for a coffeepot, and when he found it, he wished he hadn't.

"Can I get you something, Mrs. Keith? Tea? Coffee? Something stronger?"

She glared at him. "Get me my husband."

"Well, I can't do that," he said. "At least not right now."

"He didn't kill my daughter."

Keough sat down opposite her, careful not to touch any of the table's surface. "And he hasn't been charged with that crime . . . yet."

"Then why was he arrested for killing her, and those other girls? He didn't do any of those things. He didn't kill anybody!"

"He's not being charged with those other murders at all. That much I can tell you."

She brightened slightly. "Then when is he coming home?"

"I can't say," he said. "I still have to talk to the DA."

Suddenly, she reached out and clamped her hand around his wrist. Her eyes looked feverish and her grip was surprisingly powerful.

"Can you bring her home? Can you do that? I—I don't know what to do. Somebody has to make funeral arrangements."

"You haven't done that yet?"

"I—I don't know how—"

"It's all right," he told her. "They're most likely not ready to release the body anyway. You still have time."

She released his arm, and the strength that she had demonstrated just moments ago seemed to drain out of her. In the light from the kitchen window, he could plainly see some fading yellow bruises on her arms.

"Mrs. Keith—Nancy—I asked you once before if there was something you wanted to tell me about your husband," he said. "I know he beats—."

"That's between him and me, Detective," she said, cutting him off.

"But if he was doing the same thing to your daughter—"

"You don't know that for a fact," she snapped.

Keough hesitated, then asked, "Nancy . . . do you know about your husband's arrest record?"

She covered her face with one hand, then let it drop away.

"I know all about it," she said. "He told me before we were married. He's a registered sex offender."

"And you married him? And allowed him to live around your daughter?"

"Detective," she said wearily, "you can't use that to turn me against him. He never—do you hear me?—never touched Denise in that way."

Keough had never met an abused wife so adamantly—was *loyal* even the word? Could the woman's self-esteem be that low?

"Nancy—"

"I think you should go," she said.

"But I—"

"Do you believe my husband killed those first three girls?"

"No, I don't."

She looked at him.

"So isn't it your job to find out who did?"

"Yes, it is."

"Then you should be doing it."

"It's also my job to find out who killed your daughter."

"It wasn't my husband."

"What about her real father? Or any of his family?"

"He's dead, and he had no family."

"And you? Do you have any family?"

"No."

"Had you seen anyone suspicious in the neighborhood in the days preceding her disappearance?"

"No."

"Nancy," he said, "how can you be so sure Larry didn't kill Denise?"

She looked up at him, then turned her head away and said, "Believe me, I know."

She answered his questions and offered nothing beyond that. It was as if she wanted to be as little help as possible. What could you do with a mother like that?

Keough stood up and stared down at Nancy Keith, who hardly seemed to notice he was there. He decided to leave without saying good-bye.

As he was driving back to his hotel, he picked up his cell phone and checked for messages. There were two. One was from the mayor. The other was from a man named Parker, who said he was with the district attorney's office. The message was the same: "Please return this call as soon as possible."

He decided to wait until he was in his hotel room to do so.

Fifty-seven

IT WAS TIME.

Gabriel watched the girl carefully. She was walking with two others, who would not do at all. He had to wait until they reached the point in their walk home when they parted company. That was when he'd take her and sacrifice her to the angels. Once that was done, he would be free to take the "vacation" he'd mentioned to Detective Keough on the phone—to Chicago to find his missing half. Let Detective Keough and the rest of the members of the task force flounder around looking for him while he was out of the city.

He started the car—not his usual Lexus, but a nondescript car he had purchased just for this occasion. He'd used three different cars for the first three girls, all bought from different places, under different names, with cash. This one was a Ford Escort, several years old, the same color beige that was seen on cars so often these days. He did not follow the girls, but drove ahead of them to wait at the place where they'd separate. He knew where the girl lived; he knew the way she walked home each day. He also knew her name. It was always important to call them by their names. It went a long way toward getting them into the car. You could usually convince a child that if you knew their name, you weren't a stranger.

This was not a main street they were on, and there was an empty lot across from the car. He knew that at this time of day the only people who used this street were the kids walking home from school. He knew just how large a window of opportunity he had in order to coax Melissa Reid into his car. . . .

"Oh wait," Aggie Dexter said to her friend Elizabeth French.

"What is it?" Liz asked.

"I forgot to tell Melissa something."

"I gotta get home, Aggie."

"Go ahead. I'll catch up."

Elizabeth continued on while Aggie ran back, trying to catch up with Melissa. When she reached the corner, she was just in time to see Melissa get into the brown car, and the car pull away. She shrugged, assuming that someone Melissa knew had given her a ride home, and ran to catch up with Elizabeth. She'd have to talk to Melissa at school tomorrow.

In Chicago, Sariel sat in the kitchen of a small house, drinking tea and reading the newspaper. A rat quickly ran across the floor, but this was normal and no cause for alarm. There was never a job that would pay enough to allow moving out of the old Roseland neighborhood. Once it had been an acceptable place to live, but over the years it had fallen on hard times, and now it was not a fit place to live in. It was, plain and simple, a ghetto.

Sariel wondered what would have happened if Mother had been a stronger person. If she had not had to depend on men who beat her, abused her both physically and sexually, and then started on her child when Sariel was old enough—although, when was a child old enough to be abused? Mother didn't like to work, and when there was a man living with them, she didn't have to. Her child's welfare and dignity must have been a small price for her to pay.

The boyfriends got progressively worse, and more violent, until one day one of them beat Mother so badly, he killed her. He left Sariel alone with her, and then the fourteen-year-old had sat there for hours, staring at the body, savoring the quiet, enjoying the solitude. Finally, though, the police were called and told who the boyfriend was, and they took the child to a shelter. The man was convicted of killing her mother, and Sariel went from foster home to foster home—again suffering some abuse at the hands of a foster father—before finally going out on her own at seventeen.

Now, thirteen years later, Sariel was still in the old neighborhood, having inherited the old house, and every time the old memories came back, a sacrifice to the angels had to be made.

It was after the third one that Sariel noticed the same things were happening in St. Louis. Now, after the fourth one, it was necessary to check the newspapers and TV news every day, waiting for the St. Louis counterpart to strike. There was such a kinship with whoever the killer was, something never felt for anyone before.

Sariel finished the tea and folded the newspaper as another rat—or the same one—ran back the other way. What was he waiting for this time?

Fifty-eight

IT WAS AFTER 5:00 P.M. when Keough's cell phone rang. He had decided to eat dinner in the Drury Inn's own steak house on the first floor, and he had just cut into his filet when his phone sounded. He toyed with the idea of not answering it; he had already returned the calls to the mayor and the DA. The mayor had promised to set up a conference call tomorrow so he, the mayor of Chicago, the head of the Chicago task force, and Keough could talk. The DA had made an appointment to see Keough first thing in the morning, and he promised he'd review the case thoroughly by then.

Having spoken to both of those gentlemen, he couldn't think of anyone he wanted to take a call from while he was eating dinner.

Except maybe Harriet Connors.

He sighed, put his fork down, and answered the phone.

"We got a missing child," a woman's voice said.

"Who's this?" he asked, confused.

"Martha, at the task force office."

"Martha—" Keough said. "But I thought—"

"I returned to my regular assignment and they told me I was to report back here again tomorrow. I decided to come in tonight and get the computer up and running again. I knew they'd call us back."

"How did you know that?"

"Do you really want to talk about that now?" she asked.

"Who's the girl?"

"Her name's Melissa Reid. Are you ready for the address?"

"Wait, wait." He quickly took out his notebook. "Go ahead."

She read it to him and he scribbled it down.

"Who's at the scene?"

"The local police," she said. "Webster Groves."

Webster Groves, one of the most affluent neighborhoods in the city.

"Can you get ahold of Marc Jeter and tell him to get over there?" he asked.

"Sure, what about the rest of them?"

"Will they respond without asking too many questions?" he asked.

"I honestly don't know."

"See if you can get Berkery and House to respond to the scene. Just notify the rest of them to be in the office tomorrow morning at nine."

"All right."

"Martha."

"Yeah?"

"Don't say anything about what happened to Sergeant Henry."

There was a moment of silence; then she said, "I don't know what happened to Sergeant Henry."

"Oh . . . well, I'll fill you in later. Just make the calls."

"Okay."

He was about to hang up, when something occurred to him. "Martha, wait."

"Yes?"

"Why did you call me?"

"I tried Sergeant Henry and couldn't get him. I thought of you next."

"Okay," he said, "I'll talk to you later. Don't leave there until you hear from me."

"Yes, sir."

He disconnected and started to pocket the phone, then thought better of it. He dialed Nicole Busby's cell phone instead.

"Where are you?" he asked when she answered.

"I'm in that department store—what do you call it? Famous Barr?"

"The one downtown?"

"Yes, I walked over from the hotel. They have a lot of good sales, and—"

"Shopping time is over," Keough said. "Have you heard from your director?"

"No."

He explained that he'd heard back from the mayor, who had scheduled a conference call about the joint task force.

"Is this straight dope, Joe?"

"Straight dope, Nicole. And on top of that, we've got a missing girl."

"Oh God."

"Go outside and wait for me. I'll pick you up."

"On what corner?"

"I don't know," he said. "Just stand on a corner; I'll drive around until I find you."

He broke the connection and this time pocketed the cell phone.

On the table, next to his plate, were his pills. For once, he'd remembered them, but in order to take them, he had to eat something. He took two bites of his steak, one big bite of his baked potato, washed the pills down with some water, and beckoned the waiter over.

Fifty-nine

THERE WERE MANY beautiful, large homes in Webster Groves, but it still was not considered the upscale community Ladue and Clayton were. However, it was affluent enough to fit the profile of Gabriel's other victims. The parents of these girls had money; there was no doubt about that.

Keough and Nicole Busby arrived at the Jefferson Road house after the locals and their patrol supervisor, who were all standing around waiting. As they exited Keough's rental car, a man in street clothes approached them. He was fiftyish and he filled his clothes out like a man who couldn't push himself away from the dinner table. He was sweating more than the weather called for.

"You from the task force?" he asked.

"That's right," Keough said. He and Nicole displayed their IDs.

"FBI," the man said with distaste, reading Nicole's. "You, too?"

"We're with the task force, Detective . . ."

"Ford," the man said, "Detective Ford."

"We're with the task force, Detective Ford; that's all you need to know. You mind filling us in?"

"Sure," Ford said. "Melissa Reid, eleven years old. Usually walks partway home from Bristol Intermediate with two girl-friends. The other two made it home; she didn't. Mother called nine one one; a unit responded and called us. My partner and I notified you people soon as we realized what we had."

"Have you interviewed the mother?"

"Briefly," Ford said. "She's kinda pissed, thinks we're draggin' our feet." He snorted. "Think these parents would be pickin' up their kids at school, with everything that's been happenin'."

"Okay, let me have the mother's name and we'll go in and talk to her."

Ford produced his notebook and said, "Clar—wait, my handwriting sucks. Some name like that . . . Oh, wait, it's Clarise. Last name same as the kid's, Reid."

"Okay," Keough said. "You and your partner have orders to hand this off to us?"

"Yep."

"Then you've done it," Keough said. "You can go."

Keough walked past the man without another word. Nicole hurried to keep up. Ford's partner had been waiting by their car the whole time, and Keough didn't see any reason to meet him.

"That was pretty harsh," Nicole said.

"Was it?" Keough asked. "He copped an attitude as soon as he saw your ID. I just wanted to head him off."

They entered the house, a uniformed officer stepping aside to let them pass. As Keough turned to make sure the cop was letting Nicole in, he saw Berkery, House, and Jeter walking across the lawn.

"Nicole," he said, "you interview the mother."

"What?"

"I've got to talk to these guys."

She turned and saw the three detectives.

"Joe . . . I don't interview people. It's not what I do."

"It is today," he said. "Just ask her how her daughter usually got to and from school, why she didn't pick her up, where her husband is. . . . You heard me talk to the neighbor woman on Musick Avenue. You're a woman. Give her some sympathy; she'll respond to you."

"A—all right."

"I'll come back in when I'm finished," Keough told her.

She nodded, and he stepped back outside.

"What the hell is going on, Keough?" Berkey demanded as he approached all three men. "We thought the case was closed and we were disbanded."

"It's reopened, and we're a task force again," Keough said.

"By whose authority?"

"The mayor's."

Berkery looked surprised. "You spoke with the mayor?"

"He called me in," Keough said.

"Why you? Where's the sarge?"

House and Jeter were standing aside, watching the two men, listening.

"I think you know what happened with Sergeant Henry, John," Keough said.

Berkery stared at Keough for a few seconds, then looked away. He'd either been in on planting the angel pin or knew about it at least. Apparently, when he'd confessed, Henry had taken all the blame.

"So what are we doing?" House asked.

"We've got a missing girl here," Keough said. "Unlike Denise Proctor, this one is number four, I think."

"Is it like the others?" Jeter asked.

"So far," Keough said. "Went to school, didn't come home. She's eleven, which fits. If you remember, the others were eight, nine, and ten."

"Let me get this straight," Jim House said. "You're running the task force?"

"That's right," Keough said. "You can check with the mayor's office if you like, but you'll have to do it later. We need to move on this now."

"John?" House said.

Berkery looked at House and said, "He's right, Jim." Then he looked at Keough. "What do you want us to do?"

"I'm going to keep Marc with me," Keough said. "I need one of you to go to the school and talk to the girl's teachers, and her principal. Find out whatever you can—if they've seen anybody suspicious, the usual."

"And what's the other one of us supposed to do?" House asked.

"Coordinate with these locals," Keough said. "We need to do a search of the area. We're looking for a man in a car with a girl, a man walking—you know the drill. But go further. We're looking for anybody who saw a man and a girl. This snatch is only a few hours old, at best."

"Where will you be?" Berkery asked.

"Here, until I hear from both of you," Keough said. "I want to talk with the mother, and the father, if I can."

"What about Jeter?" House asked.

"I'm going to find out from the mother the girl's route home, and then send Marc to retrace it."

"We're not going to come up with this guy today," Berkery said.

"Maybe not," Keough said, "but we're going to come up with something nobody found with the first three cases."

"What's that?" House asked.

"A witness."

Sixty

KEOUGH REENTERED THE house, Jeter behind him.

"Joe."

"Yeah?"

"So what happened to Henry?"

Keough stopped and turned to face the young black detective.

"He came forward and admitted that he falsified evidence to hang all the murders on Larry Keith."

Jeter whistled.

"So Keith didn't kill any of the girls?"

"He didn't kill the first three," Keough said. "The jury is still out on Denise Proctor—so to speak."

"And this one?" Jeter asked. "Is this one our guy?"

"That's what we're here to find out, Marc," Keough said. "Come on, let's see how Nicole is doing."

They entered the kitchen as quietly as they could. Nicole was sitting at the table with Melissa Reid's mother, Clarise. Nicole was reaching across the table to cover the woman's hand with her own. Clarise Reid, a brittle-looking woman in her mid-thirties, looked as if she were about to shatter into many shards.

"Can I call Mr. Reid for you?" Nicole was asking.

"No," Mrs. Reid said, wiping tears from her face with her other hand, "he—he doesn't like to be disturbed when he's away on business."

"Not even to be told his daughter is missing?" Keough asked.

Both women looked over at him.

"Clarise Reid, this is Detective Keough. He's in charge of the task force I told you about. Behind him is Detective Jeter."

"H—hello."

"Mrs. Reid," Keough said, "don't you think you should call your husband?"

"Melissa's only been missing a few hours," the woman said. "I—I'll call him if it drags on longer."

"Where is Mr. Reid on this business trip?"

"San Francisco."

"I see."

"Excuse me a moment, Mrs. Reid," Nicole said.

She stood up and approached Keough and Jeter, then guided them out of the kitchen and into the dining room.

"What have you got?" Keough asked.

"Melissa usually walks home with two other girls," Nicole said, looking in her notebook. "Aggie Dexter and Elizabeth French."

"Do you have their addresses?"

"Yes," she said. "They usually split up about four blocks from here. Aggie and Elizabeth live on the same block, so they go one way and Melissa continues on alone."

Keough shook his head. After the first girl went missing and turned up dead, he would have been walking his kids to and from school—if he had any.

"Give Marc the addresses of the girls," Keough said. "Marc, go and find out if either one knows anything, or saw anything."

Nicole tore the page out of her notebook and handed it to Jeter.

"Okay."

"I'll be here, so when you're done, come right back and tell me what you found out."

"What if I—"

"Try to know something when you come back," Keough said, cutting him off. "It would be very helpful."

Jeter exchanged a glance with Nicole, then said to Keough, "I'll try."

Sixty-one

KEOUGH REMAINED AT the Reid house, awaiting word of a witness found . . . somewhere. The area around the school and the Reid home was canvassed, but either no one saw anything or they weren't saying. His cell phone rang every few minutes as patrol men and his own men checked in with him.

Clarise Reid finally phoned her husband in San Francisco and told him that their daughter was missing. Herbert Reid demanded to speak to the man in charge of the investigation. Keough assured him everything that could be done was being done, then asked the man when he would be returning. Herbert Reid replied that if everything was being done, there was no point in his cutting his business trip short. He would be back by the end of the week, as planned. After the phone call, Mrs. Reid went to her bedroom and locked herself in. Nicole made coffee, and she and Keough drank it as they sat at the kitchen table. There were two uniformed officers at the front of the house to keep onlookers away, but other than that, there were no others in the house. They were all out searching.

"What a son of a bitch," Nicole said.

"Who?"

"The husband. The bastard can't even bother to come home to comfort his wife."

"He's more businessman than father or husband, apparently," Keough observed.

"Are you condoning that?" she asked.

Keough shrugged. "Who am I to judge? It's his life; he can devote it to whatever he likes."

"Then he should never have gotten married, never had a child."

"*That*, I agree with."

"Will you ever have children, Joe?" she asked.

"No."

She was taken aback by the quickness of his reply.

"How can you be so sure?"

"I am," he said. "You see, I'm a cop—more cop than I could ever be a husband or a father. I wouldn't make the same mistakes Herbert Reid has made."

"Well," Nicole said, "it's a good thing you decided not to judge him."

When Clarise Reid appeared at the kitchen entryway, she startled them both.

"Mrs. Reid," Nicole said. "I hope you don't mind. We made some coffee. . . ."

"Of course not," Mrs. Reid said. "Have you . . . heard anything yet?"

"No," Keough said, "not yet, I'm afraid." He'd just had another call, but he didn't tell her.

"Would you like coffee?" Nicole asked. "Or I could make you some tea?"

Courageously, Keough thought, the woman smiled and said, "Some tea would be nice, I guess."

Keough stood and grabbed a chair away from the table.

"Have a seat, Mrs. Reid."

"Please," she said, "I'd prefer if you'd both call me Clarise."

"All right," Keough said, holding the chair while she sat.

Nicole had located the teapot earlier while looking for mugs, so she started it going while Keough sat across from Clarise Reid.

"You're probably wondering," she said, "why I allowed Melissa to walk home alone."

"That's none of our concern, Clarise," Keough said. "Our job is just to find her."

"I can't go out, you see," Clarise Reid went on. Keough didn't try to stop her. He was afraid if he did, the woman might crumble before his eyes. "I suffer from agoraphobia. I—I can't go outside."

"That's terrible," Nicole said. "But—"

Keough gave her a warning look and she stopped. He felt sure she was going to ask the same question that had occurred to him.

"It's all right," Clarise said. "I'd like to talk. Ask me what you like."

Nicole put the cup of hot water and the tea bag in front of Clarise, so the woman could make it to liking.

"I don't like it very strong," Clarise said, dunking the tea bag only a few times. "What were you going to ask me, Agent Busby?"

"Nicole, please."

"Yes, all right. It's only fair."

"I wonder why your husband would leave you alone if you can't go out . . . especially with what happened to the other three girls."

Clarise Reid stared intently into her teacup, as if the answer would be at the bottom. No tea leaves there, Keough thought.

"My husband's business is very important to him," she said slowly. "More important, I'm afraid, than his family." She looked up at both of them. "Is that unusual?"

"Too common, I'm afraid," Nicole said.

Clarise looked at Keough.

"Are you married, Detective?"

"No."

"Have you ever been?"

"No."

"Why not?"

He hesitated, then said, "Because I'm afraid I'd be the kind of husband and father your husband is."

She stared at Keough for a few moments, then said, "If only my husband were that honest about it."

Keough and Nicole exchanged a glance, but before either of them could say a word, Keough's cell phone sounded. He almost wished he could ignore it, but he answered it.

"Keough."

"Joe, it's Marc. I'm at the home of one of the girls, Aggie Dexter."

"Do you know Aggie Dexter?" Keough asked Clarise.

"She's Melissa's best friend, one of the girls she walks home with."

"What have you got, Marc?" Keough asked.

"Well, after I talked to Aggie and her mother for a while, the girl finally admitted she saw something."

"Stay put," Keough said. "We're on our way."

"What's up?" Nicole asked after he broke the connection.

"We may finally have a witness."

Sixty-two

IT WAS MARC Jeter who let them into the Dexter home, which was in a different section of Webster Groves, but very much the same kind of house as the Reids'—expensive and spacious.

"Where's the girl?" Keough asked.

"In the living room with her mother."

"Where's the father?"

"At work. Downtown."

"What'd she see?"

"She says that she and the other girl split from Melissa, but then she forgot to tell her something and ran back. When she got to the corner, she saw Melissa getting into a car."

"Does she know what kind of car?" Nicole asked.

"Did she see the driver?" Keough added.

"She's skittish," Jeter said. "I think having her mom around is making her nervous. I haven't gotten to that stuff yet. As soon as she told me she saw something, I called you."

"Okay," Keough said, "then here's what we'll do. Nicole, you take the mother aside."

She didn't look happy, but she nodded her agreement.

"Marc, you and I will talk to the girl. If it comes to it, one of us will leave the room."

"Which one?"

"Let's see who she's more comfortable with," Keough said. "You've got the inside track because you've talked to her already."

"I don't know about that."

"Why not?"

"It's not just a question of her being comfortable," Jeter said. "I'm not comfortable talking to kids."

"Why not?"

"Well, it's not kids so much as . . . little girls."

"What's wrong with little girls?" Keough asked. "Did Twain have something bad to say about them?"

"On the contrary," Jeter said. "Twain said, 'The average American girl possesses the valuable qualities of naturalness, honesty, and inoffensive straightforwardness. . . . ' "I've just never been comfortable talking to them. I think if you did it, you'd get more out of her."

"All right," Keough said. "Then you take the mother aside. Nicole, you talk to the girl with me. We'll see which of us she likes best."

"It'll be you."

"Why do you say that?"

"Marc and I have something in common."

"Wha—oh," he said. "You think she's been uncomfortable because he's black?"

"Children who come from . . . affluent homes don't usually have much contact with African-Americans, unless it's as . . . well, service people."

"Okay," Keough said, "let's try it anyway. If she is uncomfortable with you because of the color of your skin, she might confide in me even more after you leave the room."

"Okay," she said, "it's worth a try."

"This is the only witness we've had in all these cases," Keough pointed out.

The three of them entered the living room and Jeter made introductions to the mother, Helen Dexter.

"Mrs. Dexter," Keough said, "I wonder if you would go with Detective Jeter for a little while?"

Helen Dexter looked at Jeter and said to Keough, "With . . . him?" Keough immediately knew that Jeter had gotten right.

"Yes, ma'am," Keough said. "Please?"

"And leave Aggie with . . . you?" Now Mrs. Dexter cast her glance Nicole's way. The pouches of fat beneath her eyes threatened to come up and blind her. Keough wondered why the woman hadn't gotten an eye job. Wasn't that what wealthy women did as they got older? Or was he just giving way to his own prejudices in even thinking that?

"Yes, ma'am," he said, "with me and Agent Busby."

Mrs. Dexter stood up, hesitated, then said to Keough in a low voice—as if Jeter and Nicole wouldn't hear her—"You won't leave my daughter alone with her, will you?"

Keough looked at Aggie, who was seated on the sofa, staring down at her shoes. Was she embarrassed by her mother? He wouldn't have blamed her.

"I don't know, ma'am," he said, rather than giving in to her. "We'll have to see."

"But—"

"Please," he said, "follow Detective Jeter? He'll have some questions for you." Keough's phone rang at that moment and he gave it to Jeter and told him to handle the calls for a while.

Keough was always surprised that people still had these prejudices, but then he always forgot that many people considered St. Louis to be the northernmost southern city.

He looked at Nicole, who rolled her eyes, and then turned his attention to the little girl on the sofa.

Sixty-three

"BLACK PEOPLE DON'T bother me," Aggie said.

"Is that a fact," Keough said.

She looked up at him.

"They scare Mom, and Daddy calls them 'niggers,'" the little girl explained, "but Sandra's black and she's my friend . . . and her momma and daddy are way cool."

Keough sat down in an armchair across from Aggie Dexter.

"So you wouldn't be more comfortable if Agent Busby left?"

"No," Aggie said, looking at Nicole. "I think she's cool-lookin'."

"Thank you, Aggie," Nicole said. She sat in the other, identical armchair. Both were the same deep purple as the sofa, and Keough thought if he lived there, he'd have a headache all the time. The lamp shades all matched the chairs.

"Aggie," Keough said, "can you tell me what you saw today?"

"Is Melissa in trouble?" she asked, instead of answering the question.

"Well, we think she's in danger," Keough answered. "Is that what you mean?"

"No," she said. "I mean, is she in trouble with her mom?"

"She's not in trouble, Aggie," Keough assured her. "Her Mom's real worried about her, though."

"Is her dad home?"

"No, he's out of town."

"I thought maybe he was home." She looked down and shrugged.

"Aggie, do you know if Melissa's mom and dad are having . . . problems?"

"They yell at each other a lot," she said. "Mine do, too, but not as much as hers do."

"Okay," Keough said, "why don't you tell me what happened today?"

Aggie shrugged. Keough decided he was going to have to lead her through this by the hand.

"You left school with Melissa?"

"Yes."

"And who else?"

"Elizabeth."

"Is Elizabeth your best friend, too?"

"No," she said, looking at him as if he were crazy. "You can't have two best friends. Melissa's my best friend."

"Okay, sorry," Keough said. "But you and Melissa are both friends with Elizabeth?"

"Yes," she said, satisfied that he now understood.

"Aggie, is Elizabeth your second-best friend?" Nicole asked.

"Yes!" Aggie said happily, pointing to Nicole. "See, she knows."

"Yes, she does," Keough said. "I guess that's because she's a girl, too. Right?"

"Right!"

"Okay, Aggie," Keough said, leaning forward and putting his elbows on his knees, "I need you to tell me about today. You were walking home with Elizabeth and Melissa and . . ."

"Elizabeth and I turned where we always turn, 'cause she lives on this block, too."

"And Melissa?"

"She kept going. . . ."

"But you ran back to find her, didn't you?"

Aggie lowered her eyes and said, "Yes."

"Why?"

She turned her eyes toward the doorway, perhaps looking for her mother. Suddenly, Nicole was crouching next to Keough and in front of the girl.

"Aggie, is there something you don't want your mother to know?" she asked, lowering her voice. She obviously had a hunch, and Keough let her go with it.

"Well . . . yeah."

"And Melissa's mother?"

"Yes."

"Does this have something to do with . . . boys?" Nicole asked, giving Keough a sidelong glance.

Aggie raised her eyes and looked at Keough, then turned her eyes to Nicole and nodded shyly.

Nicole looked at Keough, who got the message.

"Aggie, does your mother have anything to drink in the kitchen? I'm real thirsty."

"We have some pop in the refrigerator."

"I'm going to go and get some," he said, standing up. "Would you like something?"

"No," she said, "thank you."

"I'll be back in a little while, then."

He left the room so Nicole and Aggie Dexter could have a little girl talk.

Sixty-four

WHEN KEOUGH ENTERED the kitchen, he encountered an odd scene. It was a very large kitchen, with a butcher-block island right in the center. On one side of the butcher block, Marc Jeter stood with his back against the sink. On the other side, seated at the kitchen table, was Helen Dexter. She looked as jumpy as a cat, as if she might bolt from the room at any moment. There could not have been more space between them. Jeter was on Keough's cell phone, talking to one of the cops who was searching the area.

Helen Dexter looked up when Keough entered, and the expression of relief on her face was almost comical. The look on Jeter's face said, This wasn't a very good idea.

Then, as quickly as the look of relief had come over her face, it faded, replaced by one of panic.

"Where's Aggie?"

"She's in the living room with Agent Busby," Keough said.

"You left her with that—" She half-rose to her feet, then stopped herself short and sat back down.

"I left her with Agent Busby," Keough said slowly, "because she indicated that she would be more comfortable talking to another female."

"Yes, but—" Helen Dexter stopped again and cast a meaningful glance Jeter's way. Keough assumed that he was automatically supposed to know what she was trying to say. He did, but he wasn't about to let her know it.

"Yes, Mrs. Dexter?"

"I just . . . you know . . . I mean, Aggie's not very comfortable with . . . strangers."

"Well, she seemed perfectly comfortable with Agent Busby," Keough said. "It shouldn't take long to find out what we want to know. Why don't we all just have something to drink?"

"I, uh, don't have much—"

"Aggie said there was some pop in the refrigerator." He looked at Jeter. "Marc, you want some pop?"

Before he could see if Jeter wanted to play along with him or not, Nicole appeared at the doorway.

"Joe?"

"That was quick."

She beckoned him to follow her and backed out of the room.

"We'll be back," Keough said to Mrs. Dexter, who was once again on the edge of her seat.

When he joined Nicole in the dining room, she said, "As soon as you left the room, it came gushing out."

"What did?"

"Aggie and Melissa had a bet about who would end up kissing a boy today at school. They'd be mortified if their mothers found out."

"Is that all?"

"It's a lot to girls their age."

"Okay, fine," Keough said. "Is she ready to talk about what she saw?"

"Yes."

When Keough reentered the room with Nicole, Aggie was still seated on the couch. However, her body language said she was much more comfortable now that the secret about kissing boys was out.

"Aggie," Keough said, "are you ready to tell me what you saw when you ran back to find Melissa?"

"Are you Nicole's boss?"

"No," Keough said, "we work together."

"Oh," she said, "you act like her boss."

"Well, I'm sorry if I do that," he said. "I'll try not to anymore. Okay?"

"Okay."

"Now," he said, "when you ran back to the corner, what did you see?"

"I saw Melissa getting into a car."

"And who was in the car?"

"A man."

"Was the man her father?"

"I thought he was at first, but then I saw he wasn't."

"Did he get out of the car?"

"No, he stayed behind the wheel. Melissa got into the car."

"What made you think he might be her father?"

"Because her father has a bald spot. This man had the same color hair—brown—but no bald spot."

"Long hair?"

"Not long," she said, "just a lot." She waved her hands and added, "Bushy."

"Does her father ever wear a hairpiece?"

"Oh, no," Aggie said, shaking her head.

"How can you be sure?"

"Well . . . I was over one day and her mother and father had a big fight about it." She leaned forward and lowered her voice. "Her mother wanted him to get a piece so he'd look younger."

If she could only see the back of his head, that meant she'd seen the back of the car. She wouldn't be able to describe the man's face, so they'd have to move on to the car. However, if she first thought the man was Melissa's father, that meant that he was white, and he had a lot of hair—maybe bushy and the same color as Melissa's father's. It was more than they'd gotten from the first three cases.

"Okay, Aggie," Keough said, "you're doing great. What can you tell me about the car?"

She shrugged, so once again he knew he'd have to take her step by step.

"Do you know what kind of car it was?"

"An old one."

"You mean an old model?"

"I don't know models," she said. "It was . . . old."

"Do you mean a used car, not a new one?" Keough asked.

"Yes."

"Okay, then, can you tell me the color?"

She thought a moment, biting her lip, then said, "Brown, but not dark."

"Light brown?"

She frowned.

"Was it beige, Aggie?" Nicole asked.

"Beige, that's it," Aggie said.

"Okay," Keough said, looking over his shoulder at Nicole, who was taking notes, "we have a used brown car driven by a white male with a lot of hair. We need to find out what color hair Melissa's father has."

"Brown," Aggie said, "it's brown."

"Brown hair," Keough repeated. "Aggie, did you see the license plate on the car?"

"Yes."

"Do you remember the numbers?"

"No."

"The color?"

"No."

"Do you remember a name on the back of the car?" he asked. "A sticker . . . anything?"

"There was a man's name."

Keough's heart began to beat a little faster.

"What man's name? Could you read it?"

"Oh yes, it was easy to read," she said. "It was Joe Brown."

"Are you sure?"

"Yes," she said. "I have a boy in my class named Joe, and I have a teacher named Miss Brown. That's why I remember it."

"Aggie, you're great," he said, and she beamed with pride at the compliment. "And I'll tell your mother how great you are."

Now she pouted and said, "She won't care."

"I'm sure your mother loves you and is proud of you," Nicole said.

Aggie Dexter looked up at Nicole and said, "I want to be an FBI agent like you when I grow up."

Sixty-five

KEOUGH LEFT NICOLE with Aggie, telling her to ask whatever questions she could think of that he might have forgotten, and to get everything down on paper. He went into the kitchen and decided to give poor Mrs. Dexter a break, since she was so deathly afraid of Marc Jeter, one of the nicest, mildest men he'd ever met. A man who had also committed murder in the pursuit of justice—but he decided not to tell her that. The more time he spent with Jeter now, his actions in killing Andrew Judson became more and more out of character. Keough decided that the amount of guilt Jeter had been feeling must have been tremendous.

"We're out of here," he said, sticking his head into the kitchen. "Mrs. Dexter, thank you for all your help. You have a wonderful little girl there."

"Oh, uh, thank you. Was she . . . helpful?"

"Very. Marc, do you have a business card for Mrs. Dexter?"

Jeter reluctantly dug into his pocket and brought one out. Keough took it from him and passed it to Mrs. Dexter, who hesitated before accepting it and then quickly placed it on the kitchen table.

"If Aggie remembers anything else you think might be helpful, please don't hesitate to call."

"A—all right." Jeter moved around behind Keough and left the room.

Mrs. Dexter immediately seemed to become less tense. "You will find Melissa, won't you?"

"If we do," he said, "it will be because of Aggie."

He left the room before she could reply. He heard the chair scrape as she quickly got to her feet and followed him. Maybe she just wanted to make sure Jeter and Nicole left her house.

"Good-bye, Aggie," Keough said from the entry foyer.

"Good-bye, Detective Joe," she said.

Nicole gave Keough a look, which told him where Aggie had gotten that name for him from.

"Agent Nicole, thanks," Aggie said, hugging her good-bye.

"Be good, sweetie."

Keough didn't bother looking at Helen Dexter while Nicole gave the little girl a powerful hug—or vice versa.

"That poor kid," Keough said when they got outside.

"Why?" Nicole asked.

"Look at what her parents are trying to teach her," he said. "That woman was frightened to death of the two of you."

"Children make up their own minds, Joe," Nicole said.

"Besides," Jeter said, "that's nothing new."

"No," Keough said, suddenly feeling naïve, "I suppose it isn't."

"Here's your phone," Jeter said, holding it out. "Damned thing keeps ringing."

Sixty-six

THEY WENT BACK to the Reid house, where Clarise Reid was on the verge of tears.

"Calm down and relax, Mrs. Reid," Keough said, taking her hands. "Come into the living room with me. Agent Busby and Detective Jeter will be in the kitchen."

"Why? Do you have bad news? Did you find my little girl? Is she—"

"No bad news," he assured her. "We haven't found her, but we do have good news."

"Oh my God . . ."

He hustled her into the living room and got her seated on the sofa there. Slowly, he told her what they had found out from Aggie Dexter.

"Who was this man who took Melissa?" she asked when he was done.

"That's what we have to find out, Clarise," he replied, "but I need to ask you something, and you have to answer without getting upset."

She stared at him, then took a deep breath and said, "All right."

"I need to know how things are between you and your husband."

"What? They're—well—"

"And I need the truth."

She closed her mouth, clenched her jaw, and said, "Not good."

"Are you separated? Is that why he's in San Francisco?"

"No, we're not separated," she said. "He is in San Francisco on business."

"So you have no reason to suspect that he might be behind this?"

Her eyes widened. "Kidnap his own daughter? For what reason?"

Keough shrugged and said, "Maybe he doesn't intend to come back home. Maybe he wants Melissa with him. I don't know. I'm just covering all my bases, Clarise."

She thought a moment, then said, "No, it can't—no, I won't believe that. We're having problems—we've even discussed divorce—but even if that happened, my husband wouldn't want Melissa."

"Okay," he said, "you're positive?"

"Yes, I am. Besides, he's in San Francisco. You spoke to him yourself."

But he hadn't dialed the phone. He made a mental note to have Jeter confirm that Melissa's father was actually in San Francisco at the hotel he was supposed to be in.

He asked her if she knew anyone with a car like the one Aggie had described.

"It's a fairly common color," she said, "but I don't know anyone who drives a used car."

No, Keough thought, looking around the room, you wouldn't.

"Detective? Is this the work of the same madman who took those other girls?"

What could he tell her that would make her feel any better? He couldn't very well explain that they wouldn't really know that until Melissa turned up dead, with an angel pin stuck to her clothes.

"We think it might be," he said finally, "but Aggie is the first witness we've had, so now we have something to follow up on."

"Please," she whispered, tears streaming down her face, "please find her."

"We'll do our best." Hollow words, even to his own ears.

Sixty-seven

KEOUGH RETURNED TO the task force office—*his* task force office now—with Nicole Busby, leaving Jeter in the field in case something came up. The search would continue until nightfall; then the entire team would reconvene in the office in the morning. Keough wanted to be ready to greet them all.

When they reached the office in Clayton, Martha was there, sitting in front of her computer, as always.

"We're up and running," she said as he entered.

"Good." He pulled a couple of sheets of paper from his pad and passed them to her. "Run all these names. I want anything you can find."

"Traffic tickets?"

"Those, too."

He had given her the names of Melissa Reid's parents, as well as the names of Aggie Dexter's and Elizabeth French's parents.

He went over to the desk Sergeant Henry had occupied. He considered using another, but that would entail everyone else moving over one. So he decided to deal with the issue head-on.

Nicole sat opposite him and said, "So, we're in the inner circle now, huh?"

"Sweetie," he said, "we are the inner circle."

"So what do we do now?"

"I need the Yellow Pages," he said, opening and closing drawers.

"What for?"

"The name on the back of the car Aggie said she saw?"

"Joe Brown. What about it?"

"It's got to be a dealer's name," he said. "A used-car dealer."

She sat up straight. "I didn't think of that. I thought she might have been—"

"Making it up?"

"Mistaken."

"Either might be possible," he said. "That's what a phone book will tell us."

"But . . . if it's a car dealer, then he can describe the man who bought the car."

"Hopefully." He slammed the last empty drawer. "We'll be dealing with a car salesman, remember. Very self-serving bunch."

"What about checking the other cases for the same car?"

Keough shook his head. "He wouldn't use the same car."

"You think he owns more than one?"

"He wouldn't use one he owns—at least not one with a license plate on it."

"What are you saying? He buys a car for each girl?"

"Yes."

"But that costs money."

"He has money," Keough said. "Look at the people he targets, the angel pins—he even sounded wealthy on the phone."

She frowned. "How can you—wait, you're right. Rich people sound rich, don't they?"

"Lifestyles affect speech patterns," Keough said.

"So if I won the lottery and became rich, I'd . . . speak differently?"

"Not right away," he said, "but it would happen."

"If the car dealer remembers him, we can get a full description."

"First," Keough said, "we have to make sure there is a car dealer."

"I'll see if I can find a phone book." She started to get up.

"Wait. Martha?"

"Yep?"

"Is there a car dealer in town named Joe Brown?"

"I don't know," she said. "Not one who does commercials. Wait, I'll Google it."

She used her search engine to look for a Joe Brown in St. Louis, but if there was one, he didn't have a Web site.

"Can you get me the Yellow Pages?"

"Right here," she said.

Nicole walked over, got the large book, and took it to Keough.

"This is good," he said to Nicole, leafing through it.

"Why?"

"No Web site, no commercials," he said. "He used this dealer because he was low-profile." He ran his finger down the page, then stopped. "Got it."

"Are you going to call?"

"No," he said. "I'll go over there tomorrow and talk to him."

"You're the head of this task force, now," she said. "Why don't you send Marc, or Berkery, or one of the others?"

"I was never very good about delegating," he said. "Especially when it's something I can do myself."

"What's happening with the Chicago case?"

"Glad you reminded me," he said. "I've got that conference call first thing in the morning with the two mayors and the head of the Chicago task force."

"How are they going to take it?" she asked.

"I don't know. You tell me. You met the guy running their end. What was his name?"

"Fowler," she said, "and he wasn't happy to see me, I can tell you."

"Well, if I can manage to get Harriet in a better position, I'll be happy."

He turned his attention back to the phone book and wrote down the address of the car dealership in his notebook.

"Why not call ahead now?" she asked.

"I don't want to warn anyone," he said, looking at her. "What if Gabriel works there—or even owns the place?"

"If he's got money, he's probably not a car salesman," she said, "but he could own it, I guess."

He closed the phone book. "I'll get you thinking like a cop yet."

Sixty-eight

GABRIEL LOOKED AT the girl. Her hands and feet were tied, and she was blindfolded. She was a good little girl. He'd told her not to make a sound, and she hadn't.

"Mister?" she said, speaking for the first time.

"Yes?"

"I'm kinda hungry."

"We're going to eat soon," he told her. "Now be quiet."

"Yes, sir."

He looked around the room he had rented just for this purpose. It was one of the old motel courts in town, a place hardly anyone used anymore. In fact, most of them had closed down in the past few years. There was a bed, a dresser, a small TV, a table, an extra chair, and a bathroom. Usually, he would have taken something a little better, a little bigger, but he was moving his timetable up on this one because he was anxious to get to Chicago.

Melissa Reid would be dead tomorrow, and by tomorrow night, he'd be on a plane to the Windy City.

No harm in deviating from his pattern just this once.

Sixty-nine

KEOUGH'S CELL PHONE continued to ring until he told the officers conducting the search to stand down until morning. He instructed Berkery and House to go home, and to return to the office tomorrow. Neither man sounded happy, and they would probably want some sort of explanation the next day. Keough was fairly sure Berkery knew what had happened. What he didn't know was whether or not the man had agreed to go along with Dan Henry's plan. He hoped not. . . .

He sent Nicole back to the hotel to get some dinner, and also told Jeter to go home. To his surprise, Nicole and Jeter agreed to meet for dinner. Keough had the feeling Nicole might be responding to the fact that Jeter was no longer trying so hard to impress her.

Lastly, he told Martha to shut down the computer and go home, that he'd see her in the morning.

"Can I ask you something?" she said before leaving.

"Sure."

"What happened to the sergeant?"

"The sergeant made an error in judgment, and I'm afraid it cost him his job."

She nodded, said, "Good night," and left.

Keough waited until he got back to his hotel room to call Harriet.

"Your conference call might get me inside the task force," she observed, "but they'll probably hate me even more."

"I don't think they hate you."

"Dislike, then," she said. "On top of everything else, Fowler is a chauvinist—or at least a misogynist. He won't have a woman on his task force."

There was no woman on the St. Louis task force, either—at least not while Dan Henry had been running it. Keough didn't think that was a result of a dislike for women on the sergeant's part. Now that he was running it, though, Nicole was the only woman.

"I'll call you as soon as I've finished with the conference call, let you know how Fowler reacted to the whole thing."

"Fine," she said. "I'll just sit in my hotel room and wait."

"Have breakfast in bed," he suggested.

"I've never thought of you as a decadent man, Joe—at least not until now."

Keough was about to get undressed, when his room phone rang.

"Coffee?" Nicole asked.

His first instinct was to say no, but he said, "All right. Downstairs, five minutes."

Before leaving the room, he walked to where he had Jack Roswell's chess set arranged. Roswell had tried to teach him different openings, but he'd never been able to keep the names straight, let alone the moves. The only one he ever recalled was the Ruy Lopez and he still didn't know what the exact moves were. Openings, gambits . . . Jack used to say the chessboard was a perfect metaphor for life. Not just war—as many considered chess a "war game"—but life itself.

He stared at the board for a few moments, then moved the white king's pawn forward two spaces. The simplest of openings, it gave both the queen and one of the bishops access to the board. Before leaving the room, he wondered whether in the game he was now involved in, he was a pawn or the king?

Seventy

THE BAR WAS still open. He found Nicole waiting in front of the door. She smiled as he approached, and he was struck once again at how exotically lovely she was. They'd been so busy the last few days, he'd stopped looking at her as a woman. And maybe it wasn't such a good idea to start again.

They went inside, got a table, and both ordered coffee.

"I had a message when I got back to my room," she said. "Orders from my director to put myself at your disposal."

"I guess the mayor got through to him," he said.

"I guess."

The waitress returned with the coffee. They both turned down the offer of cream and sugar. The waitress was an attractive middle-aged blonde. She gave Keough an extra smile and, in effect, put herself at his disposal, as well, if he wanted anything else.

"She's flirting with you shamelessly, right in front of me," Nicole said. "How does she know we're not together?"

"Body language?" he asked. "Besides, I don't think she was—"

"Men are so dense sometimes," she said, cutting him off, "especially about women."

"I'm sure you're right," he replied. "After all, you're the expert."

"How do you intend to use me, now that I'm assigned to you?" she asked. "I'm not a detective, you know."

"I know that," he said.

"And I suspect you don't especially care for profilers."

"I just . . . put more credence in . . . other talents when it comes to solving crimes."

"Like . . . hunches?"

"Instinct."

"Ah."

"But I want all the help I can get in these cases," he said. "You said you hadn't sent a report in yet."

"That's right."

"Can you profile both these killers?"

"To some extent," she said. "Probably the St. Louis one better than the one in Chicago."

"I want you to work on both reports for me," he said, "with an eye toward connecting them."

"Connecting?"

Keough sat forward.

"Postulate some sort of . . . relationship between them."

"I can't . . . create one."

"There has to be one," Keough said.

"Why?"

"It's too coincidental that they would be operating so close to each other."

"With so many serial killers operating in the country, why would that be odd?"

"The methods," he said, "the children—"

"Boys in Chicago, girls here."

"Same age," he said, shaking her comment off, "same method—"

"Different class of victim."

"The angel pins," he said, as if he was playing a trump card. "The goddamned angel pins are too much of a coincidence—even though they're different," he rushed to add, before she could make the comment. "The fact that there are angel pins in all the cases is too much for me to accept."

"So you think they're working together?"

He sat back. Up to this point, they had both ignored their coffee. He picked his up and sipped it, not because he wanted it, but because he needed a moment.

"I want you to tell me what you think," he said finally, "before I start voicing my hunches."

"And what if my thought jibes with your hunches?"

He smiled and said, "Well, then, we'll be on the same page."

"And will you admit then that what I do has merit?" she asked.

"I never said it didn't."

"But what you do works better."

"For me."

She changed her tack then.

"What about that remark Maurice made?"

"About what?"

"You know, Gemini," she said. "That you should beware of Geminis?"

"Maybe when we find our killer," he replied, "we'll discover that he's a Gemini."

"Maybe . . ." she said. She looked at her watch. "Well, if I'm going to do those reports, I'll have to get to it."

"You have a typewriter in your room?"

She shook her head. "Computer and printer, both very portable."

He called the waitress over and signed the check—which would go on his room tab—leaving a sizable tip. He saw on the ticket that the waitress's name was Elise.

"Thanks, Elise," he said, handing her the signed bill.

"Thank you, handsome," she said. "Come back and see me."

"I will."

As they walked out, Nicole said, "It still bugs me that she assumed we weren't together."

"Do you think it was a color thing," he asked, "or an age thing?"

Suddenly, she found the situation funny.

"Well, for your sake, I hope it was a color thing."

They walked to the elevator and rode up together. They got to his floor first, and when he stepped out, she stopped the door from closing.

"Sure you don't want to come up and see my . . . printer?" she asked.

"Not tonight," he said. "I've got some work to do, too."

"Good night, then," she said, and allowed the door to close.

He was in his room before he started to wonder if, once again, as with the waitress, he had just been dense.

Seventy-one

May 5, 2004

KEOUGH TOOK HIS conference call in his hotel room, speaking to both mayors and Commander Fowler, whom he could hear fuming on the phone. By the time he was finished explaining what he wanted to do, he didn't care how the other commander felt. Both mayors were on his team, because out of all the cases in both cities, St. Louis finally had a witness.

In the end, the mayor of Chicago gave Commander Robert Fowler very specific instructions about cooperating with Keough and his task force, which included making Agent Harriet Connor a member of his team.

"Have you got that clear, Commander?" the mayor asked.

"Yes, sir."

Keough could now tell that the commander's lips were so tight, they were in danger of cracking. "Commander," he said, "I'm sure we both want the same thing—to stop these murders as soon as we can so that the streets will be safe for children again."

"Well put, Detective Keough," Commander Fowler said. "Very well put."

Keough knew it wasn't so much a compliment as it was congratulations for saying the right things while both mayors were listening. Keough hadn't realized how condescending his remark was until he'd said it.

After he hung up, Keough knew he was going to have to have a conversation with Fowler without both mayors listening in. But that would have to come later. At the moment, he had a lead to follow up.

Nicole was waiting impatiently in the lobby when Keough came down.

"It's about time," she said. "I'm starving. Can we have breakfast?"

"Sure," he said. "We'll drive through a McDonald's on the way to Collinsville."

"Collinsville? Where's that?"

"Just on the other side of the river."

"We don't have time for a good sit-down breakfast?" she asked.

"Egg McMuffin," he said. "I'm anxious to get over to Joe Brown's, and we have to stop at the office first. I've got to get everybody squared away and on the same page."

When they took off in his car, he asked, "Did you do your homework?"

She held up a couple of folders and said, "Right here. Stayed up late to do it."

"Really? You look . . . refreshed."

"Luckily, I only need three or four hours of sleep. I work for a harsh taskmaster."

"Your director?"

"You, dummy."

"Oh."

"You know, for a brilliant detective, you don't have much of a sense of humor."

"You didn't, either, until you loosened up some."

She clasped her hands in her lap and said, "I know, but it takes me awhile to become comfortable with new people."

They drove in silence for a while, until Keough got onto Highway 40.

"You really think I'm a brilliant detective?" he asked.

"If you solve both these cases, I will," she said, hedging.

"Maybe that'll depend on what you have in your folders."

"Want to go over them now?"

"No," he said. "I know what I want to say to the troops, so let's not confuse me."

"A brilliant mind like yours? Confused?"

"Hey, you said I was brilliant," he countered, "not me."

They entered the task force's office ahead of everyone but Martha. Keough went right to her desk and handed her a Styrofoam cup.

"Tea, right?"

"Thank you, and good morning," she replied. "I have the reports from last night. John Berkery and Marc Jeter wrote them up and sent them by E-mail."

"Enterprising of them," Keough said. "I'll be doing a report myself this morning, but I'll probably just walk it over to you."

"That's fine."

"Martha, I'd like to get everybody back here who was originally with the task force. I don't want to have to brief anyone from the beginning."

"I've taken care of that," she said. "I contacted all the commands and told them the task force had been re-formed."

"You're very efficient. Next time, you get tea and a pastry."

She smiled and said, "Just keep rewarding me in the proper fashion."

Keough looked at Nicole and said, "I'm going to take a few minutes to type out a report on yesterday's incidents. Why don't you grab a desk and have your breakfast?"

"I'll fine-tune my reports, as well," she said. "We can go over them in the car."

Keough went to the desk formerly used by Dan Henry and sat down. He hadn't expected to be in this position when he first came to St. Louis, but now that he was, he'd make sure he ran a tight ship.

Seventy-two

KEOUGH SAT BACK in his chair and regarded the roomful of people. He'd worked most closely with gold shields Jeter, Berkery, and House. The other two, O'Doul and George, were silver badges, working as plainclothes officers. He hadn't worked much with them at all. The other men in the room were cops who had worked door-to-door, canvassing and searching, jobs that required footwork rather than a knowledge of detection. With Busby and Martha included, there were about twenty people in the room. All of them were staring at Keough, waiting to hear what he had to say. Most of them wanted an explanation about the change of command.

"By now, you all know that I've replaced Dan Henry as head of this task force. We're also coordinating with the Chicago task force that's been working on their version of these crimes. In their case, it's been boys who have been kidnapped and killed, but the same age as the girls here. So I guess what we have now is a sort of multicity, multiagency task force on our hands."

"What happened to Sergeant Henry?" someone asked.

"Well, we made an arrest a couple of days ago, a man named Larry Keith. Now, while Mr. Keith may still turn out to be guilty of his stepdaughter's murder, we have good reason to believe he's not our serial killer. For some reason, Sergeant Henry took it upon himself to . . . fabricate some evidence against Keith to make it look like he was guilty. In the end, he came forward and owned up to what he'd done. He's no longer part of the St. Louis Police Department."

"Did they take his pension away?" another cop asked.

"That, I don't know," Keough said. "You'll have to ask around about that. All I know is, we still have a killer on the loose, and he struck again yesterday. A girl named Melissa Reid was snatched on her way home from school. She's eleven. Most of you are going to be on the streets today, trying to find her, hopefully still alive."

"And the rest of us?" Jim House asked.

"Well, Jim, we've got a witness, which is something we never had before," Keough explained. "So we have some leads to work. I'm going to want you three detectives to stay behind while everyone else hits the streets. Use whatever sources you have, work the area where the girl was taken, and see what you can find out. Martha's got all the information written down for you. Just grab your assignment on your way out."

Nobody moved. Keough stood up as the members of the task force shuffled to their feet and exchanged glances.

"We might as well get this out of the way right now," Keough said. "If any of you think that you'd rather see a murderer go free than work for me, you're invited to leave. If you'd rather see him go free than think you're being disloyal to Dan Henry—a man who faked evidence to arrest an innocent man—then leave now. There's the door."

Again they exchanged glances, but nobody said anything until John Berkery stood up, surprising Keough.

"We still have a job to do," he said, turning to face the others. "Dan Henry made his own decision, and it was a bad one. He has to live with that. I, for one, don't want to live with the knowledge that I let a killer go free." He pointed at Keough. "This man's in charge now, and he's got a lot of experience catching serial killers. He's going to see us through this." He turned to face Keough. "You tell me what to do, Detective Keough, and I'll do it."

"Thanks, John," Keough said, surprised at the support and where it was coming from. "Thanks a lot. Now, what about the rest of you?"

There was a moment of silence; then a couple of men stepped over to Martha's desk and picked up their assignments. Another followed, then two men, and then they were all filing by her desk on the way to the door. No one accepted the invitation to leave.

Finally, Keough was there with just Jeter, Berkery, House, Busby, and Martha. Berkery stepped to the desk and stuck his hand out.

"Dan Henry was my friend, and my sergeant," he said, "but he made a bad decision. I had nothing to do with it."

"I believe you, John," Keough said, shaking his hand. "And thanks for the vote of confidence. I don't know how many of them I would have lost if you hadn't spoken up when you did."

"Probably not many," Berkery said. "They're all good men."

"I don't doubt that," Keough said. "Not for a minute."

Berkery backed away from the desk and joined the others.

"Guess we're ready for our assignments," Jeter said.

"Anybody know anything about a car dealership called Joe Brown's? . . ."

Seventy-three

KEOUGH HAD TAKEN Highway 40 from downtown to Clayton, then got back on it to go through downtown again, crossing the river to Collinsville.

"You know, Marc wasn't very happy this morning," Busby told him.

"I know that," he said.

"He thinks of himself as your partner."

"Marc's a good young detective," Keough said. "He'll get over it. You and I need to talk this out, and there was no point in three of us going to Collinsville."

"You want to hear my reports, then?"

"Sure," he said, "unless it'd be easier just to talk it out."

"Well, the first part of each report is pretty standard, meaning that I feel pretty certain both of these killers fit the usual profile of the serial killer: They're probably in their late twenties to early thirties, products of abuse and/or broken homes."

"Oh, I see," Keough said, "the usual stuff."

She looked up from her reports at him. "The usual mumbo jumbo, you mean?"

"What?"

"That's what you think of profiling, isn't it?"

"Would you be sitting here next to me if that was what I thought?"

Partially mollified, she said, "I suppose not."

"But what I want is more than the usual stuff," he told her. "We've got two serial killers operating within three hundred miles of each other, with a very similar MO. Now either they're working together, coordinating their efforts, or . . ."

She waited a moment, then asked, "Or what?"

"That's what I'm asking you," he said. "Give me some other possibilities."

"Well, I can only think of one, but I can't endorse it."

"Why not?"

"It doesn't fit any profile."

"So maybe we're about to invent a new one," he said. "What are you referring to?"

"For both of them to be doing the same thing at the same time, they could be related to each other."

"Brothers, you mean?"

"Brother, father and son—" She stopped short.

"Okay, so if they're brothers, they were raised together in the same family, the same environment."

"The way these two are operating indicates they were raised differently; that's why I don't feel I can endorse this school of thinking."

"Keep explaining it to me."

"The St. Louis killer appears to be a product of a higher social class," she said. "The Chicago killer is going after children from low-income families. This is an indication of how each was raised."

"Okay," Keough said, "what if they're related, but they were separated and raised differently?"

"If these serial killers were created by their environment . . ." She trailed off, pausing to rethink her statement.

"What if it's not environment?" he said. "What if they're related but were brought up differently, and something inside them— something genetic—caused them to become serial killers at the same time."

"The very same time?" she asked. "I don't see it, Joe."

"So two brother are raised differently, but they become serial killers at the same time. How is that possible?"

She paused again and turned her head to look out the window.

"Don't you believe that serial killers can be genetically shaped?"

"They're usually a result of their upbringing," she said, "their environment."

"What if our killer was brought up with a silver spoon in his mouth?" Keough asked. "What if he was never abused, and not the product of a broken home?"

"Why is he a serial killer, then?" she asked. "Why is he choosing young girls from well-to-do homes for his victims?"

"I can't answer the second question," Keough said, "but he could have become a serial killer because of something in his head, something he was born with—call it a time bomb—that just went off."

"And you're saying this time bomb went off in both of them at the same time?"

"Why not?"

"For that to have happened, they'd have to be . . ."

"Related?"

She looked at him and said, "Gemini."

Now he looked at her and frowned. "What?"

"Geminis," she said again, then added, "twins."

Seventy-four

THEY LET THE discussion drop when they got to Joe Brown's Pre-owned Cars in Collinsville, right off of Highway 255. There were quite a few car dealerships in the area. Keough figured they weren't going to be lucky enough to find that their serial killer had used the same one all four times.

They parked in a lot filled with used cars, many of them the color of the one they were interested in. Also, each car had the name Joe Brown on the back, a stylized signature in metal.

The office had the feel of a building that used to be a fast-food place—maybe a McDonald's or Burger King—that had gone out of business and was reincarnated as a car lot.

"These are used-car prices?" Nicole asked, looking at the big numbers painted on the windshields. They were big and white, and they were high.

"Can't get much cheaper anymore," Keough commented, "except maybe the jacket this guy's wearing."

The salesman approaching them looked like he was dressed to play the part in a commercial. His jacket was vivid yellow, and the belt on his brown pants matched, as did his shoes.

"You folks lookin' for a nice family car?" he asked, rubbing his hands together.

"We're looking for Joe," Keough said, flashing his ID. Nicole did the same, and the man caught sight of the FBI designation on hers—that's all he saw.

"Ooookay," he said, "but you gotta tell me which Joe. We got a few."

"Brown?" Keough asked. "There is a Joe Brown, isn't there?"

"There sure is," the salesman said. From the degree of relief on his face, his name must also have been Joe. "I'll get him for you."

"Why don't you just take us to his office?" Keough suggested.

"Whatever you say. Follow me, then."

He led them down a corridor to a back office; they didn't pass any others along the way. Apparently, the boss was the only person to have one. Keough thought he could still smell french fries in that hall.

"Boss?" the man said when he got to the door.

"What is it, Joe?"

"Some folks from the FBI are here to see you."

"From where?"

Salesman Joe waved them in and then slithered off back along the hall.

Keough let Nicole enter first. The man behind the desk stood up, almost knocking his chair over as he did. He was too tall and bulky for the room, but Keough put his clumsiness down to nerves. There might have been some cars out in the lot that weren't exactly kosher.

"Hello, folks," he said, plastering a big smile across his face. "I'm Joe Brown, the proprietor. What can I do for you? FBI, did Joe say?"

"We're with a task force that is investigating the deaths of several little girls. I'm sure you've seen it on the news."

"Oh, right, right," Brown said, "three or four, isn't it?"

"Four right now." Keough looked around, saw two chairs against the wall. "Mind if we sit?"

"Hey, of course," the man said. "Sorry I didn't ask, but I'm kinda nervous. It's not every day you get a visit from the FBI, is it?"

Keough pulled over the two wooden chairs.

"Do you have some reason to be nervous, Mr. Brown?" he asked when he was seated.

"Well, let's be honest," the man said. "You could really jam me up if you wanted to. I mean . . . you are the FBI."

Keough still didn't correct him, but he hoped they could get beyond that now.

"Well, we're not here to cause you any difficulty, sir," he said respectfully. "We just need your help with something."

"Anything I can do, I will," Joe Brown said. "Just tell me what it is."

"Another little girl was kidnapped yesterday," Keough said, "and a witness saw your name on the back of the car that was used."

"My name?" His voice went up an octave.

"You know," Keough said, "that metal signature . . ."

"Oh." Brown looked relieved. "Yeah, we put that on all our cars. So you mean the kidnapper was driving a car that was bought here?"

"That's what I mean."

"I see. Well, how can I help?"

"We'd like to try to find out who bought the car."

Joe Brown frowned. "Do you have a license plate?"

"Our witness was another little girl," Keough said, "and she didn't get that. We know it was beige, not new, not very big." Keough went on to give Brown as much of a description as they had of the driver. Before he was done, he noticed the car dealer becoming excited.

"Now, wait a minute," he said, wagging a finger at them, "wait a minute. . . . There's a guy who's buying cars—I mean, he's bought three or four in the last few months."

Now Keough started to get excited.

"Who is he?" he asked. "How many times has he been here? You must have a—"

"Wait, wait," Brown said, waving both hands. "I knew this guy was up to no good!"

"How did you know that?"

"I just had a feeling. But he didn't buy all the cars from me. He bought the others from different dealers."

"How do you know that?"

"I'm a small business," he explained, "I don't do commercials like the big guys do. Well, there are a lot of us small dealers, and I drink with a few of them. We meet a few times a week after work to bitch and whine, or brag if we had a big day. One night, we're talking, comparing notes, and we realized that we'd each sold a car to the same guy, within months of each other."

"Do you have the guy's name? Do you remember what kind of car he bought?"

"Seems to me he didn't want a good one, but he paid with cash."

"Look," Keough said, "this had to be in the past week or so. . . ." He looked at Nicole for help.

"Unless he bought them all at one time," she said, "before he picked up the first girl."

"No," Keough said, "he'd have to store them then. I think he bought a car before each girl, and then got rid of it."

"How?" Brown asked, caught up in Keough's logic. "You don't think he sold my car to another dealer, do you? Maybe traded it in?"

"That's a possibility," Keough said. "Can you check on that with your friends?"

"No problem," Brown said. "I could call around right now and—"

"Not just yet," Keough said, stopping him. "I want to talk a bit more first."

"Okay. I'm glad to help catch this guy, and I know my colleagues will be, too."

"If we catch this guy with the help of all of you," Keough said, "I'll have a monument erected to used-car salesman everywhere."

"Preowned," Brown said.

"What?"

"They're preowned cars," the man said, "we don't say used anymore."

Seventy-five

SINCE THE CAR used in the kidnapping of Melissa Reid was the most recent one purchased, Joe Brown agreed to go looking in his files to see if he could find the purchase order. Keough and Nicole Busby waited anxiously in his office. They didn't speak, because they were both afraid to. They thought if they just waited in silence—and, in Nicole's case, said a silent prayer—Brown would come back with the name and address of their serial killer.

"Well," the man said, reentering the office and shaking his head, "I've got three purchase orders for cars like that." He sat down. "They're all Toyota Corollas. If you look on the road these days, that's about all you see."

"And you don't remember which one is the guy who has been buying all the cars?"

Brown looked down at the purchase orders, then said, "Detective, I can't be sure, and I don't want to tell you this is the guy."

"Well," Keough said, "if you can photocopy those orders, we can just go ahead and check out all three customers."

Joe Brown hesitated, then asked, "Uh, is this legal? I mean, don't you need a warrant . . . or something?"

"I can get a warrant, Mr. Brown," Keough said, "but that would just slow us up. If you give us these three purchase orders, in the spirit of cooperation, it's very legal, I assure you."

"Well . . . okay, give me a minute."

He left the office again, and Keough hoped that somewhere in this fast food–sized operation there was a copy machine.

"So now we have to check out all three of these men?" Nicole asked. "That little girl doesn't have much time, Joe."

"I know it, Nicole," Keough said. "I've got an idea that may save us some time."

When Brown came back again, he handed Keough the three purchase orders.

"Mr. Brown, I wonder if you could do me a favor?"

"Sure."

"Since you say you are drinking buddies with the other dealers, could you call them, give them these names, and ask if they come up with a match? If all four of you have sold a car to the same guy, then he's our man."

"Hey, that's a great idea," Brown said. "And you can just call me Joe."

"Okay, Joe."

"And what's your name?" the man asked as he picked up the phone to dial.

"I think," Joe Keough said, "it would be easier if you just kept calling me 'Detective.'"

Brown placed calls to three other dealers, who all promised to check it out and call back. After the third call had been made, it became awkward in the little office.

"Can I get you something?" Brown asked. "There's a Dunkin' Donuts a few exits down. I could send somebody out for coffee and dough—oh, uh, hey, I wasn't trying to be funny or anything—I mean about the doughnuts," he stammered.

"It's okay, Joe," Keough said. "No offense taken, and we don't want anything. We really just need to get this information."

"I can understand that," Brown said.

"If you have some work you want to do while we're waiting, go right ahead."

"Well," Brown said, "in light of what's at stake, nothing else seems to be very important. My wife and me, we got two girls of our own, and we're trying for a third child—we want a boy this—"

He was interrupted when the phone rang. He picked it up, listened, wrote something down, and then hung up.

"We got a match," he said excitedly. "Now, if the others would call—"

The phone rang, interrupting him again, and he went through the same thing.

"Another match—" he said.

"Great!" Keough reached out for the slip of paper Brown had written on.

"But it's a different name."

Keough snatched his hand back. "Shit!"

"Maybe," Nicole said, "it'll get clearer when some of the others call back."

Keough sat back. "Maybe."

"Besides," she added, "cutting it down from three to two helps us."

Not as much as having the perp's name and address, Keough thought.

Fifteen minutes later, all of Joe Brown's dealer buddies had called in. They had the names of two men who had bought more than one car, but only one matched the name that Brown had.

"This is our guy," Keough said, showing the name to Nicole. "Three cars. He must have bought the fourth from someone who isn't part of Joe's circle of friends."

"Michael Delacorte," she said, looking at the piece of paper.

"Hey!" Joe Brown said.

"What?" Keough asked.

"When she just said it out loud, I remembered," Brown said. "I called him Mike and he got upset. He said his name was Michael. He was real particular about that."

"Joe," Keough said, standing, "I want to thank you for your help."

Brown stood and shook hands. "I'm glad I could do it. I hope you catch this guy."

"Believe me," Keough said, "nobody hopes that more than I do."

Brown exchanged good-byes with Nicole Busby and then watched them both walk down the hall.

Outside, Nicole asked, "Are we going straight to his house?"

"We are, yeah," he said.

"No backup?" She'd read his tone correctly.

They got in the car before he answered.

"If we call for backup, we'll have locals driving over there as well as our guys. Even if we keep them silent and don't let them approach the house, they'll congregate at each end of his block. Word gets around when that happens in a neighborhood."

"So what now?"

"I'm going to call this in to Martha and keep it off the air. She can check this guy out in her computer while we drive over there. By the time we arrive, we should know everything about him, including his shoe size."

"Joe, you'll need backup to go in after him," she said.

"You have a gun, don't you?"

"Well, yes, but . . ."

He turned his head to take a quick look at her and saw how agitated she was.

"Okay," he said. He used his cell phone to call Martha, gave her the name and address of the suspect, and then asked her to have Marc Jeter, John Berkery, and Jim House meet them at that address but not to go in until he and Busby got there. By the time he hung up, Agent Nicole Busby was much less agitated.

Seventy-six

GABRIEL PAUSED IN the middle of his living room to go over a mental checklist. Things to do today: *Kill the girl. Get rid of the body. Dispose of the car. Fly to Chicago.* All that was left to do was the last—fly to Chicago.

He left the house, making sure the alarm was set and the doors were locked, went to his three-car garage, chose the Lexus, and drove himself to the airport, satisfied that he had left enough behind to occupy Detective Keough and the rest of the task force until he returned.

Seventy-seven

"I HAVE TO tell you something."

Keough didn't take his eyes off the road. He thought it was ironic that they had to go back to Clayton to get to Michael Delacorte's house.

"What's that?"

"My thesis was based upon the fact—the belief—that serial killers are made, not born."

He hesitated a moment, then said, "Well, that puts us at odds, doesn't it? Because I believe the opposite."

"Based on what?"

"Based on the fact—the fact—that I've met many men—and women—who were products of a broken home, and of child abuse, but did not grow up to be serial killers."

"But all of the serial killers who have been studied have been," she said. "That fact is indisputable."

"Maybe so," he said, "but all that means is all serial killers have been abused, but all victims of abuse do not become serial killers."

"You're looking at it backward."

"The academics are looking at it backward."

"And I'm an academic?"

"Nicole, I don't think this is the time to debate genetics versus environment."

"When *will* be the time?"

"Maybe when we catch these two killers," Keough said, "then we can ask them."

When they reached the Clayton residential area, which was lined with large and expensive homes, Keough parked his car a few houses down from the address they wanted.

"Stay here," he said, undoing his seat belt. "If anyone approaches you—residents, private security, or local cops—show them your ID. The others should be here soon. If you see them, flag them down and make them wait for me."

"What are you going to do?"

"I just want to take a look around."

"You won't try to go in without backup?"

"No," he said, "don't worry. I just want to check his garage and see if he's home. I'll be right back."

"A—all right."

"Here." He gave her his cell phone. "In case somebody tries to contact us."

"Too bad we don't have a radio."

"In a few years," he predicted, "these will probably replace radios. We won't have to deal with all that static."

He opened his door, put one foot outside, then turned back to her and asked, "What kind of gun you got?"

"Nine-millimeter."

"Glock?"

"Yes."

"You qualify with it?"

She bit her lip, then said honestly, "Just barely."

"Okay, stay in the car and don't shoot anybody."

"I think I can do that."

"I think so, too." He stepped out of the car, closed the door, and crossed the street.

* * *

Keough found the house, an impressive structure with white columns and a huge wraparound porch. He'd seen B and B's that weren't as large.

He circled the house, looking in windows, staying aware in case a neighbor saw him. It was midday, but he knew some of these people might have so much money they didn't work, or they worked at home. If someone spotted him, they'd probably just call their private security firm, or the cops, instead of approaching him. He'd seen a sign for private security, but sometimes that was all neighborhoods did—put up signs.

He worked his way around to the three-car garage and peered in a window. There were two cars inside, small sports cars he wasn't privileged enough to recognize. All he knew was that neither was the one they were looking for. The empty space worried him. The perp could have taken that car out, meaning he wasn't home. Maybe he'd driven it to wherever he had the girl stashed.

Satisfied that he'd done all he could until backup arrived, he returned to the sidewalk and made his way to Nicole and the car. When he got there, she was sitting inside with three men—two in the backseat and one in the front. Jeter, Berkery, and House had arrived.

"We left our cars up the street," Berkery said when Keough opened the driver's door. He didn't attempt to get in; there were too many bodies. "Agent Busby has briefed us on this guy Delacorte."

"Is he home?" Jeter asked.

"I don't know," Keough said. "I didn't see him inside, and there's a car missing from the three-car garage."

"Let's go in and get him, then," Berkery said.

"Agent Busby filled us in on how you got his name," House said. "That was good work."

"We got lucky with that little girl as a witness," Keough said. He looked at Nicole. "Did Martha call with our make?"

"Yes," she said. "Michael Delacorte inherited a ball-bearing company from his father when both parents died. He then sold it for millions, and apparently he doesn't feel the need to work."

"It would cramp his serial killer style if he had to go into an office," Jim House said.

"And wants or warrants? Past arrests?"

"He's clean, apparently," Nicole said. "Not even a speeding ticket."

"When he finally decided to break the law, he went whole hog, didn't he?" Berkery asked.

"We don't know that this *is* the guy," Keough said, "but we're going to go in and find out."

"No warrant?" Jeter asked.

"We've got probable cause," Keough said, "and besides, we've got carte blanche from the mayor to do whatever we have to do."

"Well then," Berkery said, "let's do it."

"I don't want to go crashing in," Keough explained. "There's the slightest chance he might have the girl inside. I'll take Nicole to the front door with me. The house is huge and there are exits on all sides. Marc, take the back; John and Jim can take either side. I'll give you five minutes to get in place, and then I'm going to ring the doorbell. Got it?"

They all nodded.

"Okay, then," Keough said, "let's do this."

Seventy-eight

KEOUGH AND NICOLE approached the front door. He motioned
for her to stand to the left while he stood to the right. When he figured everyone was in place, he rang the doorbell. It was loud and
they could hear it echoing inside. When there was no answer, he
rang it again. Still no response.

"What now?" Nicole asked.

"We go in." Keough drew his gun and looked at Nicole, silently
telling her to do the same. She took hers from beneath her jacket
and held it properly.

"You've done this before," he said.

She shook her head and said, "TV and movies."

Keough tried the knob but found the door locked. It was heavy
and he doubted he'd be able to kick it in. They'd probably be able
to get access from a side or back door, or a window, but for him to
go and join one of the others, he'd have to leave Nicole here alone,
in case Delacorte came out the front door. He didn't want to do
that, since she wasn't actually a trained field agent, but before he
could make up his mind, the doorknob turned and the door started
to open. Both he and Nicole took a step back and pointed their
guns at the door.

"Don't shoot," Jim House said with a grin.

"How'd you get in?" Keough asked.

"French doors are the easiest to force," he said. "I figured one of these heavy front doors would be rough."

"Good work," Keough said. "You see anybody inside?"

"No, but I just walked from the dining room to here."

"Okay," Keough said. "Go and let the others in. I don't think he's home, but Nicole and I will check the upstairs; the rest of you look downstairs. Once we're clear, we're going to need a forensics unit in here. There's got to be something to tell us if we've got the right guy."

"Okay."

House backed up, allowing Keough and Nicole to enter. They found themselves in a huge entryway, facing a staircase to the second floor.

"Wow," Nicole said.

"Yeah, I know," Keough said. "You'd think a man this rich would have better things to do than kill people."

"Children," she said, with distaste. "He kills children."

"Yeah," Keough said, "maybe. We're not sure this is the guy, Nicole, so don't get trigger-happy on me. In fact, put your gun away."

"What?"

"You're with me; it's all right," he said. "You don't need to have it out."

She looked for a moment as if she was going to argue, but then she simply shrugged and replaced the gun beneath her jacket.

"Okay," Keough said, "let's wait for the others before we go upstairs."

In moments, they were joined by Jeter, Berkery, and House.

"Okay, in twos, but be careful," Keough said, keeping his voice low. "If you find the little girl, sound off."

"What about the guy?" House asked.

"If any of us find him, the rest will know about it," Keough said. "Marc, why don't you stay outside, just in case."

"But I want to—"

"Marc," Keough said, "he might still be in the house, planning to slip outside while we're searching. Also, I noticed a keypad by the door. We tripped a silent alarm getting in here, so security should be along shortly. You can identify yourself to them and explain what's going on."

"All right," Jeter said, "but I hope he does try to get by me."

"Marc," Keough said, giving Jeter a meaningful look, which he hoped the young detective would take to heart, "be careful."

By the time the security service arrived, the agents had checked the entire house and found it empty. Michael Delacorte was a very neat person, but there were indications in the bedroom and the master bath that he had done some packing.

"Nicole," Keough said, "you and I are driving to Chicago."

"Chicago? But why?"

"Because I think that's where he went."

"But . . . why? How . . ."

"Remember my conversation with Gabriel? He said he was going to grab one more girl and then take a vacation."

"So? How does that mean Chicago?"

"He said he had a 'family matter' to attend to."

She studied him for a moment before speaking. "You took our discussion about brothers—twins—seriously."

"You said yourself that it's the only way two people could take the same path in their life at the very same time. There would have to be an even closer connection than brothers."

"Maurice's 'Gemini' warning."

"Yes, that, too."

"But why drive? He would fly."

"By the time we get to the airport, find out when the next flight is, get tickets, and wait for it to take off, we could be halfway there. It's four hours, maybe less if we floor it."

Keough had also never liked flying, and it was even less fun now with stepped-up security measures after September 11—security measures that seemed to inconvenience the average traveler more than root out potential terrorists.

"We could get stopped along the way by the state police."

"I'll get the way cleared," he said. "No one will stop us."

"When do we start, then?"

"As soon as I get things in motion here in the house."

Things in motion meant forensics checking everything from the attic to the basement and the garage, and even the laundry in the bathroom hamper. By the time the house was overrun with cops and technicians, Keough pulled his task force detectives aside to tell them he was going to Chicago and taking Nicole with him.

"John," he told Berkery, "you're in charge. Get in touch with me as soon as you find that girl, dead or alive."

"Most likely dead," Berkery said. "He wouldn't leave town unless he'd killed her already.

"I agree," Keough said, "but let's make this the last dead girl. We need to find something in this house that connects him to at least one of those girls."

A supervisor from the Clayton Police Department arrived at that moment, and Keough sent Berkery over to deal with him.

"Jim," he said to House, "stay on these techs. Make them find something."

"You got it."

As Jim House walked away, Jeter asked, "What about me? Can I go to Chicago with you?"

"No," Keough said, "I need you here, Marc."

"To do what?"

"There's a computer in the den," Keough said. "Get on it and find something that tells me I'm not wasting my time going to Chicago."

Jeter snapped his fingers. "Like an electronic airline ticket?"

"I don't care what you find," Keough said, "I just don't want to be driving to Chicago for no reason."

"Why don't you wait until—"

"No time," Keough said. "I've got to follow my instincts on this one, and they tell me he's going to Chicago to look for a twin brother—something he may not even be aware of yet!"

Seventy-nine

WHEN HE FELT that all wheels were turning in the proper direction, Keough and Nicole got in the car and started for Chicago. He stopped for gas and used the opportunity to call ahead to Harriet Connors.

"I just hope you're doing the right thing, Joe," she said.

"So do I."

"I mean, I'm happy to have you coming here, but if he's still in St. Louis—"

"I've got to follow this hunch, Harriet."

"I know you do," she said. "Now let me give you directions to the task force's office. . . ."

After he'd memorized her directions, he said, "Make sure Commander Fowler knows I'm on my way."

"I'll tell him. Where are you going to start looking when you get here?" she asked.

"I have no idea," he said, and hung up, hoping he would by the time he got there.

They had just passed Springfield, Illinois, when Keough's cell phone rang.

"Talk," he said into it.

"Joe, you were right," Jeter said to him. "I found an electronic ticket he got on the Internet."

"A rich guy like him uses a discount Web site?"

"It's not so much that it's cheaper as it's easier," Jeter explained. "Anyway, he's landing at O'Hare at about four P.M."

Keough checked his watch. They'd be driving into Chicago around six o'clock. Only two hours' difference.

"Did you find anything about hotel reservations?"

"No, nothing."

"Maybe he keeps an apartment there. Check that out, Marc. If he's got a place, you might find his name with the gas or electric company—unless he's using a phony name."

"Why wouldn't he book his flight that way?"

"He'd need proper ID because of security."

"That's right."

"What about forensics?" Keough asked. "They find anything?"

"Not yet," Jeter said. "They took a bunch of clothes and shoes to the lab."

"Well, let me know when they do."

"Gotcha."

"Good work on the ticket, Marc. See what else you can find in his computer and—wait a minute. Here's Harriet Connors's phone number in Chicago. Call her and get an E-mail address at their task force; then send along anything you find. Also send a copy of Delacorte's birth certificate."

"That's a good idea," Jeter said, "but I've got to tell you: I took a close look at it. It might have been altered."

"I thought of that, but it's all we have. Oh, and see if you can get us a good description of Delacorte, maybe from a neighbor. Send that to the Chicago office, as well."

"Right. Talk to you later."

Keough broke the connection and put the cell phone down in the change tray between him and Nicole.

"That was a good idea, the E-mail thing," she said.

"I get a good idea once in awhile."

"So he did book a flight to Chicago?"

"Yes."

"Good thing you followed your instincts."

"It usually is," he said. "Not always, but usually."

"Must be nice to be that sure of yourself," she commented.

"Not always."

Keough called Harriet and told her to have detectives go to O'Hare and look around discreetly. Maybe using whatever description they had, they could spot him and tail him. He also told her to make sure no marked units would be at the airport. They didn't want Delacorte to be tipped off.

They were approaching the Dixie Truck Stop and Keough was entertaining thoughts of making a pit stop, when his phone rang again. He had been doing eighty to ninety most of the way, but word had obviously gone ahead of them to the state police, because when he'd passed a couple of their cars—one of them unmarked— it had looked like they were tied to a post.

"Go ahead," he said into the phone.

"I'm surprised this guy doesn't have one of those programs like History Kill on his computer," Jeter said to Keough. "You'd think he'd want to hide his cybertrail."

"That's what this History Kill does?"

"Yes."

"Well, he's arrogant enough never even to entertain the thought that we might find his home, let alone get into his computer," Keough said. "What did you find? Porn?"

"No porn at all," Jeter said, surprised. "Everybody looks at a little porn sometimes, but not this guy."

"So what did you get?"

"He's been searching birth records in Chicago."

"Bingo!" Keough said. "He's looking for a brother—probably a twin."

"You'd think a twin birth would be easy to find," Jeter said. "If he's in his late twenties, early thirties, we're talking about the seventies. Even if the hospital wasn't computerized then, you'd think seventies and eighties births would have been put on computer later."

"Okay, maybe it's not a twin," Keough said. "Just keep looking."

"Will do."

"Anything from forensics?"

"Not yet."

"Talk to you later."

They were outside Joliet when the phone rang again. Keough had stopped once for gas, and they'd grabbed a couple of microwaved sandwiches that they'd eaten in the car, washing them down with Cokes—diet coke for him. He also remembered to take his pills, which, with everything else he had on his mind, was a feat in itself. Sometimes he forgot for a couple of days, and Harriet was always ragging him about it. She said she couldn't always be there to remind him and that one day he was going to wake up in a coma.

"Marc?"

"Harriet. I got that stuff your Detective Jeter sent along—the birth-record searches and all."

"What about utilities?"

"If your man has an apartment here, he's subletting, or using an assumed name. Where are you?"

"Joliet."

"You're less than half an hour away," she said. "I'll see you soon."

He nodded, even though she couldn't see him, and hung up.

They had passed the Joliet exit on I-55 and were approaching the I-80 exit—which they would not take—when the phone rang yet again.

"Keough."

"We found something, Keough."

It was Berkery. "John, what'd you find?"

"A strongbox with some personal papers in it."

"Like what?"

"A birth certificate."

"I don't believe it."

"Imagine this guy leaving stuff like that around," Berkery said. "The smartest sons of bitches are as stupid as the rest of them."

"What hospital was he born in?"

"Roseland."

"Parents named Delacorte?"

"Nope," Berkery said. "Parents named Shur."

"He was adopted."

"Looks like it."

"Either scan that into a computer and send an E-mail to Chicago or fax it, whichever is quickest."

"Right."

"What else was in that box?"

Nothing relating to this," Berkery said. "Stock options, deeds, corporate papers—"

"John," Keough said, "have Jeter run the corporate name through the computer and see if the company maintains an apartment in Chicago. Even though Delacorte sold out, maybe he maintains use of an apartment."

"Good idea. I'll tell him. You in Chicago yet?"

"Outskirts. Should be at the office there soon. John? What about a phone book?"

"We're on it," Berkery said. "We're going through it, looking for friends, girlfriends, booty calls, whatever. Somebody's got to know this guy well enough for him to have told them he'd be out of town."

"Maybe," Keough said, "but the profilers would say he's a loner."

He looked at Nicole and she nodded.

"I'll call in when I get to the office," Keough said.

"Right. Talk to you later."

As Keough put the phone down, Nicole said, "I feel like we're accomplishing more during this car ride than we have for days."

"We got to the top of the hill, Nicole," Keough said excitedly. "Now we start down the other side." He glanced at her. "This is when it starts getting good."

Eighty

GABRIEL HAD ARRIVED in Chicago on time and immediately taken a cab to the apartment his father's old company maintained on Lakeshore Drive. One of the conditions of the sale was that Gabriel—or Michael Delacorte, as he was known to them—would retain all the perks of being owner and CEO of the company.

The apartment was in one of the more luxurious buildings on Lakeshore Drive, with a beautiful clear view of Lake Michigan and the yacht club.

Upon arrival, he did not unpack, but simply tossed his suitcase into the bedroom. He poured himself a drink and then called Roseland Hospital to see how much information he could get on the phone before actually going over there. It was not in a good part of town, and he wanted to avoid going there if possible.

But the information was not to be had over the phone. The person he spoke to quoted hospital policy to him, saying she could not give out names or addresses.

"I only want to know if this doctor still works there," Gabriel told the woman on the phone. "I'm not asking for an address."

"I'm sorry, sir," she said, "I simply cannot answer any questions over the—"

He slammed the phone down. He was sure if he went down there and flashed a few bills around, somebody would be only too happy to answer his questions. It always came down to money, didn't it?

One of the other perks of his agreement with his father's old company was that there would always be a car in the basement garage, gassed up and ready to go. He knew where the keys were, so he finished his drink to calm himself down. He took the elevator to the basement garage. The car was a Lexus, much like the one he preferred to drive at home.

He got in the car and started the engine, then used the automatic system in the car to get directions to Roseland Community Hospital. As he pulled out of the garage, it was just starting to get dark. He hoped he had enough hours left in the day to accomplish what he wanted. He was afraid that if he had to wait until tomorrow, he would not be able to sleep all night.

His goal was within his grasp. He could taste it.

Eighty-one

THE OFFICE OF the Bureau of Investigative Services of the Chicago PD was located at 3510 South Michigan Avenue. It was also the building in which the task force was housed. Keough parked his car by a hydrant down the street because parking was the least of his worries. He didn't particularly care if he got a ticket, or if the car got towed. He was more concerned with catching two serial killers.

When he got off the elevator with Nicole, the first person he saw was Harriet. He had rung her cell phone from the street to say they were on their way up. The first thing she did was hand him a printout of the birth certificate Jeter had sent.

"You may not remember Agent Busby," Keough said.

The two women shook hands and Nicole said, "We didn't get much of a chance to talk."

"I've heard good things about you from Joe," Harriet said.

"Same here."

"Okay, now that we're all friends," Keough said, "did they spot him at the airport?"

"No," Harriet replied, "and they didn't want to guess and tail the wrong man."

"I kind of wish they had," Keough said.

"There were two detectives at the airport, and they said three guys got off the plane who could possibly have been Gabriel."

"Okay, okay. Who's inside?"

"Commander Fowler and three of his task force detectives."

"No politicians?"

"Not right now. The deputy superintendent of the Bureau of Investigative Services was here earlier. The task force is operating under him. He wants to be kept informed."

"Let's go in and you can introduce me," Keough said. "Is Fowler still balking at our participation?"

"Let's just say that if he gets any redder in the face, his head will explode," she replied, "but he's heard from the deputy superintendent, the superintendent, and the mayor that he's to cooperate."

Commander Fowler was very polite when introduced to Keough and Nicole, who said she'd met him earlier in the week. He didn't react to that, so they didn't know if he'd forgotten or was just playing ignorant.

The three Chicago detectives all shook Keough's hand and nodded. They looked as if they might have gone through the Academy together, ten or fifteen years after their CO. In an attempt to remember their first names, Keough replaced the famous double-play trio of Tinker to Evers to Chance with their last names—Davis to Johnson to Vance. It was Vance's name that inspired this technique to recall names.

There were many more men in the field, Harriet told him.

"If you'll allow me, Commander," Keough said after the introductions, "I'll tell you and your men what brings me to Chicago."

"I wish you would, sir," Fowler said.

Keough took up a position in front of the room, which was easily twice the size of the office in St. Louis. There were several computer terminals, with a different civilian employee at each, two men and a woman. He stood just in front of a large cork bulletin board and a clear erase board.

Slowly, he went through the train of logic that had led him to jump in his rental car and drive to Chicago at high speed—a drive he hoped had put him in town just two hours behind Michael Delacorte. When he was finished, all of the people in the room stared at him for a few moments. Then Detective Vance cleared his throat. He didn't speak, just cleared his throat, which seemed to break the spell.

"If you'll forgive me, Detective Keough," Commander Fowler said, "that doesn't strike me as sound police procedure, but, rather, as a seat-of-the-pants decision based on wild assumption."

Keough had expected the man to denigrate his conclusions, so this came as no surprise.

"Commander," he said with a small smile, "the seat of my pants has served me very well in the past."

"That may be, but you're asking me to commit my men to action based on your hunch."

"Commander Fowler, we have a legitimate suspect in the murders of four St. Louis children." That wasn't exactly true, but Keough had pretty much decided that the still-missing Melissa Reid was dead. "Can you say the same about your four dead Chicago children?"

Fowler clenched his jaw and said, "No, we can't."

"I—we have followed his trail here," Keough went on. "We have a birth certificate from Roseland Community Hospital. We found that he has used his computer to check birth records at that hospital. It is my belief he's going there in person. I'll need some of your detectives to take my partner and me over there, and back us up."

Fowler looked pointedly at Harriet, then at Nicole, clearly wondering which partner Keough was talking about.

"Now, I don't particularly care if you assign these men or they volunteer, and I don't care if you support my theory or not. I'm asking you for two men, because I don't want to panic this killer by having police cars with lights and sirens pull up in front of the hospital."

"You think he's going to Roseland looking for what, a brother?" Detective Vance asked.

"Not only a brother," Keough said, "but possibly a twin—and I think that twin will turn out to be your serial killer."

"How did you come to that conclusion?" Vance asked.

"Take us to the South Side and I'll tell you on the way."

Vance looked at Fowler and said, "I'll take them over there, sir."

"Fine. Anybody else?"

"I'll go, sir," Detective Davis said, grabbing his jacket from the back of his chair."

"Go, then," Fowler said.

"Commander, someone from St. Louis will be calling, sending an E-mail, or faxing us an address for an apartment here in Chicago. It may be where Delacorte is staying. I'd like you to send backup with Agent Connors to check it out."

"I said I'd cooperate, and I will," Fowler said. "Detective Johnson and some other men will go with her."

Keough looked at Harriet. "We have to split up."

"Okay," she said without argument. "Hopefully, one of us will catch this bastard."

He turned and found himself faced with Vance and Davis—one tall, one short; one white, one black. Easy to tell them apart. Both men's eyes were shining, as if they had more enthusiasm for his logic than their commander did.

"We're ready," Vance said.

"Lead the way," Keough said. "We'll keep in touch by cell phone, Commander."

Keough turned to follow the two Chicago detectives out, but he stopped short when Nicole tried to go with him; he obviously had changed his mind about taking her along.

"Stay here, Nicole."

"But—"

"The detectives and I will handle this," he said. "It's time for you to stay inside. Find out which one of these computer operators is getting E-mails from Marc. Work with them. I don't want to take any more chances with you in the field. Do you understand?"

"Yes, all right," she said.

"We need you to pick their brains when we bring them in."

"Elevator," Vance said, sticking his head in the door.

"Harriet . . ."

"I know," she said. "Be careful. You, too."

Eighty-two

IT WAS DARK when Gabriel left Roseland Community Hospital several hundred dollars poorer but with information written on a slip of paper in his pocket. Money always did the trick, no matter how honest or loyal the people involved were. It was simply a matter of finding the right person in the right situation and offering the right amount of money.

In this case, it was a front-desk nurse with two mortgages, three kids, and an ex-husband who did not pay child support.

The plaque next to the doorbell on the wall said DR. HAROLD T. BOYLE. This had been the doctor's name on Gabriel's birth certificate, but he had been unable to find a listing anywhere for a Dr. Boyle. The plaque next to the door looked worn and faded. The nurse at the hospital had told Gabriel that Dr. Boyle was no longer practicing. Of course, this did not explain why there was no phone listing for the man. With third hundred dollars came the information that Dr. Boyle could no longer practice because several years before his license to practice medicine in Illinois had been revoked for treating gunshot wounds without reporting them. This might also explain why he ended up living in Roseland, a neighborhood the likes of which Gabriel had never seen. He'd seen more rats during his walk from the car to the house than he'd seen in his whole life.

Gabriel rang the bell, and the outside light came on. The bulb was yellow, for some reason, and the light made the plaque look even older and more faded. The man who opened the door looked like a perfect match for the plaque.

"Dr. Boyle?" Gabriel asked.

"I—I don't practice medicine any longer," the old man said. His eyes were rheumy, but otherwise he was fairly dapper-looking, with a well-tended gray mustache and a full head of gray hair. He was tall, but he did not quite fill out his clothes—he looked as if he had suffered a recent weight loss.

"I don't need to be treated, Dr. Boyle," Gabriel said. "In a way, I was already treated by you. You delivered me back in 1974."

The doctor blinked, then said, "I delivered a lot of children over the years, sir. Even if you were to tell me your name—"

"It's Delacorte," Gabriel said. "My name is Michael Delacorte."

The man stared at Gabriel for a few moments, then nodded to himself and said, "I suppose you had better come in, then."

Sariel was getting the urge again. These feelings were coming much closer together lately. When would the time come when the urge was totally out of control?

Sariel left the disheveled kitchen and walked into the immaculate bedroom. This room was kept neat because this was where the altar was. Kneeling down in front of it, Sariel lighted a red candle and then began to pray to the Angel Lilith.

Lilith had been described as Satan's favorite Bride of Hell, but to Sariel, she was a savior. It was to Lilith the sacrifices were made, and from Lilith guidance was taken.

Tonight, prayers were said to Lilith for a sign, for a direction to life, for deliverance from a life of poverty and suffering, and from the memory of neglect and abuse.

Prayers were offered to Lilith, the most evil of angels, for something good to come in an otherwise dismal life!

Eighty-three

WHEN KEOUGH ARRIVED at Roseland Community Hospital with Detectives Vance and Davis, his cell phone rang as they entered the lobby.

"Excuse me," Keough said.

"We'll find someone in charge," Davis said, and Keough nodded. "Hello?"

"Joe, Harriet. We've come up with two things—well, your boy Jeter did, actually."

"Shoot."

"He sent us a photo of Michael Delacorte."

"That's great! Get copies made."

"We're doing that now. It was apparently found in Delacorte's house."

"Anything from forensics yet?"

"No."

Keough was impatiently waiting for the CSIs to find a fragment of something in Delacorte's house to tie him to at least one girl.

"What's the other thing?"

"Jeter sent us the address to an apartment on Lakeshore Drive maintained by Delacorte's former company."

"Well, take some people and get over there."

"Can't."

"Why not?"

"Fowler won't move without a search warrant."

"Then get one."

"It's late, and he doesn't want to wake a judge. Especially since he doesn't really agree that we have enough to warrant—excuse the pun—a search."

"Jesus Christ! What the hell does he—Okay, wait." Something occurred to him. "Forget about a warrant. Just stake the place out. You've got a photo of him now. Keep watch and let me know if you see him there."

"Okay," Harriet said. "I can do that."

"No, Harriet, don't do it alone. Take somebody."

"Like who? Fowler's not going to okay—"

"Take Nicole."

"Busby? She's not a field agent."

"She's been trained. Besides, it'll give you somebody to talk to."

"Okay, I'll take her," Harriet said, "but I'll also talk to Johnson. I gotta tell you, Joe, these three detectives—Vance, Davis, and Johnson—have been carrying the weight here and doing all the work. Fowler's an administrator; he never leaves the office."

"That's no surprise," Keough said. "Okay, maybe Johnson will volunteer the way these two guys with me did. Keep in touch, Harriet. Check with whoever manages that building and see if the company also keeps a car on the grounds. A lot of big companies supply an apartment and a car."

"Good idea," she said.

"Don't ask the doorman any questions," Keough said as a parting shot. "They're usually more loyal to the people who tip them than to the police."

"Gotcha. Talk to you later."

He broke the connection as Detective Davis approached.

"We found the hospital administrator."

"What's he doing here after hours?" Keough asked.

"He just happened to still be in the building. His office is this way."

As they walked, Davis asked, "What was the call about?"

Keough repeated the entire conversation, including the comment Harriet had made about the three Chicago detectives.

"She said that?"

"She did."

"Well, she's right," he said. "None of us were thrilled with Fowler as the CO of the task force, and for the most part, we've been trying to work around him. He's the one who told us to freeze your partner out."

"I guess you needed to follow orders."

"Maybe not," Davis said. "We should have used our initiative and worked with her. If we had, we might be further along right now."

"Well, you're working with us now," Keough observed.

"The commander's not going to be happy about us volunteering to come here with you," Davis said. "I'm sure Johnson will go on stakeout with your partner, and Fowler won't forget that, either. He'll consider us traitors and find some way to make us pay."

"Well," Keough said as they turned down a new hallway, "the antidote to that will be finding both of these killers."

"Are you sure this Delacorte is your man?"

"Honestly?" Keough asked. "I'd feel better if we could find something in his house to connect him to the four girls. My gut tells me it's him, but I can't prove it yet."

"Well, I'd rather go with your gut," Davis said, "than Fowler's head."

Eighty-four

WHEN THEY REACHED the administrator's office, Detective Vance was sitting in a chair, facing a man behind a desk. Their conversation broke off as Keough and Davis entered.

"Mr. Vogel," Vance said, rising, "this is Detective Keough. He's with the Federal Serial Killer Task Force, and he's running this investigation."

"Well," Vogel said, extending a bony hand for Keough to shake, "anything I can do to help catch this madman. Terrible thing, killing these young boys."

"Yes, sir, it is," Keough said.

"My wife and I have been married twenty years," Vogel said, running a hand over his thinning gray-brown hair. "We never did have children of our own, but I can imagine what these parents must be going through. What can I do for you, gentlemen?"

He was so tall that when he sat, it was almost as if he had to fold himself into his chair. The three detectives remained standing.

"Mr. Vogel—or is Dr. Vogel?"

"It's Mr.," Vogel said. "I run the hospital, but I'm not a physician."

"Well, Mr. Vogel, here's our problem. The man we believe has been killing little girls in St. Louis was born here in this hospital in

1974." Keough took out his notebook. "May twenty-fifth, to be exact."

"My God."

"That's not all. We believe there may have been a second birth."

"On the same day?" Vogel asked. "You mean twins?"

"Yes, sir. Would that be reflected on both birth certificates?"

"Well, no, only individual births are recorded on a birth certificate. In fact, some parents request a third one—a joint birth certificate—but I think that's a complete waste of paper."

Mr. Vogel had some very definite opinions, it seemed.

"So, what would you like from me?"

"We have a copy of a birth certificate, but we don't know if it's the original. It's missing several pieces of information. We would like to check the original birth certificate, see if we have an altered copy. We'd also like to see if there was a second birth, and we need to interview the doctor who delivered one or both babies. We'd also like to know if you have any employees working here who were working back then."

"Thirty years ago? Hmm, I'm not sure we have anyone who has been here that long—certainly not a doctor."

"Would birth records from that time be on your computer?"

"We've transcribed a lot of material onto the computers," Vogel said, "but I'm not sure if we go back that far."

"How can we find out, sir?"

All eyes turned to the computer on Vogel's desk.

"Well . . . I'm not very well versed in use of the computer, I must admit."

"Who is?"

"Our clerical staff, but I'm afraid they went home at six o'clock."

"You mean to tell me there's no one in the building who knows how to run the computer?"

"I'm sure there is, but . . . offhand . . ."

"Okay, here's something else for you to digest, then," Keough said. "We think the St. Louis killer is also looking for the same information. We believe he was probably here before us tonight, if he's not still in the building."

"My God!" Vogel almost came out of his chair. "In my hospital?"

"Has anyone else been here today looking for information?"

"No, of course not!" Vogel said. "If they had, I would have told you."

"Maybe he'll come in tomorrow," Davis offered.

"I don't think so," Keough said. "He flew here today, and I don't think he'll have the patience to wait—and I got here about two hours behind him. I'd like to think I'm still at least that close."

"Are you even sure this is the right man?" Vogel asked.

Keough looked at Vogel, then at Davis and Vance, who seemed to be wondering the same thing.

"Sir," he said to Vogel, "this is the lead that we're following. Is there someone else in the hospital Delacorte might have spoken to?"

"Not about this," he said. "He would have had to come and see me—and if, as you say, you're two hours behind him, then my clerical staff would still have been gone for the day."

Keough stared at Vogel, and then at the man's dormant computer.

"Either of you know how to run a computer?" he asked Davis and Vance.

Both men shook their heads.

Eighty-five

VOGEL CONTINUED TO insist that no one had been in the hospital that day asking questions; that he could not run the computer; and that there was no one in the hospital who could.

"What about your staff?"

"I—I'd have to call someone to come in on overtime," Vogel said, sounding like a true bureaucrat.

"Well, do it."

Vogel hesitated.

"Does somebody have to okay that?"

"Well, yes . . . I do."

"Then do it," Keough said. "Start making calls. Find somebody who can run the computer and get them in here."

"That could take hours."

"Yeah," Keough said, "I guess it could."

Vogel still didn't move.

"Mr. Vogel, is there a problem?"

"Well," the older man said, "I believe you'd actually need a search warrant for me to do everything you're suggesting, Detective."

"Sir, did you understand what I said about being two hours behind a killer?"

"I understand that you *believe* you are two hours behind a man you believe to be a killer," Vogel said. "If you had a search warrant, then I would know a judge agreed with your assumptions. At this time, however, they are just that, *assumptions*."

"Let me get this straight," Keough said. "You're going to make me get a warrant to look at your records even though you know you might be helping a killer get away."

"Sir," Vogel said, spreading his hands, "I am just trying to follow the letter of the law."

Keough looked at Vance and Davis, who each shrugged helplessly.

"Let's go," Keough said, standing up. He looked at Vogel and said, "We'll be back with a warrant."

Vogel looked at his watch but said nothing. The inference was clear: He would not be there if they returned tonight with a warrant; he would be home. Well, if he was willing to have them roust him out of his home, Keough was willing to do it.

Outside in the hall, Davis said, "He took a payoff, didn't he?"

"Oh yeah," Keough said. "Delacorte was here and paid him for the information. So now he knows where the doctor lives, and we don't."

"We have the doctor's name, though," Vance said. "It's on the birth certificate."

"If the birth certificate we have is not an altered copy," Keough said.

"What about the phone book?" Vance asked.

"If the doctor was in the phone book, Delacorte would not have had to pay off Vogel."

"So what do we do?" Davis asked.

Keough stopped in the middle of the front lobby, his body vibrating with frustration.

"We could go back and beat it out of him," he said, only half-kidding.

Davis and Vance exchanged a look.

"Uh, we'd be out of a job, then," Davis said.

"I could go back and beat it out of him."

"How would that affect your job?" Vance asked.

"I'm not really sure," Keough said. "I've got the mayors of two cities telling me to do whatever it takes to catch these killers."

"Well then, we'll wait outside," Davis said.

"Don't kill him," Vance added.

Keough looked past the two detectives at the nurse behind the front desk. It seemed to him that she was making every effort not to look at them, all the while stealing glances in their direction.

He remembered that when they had first entered the lobby, his intention had been to go up to her and ask some questions. He'd been interrupted by the cell phone, at which time Davis and Vance had gone looking for an administrator, or supervisor. He was an out-of-towner, and he would have gone straight for the front desk. Delacorte was an out-of-towner, too.

"I think that's a good idea," he said. "Wait for me outside."

Davis laughed nervously.

"You're not really going to—"

"No," Keough said, "I'm not going to beat anyone, but I do have an idea."

"Anything we can help with?" Vance asked.

"No," Keough said, "I've got it."

He watched them walk out the front door, then turned to look at the nurse again. He caught her looking at him, but she turned away quickly. Slowly, he walked over to the desk.

Eighty-six

As Keough approached the nurse, she suddenly found something very interesting on the top of her desk.

"Ms. Miller?" he asked, reading the name on her tag.

"Yes?" She looked up at him, trying very hard to keep her eyes innocent. Instead, they looked tired and defeated. She appeared to be someone who had twenty years on the job and dreaded coming to work every day.

"I couldn't help noticing you from across the lobby," Keough said. "Was there something you wanted to tell me?"

"What?" She seemed shocked. Apparently, she thought she had been doing a very good job of being invisible.

"It occurs to me that normal procedure for someone coming through that door would be for them to present himself to you. Did a man come in tonight looking for information? Maybe a former doctor's address?"

"I don't—"

"And maybe you passed him on to Mr. Vogel? Or gave him the information yourself in exchange for a few dollars?"

She bit her lip and remained silent, but her reaction was enough for him.

"This doesn't have to go any further than the two of us . . . Amy, is it?"

"Amy," she said, shaking her head. "Stupid damn name for a fifty-year-old woman, ain't it?"

He didn't know what to say to that. Apparently, this woman had many issues to deal with, and she chose to make her parents' choice of name one of them.

"I could get fired, you know. . . ."

"You and me, Ms. Miller," he said. "No further."

She pondered her decision a moment, then nodded and said, "Fuck it. Crap job anyway, in a crap hospital, and Vogel's the biggest piece of crap here. Yeah, a man came in tonight, said he needed some information on a birth thirty years ago."

"So what happened?"

"I've got bills, Detective. . . . responsibilities . . ."

"So you're telling me you took money from the man for the information?"

"Yes," she said, embarrassed. "I was able to bring it up on the computer and run off a copy."

"And you could run off a copy for me right now?"

"Sure, Detective," she said, "why not?"

It only took a few minutes for the printer to whir to life and print out a sheet of paper. Keough took out the copy he had gotten at the task force office from Jeter's E-mail and compared them. The difference was obvious.

"Can you explain why they have different parents' names on them?"

She studied them both. "Yours is a bad copy of a copy, but it looks like the original. The one I printed out is the one we have on file."

"So this one has the names of the original parents? And then the one you just gave me was changed?"

"Obviously."

"Can you think of a reason for that?"

"Just one."

"And that would be?"

She hesitated, looked around, then said, "There was a time, back then, when some babies were being . . . sold. I don't know that happened here, but it's one possible explanation for this." She tapped the two certificates.

"Okay, Ms. Miller," Keough said, folding them both and putting them in his pocket. "Thanks for the information."

"I'm not in any trouble?"

"I'm not here to judge you. I know how hard it is to be—"

"Single," she said, cutting him off, "trying to raise my kids on the crappy salary they pay me."

"Exactly."

"So, do you want the doctor's address?"

Keough tried to hide his own embarrassment. He'd been about to walk away.

"That hasn't been erased from the computer?"

"Everybody here knows his address," she said. "He was a big wig here, once, but he got caught trying to make some extra cash. State took his license to practice medicine away from him and he was never able to leave this crummy neighborhood."

"We're talking about Dr. Harold Boyle?" Keough asked.

"We are."

She wrote the address down for him, and even supplied directions.

"You've been very helpful, Amy."

"And no trouble?"

"No trouble. Thanks."

If the birth certificate found in Delacorte's house was the original, then that would mean that everything on it was true—doctor's name, parents' names, time, and date. If Michael Delacorte's parents had adopted him, no adoption agency would have given them a copy of the child's birth certificate. So the child hadn't been adopted. Given the wealth of the parents, and what Amy Miller had offered, it was more likely they'd bought the child. Still, if that was the case, why would his parents keep a copy of the real certificate?

As Keough stepped outside the hospital, he held up a hand to the two Chicago detectives and dialed Harriet's cell.

"Where are you?" he asked.

"Outside the building on Lakeshore Drive. I've got Agent Busby and Detective Johnson with me," she told him. "What about you?"

"Outside the hospital," he said. He told her about his conversation with Vogel, and Amy Miller.

"We're going to go check out the doctor," Keough said. "He should be able to confirm my theory that, as a newborn, Michael Delacorte was purchased from the Shurs. See if you can find out anything about them—like a current address. Also find what you can on Dr. Boyle." He gave her the doctor's complete name from the birth certificate.

"How am I supposed to do all this?"

"Either leave Johnson and Busby at the building and go back to the task force office or send Nicole back. Keep Johnson there, though; he's the one with local ID."

"Okay. We'll check the Yellow Pages, but Delacorte probably already did that."

"Then he's going to want the information from Dr. Boyle, and he's going to get there first."

"Maybe he'll still be there when you arrive," she said.

"What about that warrant?"

"Not yet," she said with a sigh. "Be careful, okay? In case he's still there."

"I will," Keough said, although they both knew it was more likely he'd get there and find Dr. Boyle dead.

Eighty-seven

KEOUGH, VANCE, AND Davis approached the house carefully, quietly, guns drawn. It was a less than modest home in an apparently quiet neighborhood, not something you'd expect a successful doctor living in—unless he'd been forced to retire from practice.

As they reached the front porch, Keough quietly directed Davis to cover the back. He waited a couple of minutes, and then he and Vance approached the door. He briefly eyed the faded plaque and was about to ring the bell when he noticed the door was ajar. He made a high sign and pointed to himself, then a low sign and pointed to Vance, who had obviously gone through enough doorways to understand.

Keough counted off three with his fingers and then they went in. They found themselves in a darkened living room, and Keough cursed because neither of them had a flashlight.

"Dr. Boyle?" Keough called out. "It's the police. Answer if you can."

No reply.

Their eyes were adjusting to the dark interior. They could see the shapes of the furniture, but no human forms. Vance closed the door and locked it so no one could come in behind them. Keough found a lamp and turned it on. The room was now illuminated and they could see that there was no one inside.

"Okay," Keough said, "let's stay together and check out the house."

"Right."

They found the kitchen, and the back door, which they opened to speak to Davis.

"We're going to check the rest of the house," Keough said. "Stay out here and be careful."

"Got it."

They went back in and started moving through the house, opening doors and entering rooms the same way they had entered the house. Finally, they saw a light from beneath a door at the end of a hallway.

They approached the door, which Keough opened. They moved into the room, high and low, and found Dr. Harold T. Boyle sitting behind a desk, holding a bottle of whiskey in one hand and a glass in the other.

"Dr. Boyle?"

The old man had been staring into space, but now he looked up at them.

"Sir, we're the police."

"He's gone" was all Boyle said.

Keough holstered his gun and turned to Vance, who was doing the same.

"Might as well let Davis in," he said.

"Right."

As Vance left the room, Keough moved closer to the doctor to see if he was drunk.

Boyle held the bottle out to Keough and said, "I wanted to have a drink . . . lots of drinks . . . but my damned hands . . . I couldn't get the bottle open."

Gently, Keough took the scotch bottle, twisted the top off, and, as Boyle proffered his glass, poured in two fingers' worth. Gratefully, the doctor drank it down in one gulp, then held the glass out for more.

"No," Keough said. "You've got to answer some questions first, and then you can drink all you want."

The older man looked at him sadly. "More questions?"

"There was a man here asking you questions, right?"

"Yes." The doctor was too weary to hold his head up.

"Did he hurt you?"

"Hurt me? No, he didn't hurt me, but he . . . frightened me."

"Did he threaten you?"

"No," the doctor said, "but he frightened me nevertheless. I mean . . . just looking into his face, his eyes, was . . . terrifying." Dr. Boyle shuddered, as if to illustrate his point.

Keough looked around for a chair, spotted one, and pulled it over so he could sit across from the doctor. At that moment, Detectives Davis and Vance entered and took up positions by the door. Boyle looked past Keough at the two men, the weariness in his eyes replaced by fear.

"They're Chicago detectives," Keough said. "They're here with me."

The doctor seemed to relax, but not by much.

"Dr. Boyle, we believe the man who came to see you was Michael Delacorte. Is that correct?"

"Y—yes."

"And he came because you are the man who delivered him thirty years ago?"

"Yes, th—that's right."

"Dr. Boyle, we need to know everything that happened that night," Keough said. "Michael may be killing small children, and we think he has a brother who is doing the same thing—possibly a twin. Are we right?"

"Yes," the doctor said, "and no."

"You'll have to be clearer than that," Keough said, "a lot clearer. . . ."

The amount of money the man was offering him was obscene, just for a piece of paper. Hand over the birth certificate, and then make sure the dual birth does not show up in hospital records. And look the other way while the father sells one of his children. . . .

"So for you, it was all about money?" Keough asked.

"Oh yes," Boyle said. "Isn't it always?"

"And yet . . . the birth record does exist in the hospital," Keough pointed out. "In fact, it's been updated and put on computer files."

"I thought, How would anyone ever know I didn't expunge the two births from the records? Dr. Boyle said. "I took the money, but I didn't really do anything wrong."

"You changed the name of the parents from the Shurs to the Delacortes. And you looked the other way while a father sold one of his children."

"That child was better off," Boyle said. "He would have a better life than the other one. Who was I to keep him from that?"

"And what happened to the other child?"

"I tried to make up for what I did," Boyle said. "That child was my patient for years."

"So you were the second child's GP?" Keough asked.

"That's right," Boyle said. "Chicken pox, measles, strep throat—unwanted pregnancies."

"Pregnancies?" Keough asked. "What are you talking about?"

"I thought you knew," Boyle said. "You seemed to know when you came in . . ."

"Know what, Doctor?" Keough said. "Spell it out."

"The second child—the twin—was a girl."

Eighty-eight

KEOUGH WAS STUNNED. If the second child was a girl, then the second serial killer was a woman—and she was killing boys! Nicole Busby would have a field day with this.

"Did you tell Delacorte this?"

"Yes."

"How did he respond?"

"He was . . . excited."

"Dr. Boyle, why did you leave your name on the birth certificate thirty years ago?"

"The man paid for it," the doctor said. "He had a right to all the information on the document. How was I to know that thirty years later the boy would come looking for me?"

"So you tried to make the little girl's life easier?"

"Yes," Boyle said, "but it was not an easy one. There were injuries—many, many injuries—that were not accidental."

"Abuse?"

Boyle nodded.

"By the mother?"

"The mother, men in the mother's life . . ."

"What kind of abuse?"

"All kinds, I'm afraid," he said. "Mental, physical . . ."

"Sexual?" Keough asked.

"Yes." Boyle nodded his head, ran a liver-spotted hand over his face. Keough thought the man might be in his sixties, but he looked twenty years older. "So you see, I saved the boy from all that."

A real humanitarian.

"Who raised the girl?"

"Her birth mother."

"And the father?"

"He took the money Delacorte senior paid him and abandoned his wife and daughter."

"And she grew up here, in this area?"

"Yes," he said. "Sally Shur—the children's mother—was never able to afford to move away, and after Sally died, the girl couldn't move, either. She still lives in the same house."

"Did you give Delacorte the address?"

"Yes." Boyle reached for an empty folder and pulled it over to Keough, who saw the name Sarah Shur on it. "He took her records."

"Dr. Boyle," Keough asked, "do you remember the home address?"

"Of course."

Keough grabbed a pen and an old prescription pad from the desk and pushed them toward Boyle.

"I need a drink," the old man said.

"I don't wonder," Keough said. "Write down Sarah Shur's address; then you can have a drink."

With a shaky hand, the doctor obeyed, and Keough tore the sheet from the pad, read it, and passed it back to Detective Vance.

"You know where that is?"

"No," Vance said, showing it to his partner.

"I do," Davis said.

"Okay," Keough said, standing up. "Vance, take the doctor in."

"In . . . to where?"

"The task force office."

"And charge him with what?"

"Take him into protective custody for now," Keough said. "We'll figure out what we're going to do with him later, but now Davis and I are going to this address."

"You better call for backup."

"On the way," Keough said, although he had no intention of doing so.

He didn't want to panic Gabriel/Michael—although the man was very likely unflappable. There was also the fact that there was no evidence against either of them—brother or sister. They could take them into custody, but what would they charge them with? As far as he could see, all they knew now was that crimes had been committed against the two of them, but not *by* either of them.

"Come on," Keough said to Davis. "Let's get over there."

As they went out the door, he was dialing Harriet on his cell phone. . . .

Eighty-nine

GABRIEL HAD NEVER been nervous in his life—until now.

He sat in his car in front of the old house in the run-down neighborhood and hated to think that a sister of his—his twin—had grown up in this environment, while he had been taken away to a life where he had been given everything. It made him want to weep, carry her away from here.

He checked his watch and decided not to waste any more time procrastinating. He got out of the car and walked up the cracked walk to the wooden porch, which had fallen at some time in the past years and was leaning precariously to one side. He mounted the steps, approached the door, took a deep breath, and rang the bell. It didn't work, so he had to knock.

And then he waited.

When Sariel—Sarah Shur—opened the door and saw the man standing on the front porch, she knew. It was his face she recognized, because it was her own.

"It's you," she said, and they embraced. For the first time in their lives, each was whole.

Ninety

KEOUGH GAVE HARRIET the address and told her that she and
Detective Johnson should meet him and Davis there. She took a
moment to ask Johnson if he knew where the street was.

"Okay," she said. "Don't go in until we get there, Joe."

"We won't."

"Hey, wait!"

"What?"

"What about Nicole?"

"Leave her there, watching the apartment—and give her your
cell phone."

More mumbling. "She has her own. I have the number."

"And call the office, get somebody to drive out there to wait
with her so she has a car."

"Okay."

"And make damn sure she doesn't do anything but watch and
call us."

"Right."

Davis parked down the street from the address they wanted.

"Now what?"

"Wait here."

"Where are you going?" Davis asked. "You told Agent Connors you wouldn't move until she got here."

"I'm not going in," Keough said. "I just want to see if he's in there."

"That's a Lexus parked in front of the house," Davis said, "and it ain't hers."

"I'm just going to look."

"Fine," Davis said. "I'll wait here and flag Connors and Johnson down."

Keough approached the house from the side, noticing that the lights were on inside. The yard was strewn with junk—what looked like old wood and pieces of metal—not to mention weeds. He almost stepped in some kind of hole and barely avoided twisting his ankle, and at least one rat ran across his feet. He made it to a side window and peered inside. There was a curtain covering the window, but it was worn so thin he could see right through it. He found himself looking at a man and a woman sitting on a sofa, embracing. The man was facing him, and he certainly looked like Michael Delacorte. He couldn't see the woman, but it was a pretty safe bet she was his twin, Sarah Shur.

He finally had the man who called himself Gabriel within his grasp. Now the question was, What could he do about it?

Keough got back to the car and waited with Davis for nearly another half hour before Harriet and Johnson pulled up behind them. No one had moved from the house, and the lights were still on.

Harriet and Johnson joined them in their car.

"Is he in there?" she asked excitedly.

"Both of them."

"Both?" Johnson asked.

Keough gave them an shortened version of what Dr. Boyle had told them, the most stunning piece of information being that Michael Delacorte's twin was a woman.

"A female serial killer?" Johnson asked. "Isn't that unusual?"

"Not as unusual as it once was," Harriet said, "but I didn't expect it in this case."

"Neither did I," Keough said.

"You were right about a twin, though," Harriet said. "Why aren't you happy?"

"Because I've been thinking while we've been waiting for you."

"And?"

He turned in his seat so he could face all three of them.

"We could go in there right now and grab both of them," he said.

"But?" Davis asked.

"But we can't charge them with anything," he said.

"We can question them," Johnson said.

"And let them know we're onto them?" Keough said. "And we can't prove anything," he added.

"So what do you want to do?" Harriet asked. "Let them go?"

"They don't know we're onto them," Davis said.

"Right," said Harriet, "so they'll probably go back to Lakeshore Drive, or . . ."

"Or he'll take his sister home with him."

"Would she go?"

"Look where she grew up," Keough said; "look where she ended up. And then look at what he can offer her. He's wealthy, and he can change her whole life."

"Busby would say she's in the middle of her sequence," Harriet said.

"What?" Davis asked.

"They've both established their patterns," Keough said. "He in St. Louis, she here. He told me he was going to continue when he got back."

"So she'd want to continue hers, too," Harriet said.

"Unless they just stop," Davis suggested.

The other three looked at him.

"Don't they do that? Sometimes just stop?"

"Sure," Harriet said, "sure they do."

"Maybe she'll go with him," Keough said, "and she'll stop, and he won't. My main point is, we can't charge them. We have no evidence. We'd eventually have to let them go, and then they might run."

"So what are you suggesting?" Harriet asked.

"Let's just tail them."

"Why not go back to St. Louis and wait for them?" Harriet asked.

"Well," Keough said, "that would be just a little too optimistic, wouldn't it?"

"You mean you're admitting you might be wrong?" Harriet asked, feigning shock.

"There's always a small chance."

They were all silent for a few moments, staring at the house, waiting for something to happen; then Davis spoke.

"I don't buy it," he said.

"What?" Harriet asked.

"Danny?" he said, looking at Johnson.

"Yeah, right," Johnson said. "Our jurisdiction. We're gonna take 'em."

"Hey, wait—" Keough said.

Davis opened his door to get out, but Keough grabbed his arm.

"Look, Keough," Davis said, "you did it. I admit it. You found not only your killer but ours, too—and we want her. We'll give you all the credit in the world, but we want her off our streets."

"You won't be able to hold her," Harriet said.

"Maybe not," Davis replied, "but it's like you said: They'll know we're onto them, and they'll stop."

"Or go someplace else," Johnson said.

"And that would be good enough for you?" Keough asked.

"Our job is to protect the public—our public," Davis said. "Come on, Danny."

Johnson opened his door.

"Goddamn it, wait!" Keough said.

"You want to fight with us on this, Keough?" Davis demanded.

"This is Fowler's idea, isn't it?" Harriet asked. "Yeah, I can see his fingers all over this."

"He's our boss," Johnson said, getting out of the car. The two Chicago cops took out their guns and started for the house.

"What do we do?" Harriet asked Keough.

"We could shoot them."

"Joe . . ."

"All right," he said in disgust, "let's back them up. We'll never forgive ourselves if they get killed."

As they got out of the car, she said, "I'm sorry. I liked your way."

"Yeah," he said, shaking his head, "I did, too."

She wrinkled her nose and asked, "It's always the by-the-book types who don't, isn't it?"

Ninety-one

"HEY, HEY, HOLD on," Keough called after the two Chicago detectives, trying to be heard while keeping his voice down.

They both turned.

"You decide to help?" Davis asked.

"If we can't talk you out of it," Harriet said, "we might as well keep you from getting killed."

"We're the primaries," Johnson said. "We'll go in the front."

Keough decided not to do his song and dance about being authorized by two mayors.

"Fine," Keough said, "we'll take the back—but go easy."

"We'll give you three minutes."

Keough took Harriet past the window he'd looked through earlier, where he'd seen Delacorte and—apparently—Sarah Shur sitting on the sofa. He looked in the window now and saw nothing.

"Uh-oh," he said.

"What?"

He quickened his pace to the back door and found it wide open.

"Uh-oh," he said again.

"Damn," Harriet said. "Nobody covered the back?"

"The car was out front," Keough said angrily. "I didn't think he'd leave it."

"Maybe they're still inside."

Keough's anger was directed at no one but himself. He took a few steps into the backyard, saw several holes in the back fence large enough for a person—or persons—to slip through.

"They could be long gone," he said.

"Let's go inside," she said as they heard knocking on the front door, "see what we can find."

"Damn," he said again under his breath. They took out their guns and entered the house.

David and Johnson were now pounding on the front door, yelling "Police" and "Open up."

So much for going easy.

The house was very small, maybe four rooms to it, and it was obvious that it was empty.

"Might as well let them in," Harriet said. "I'll check and see if she packed anything."

"How will you know?'

"A woman knows."

He shrugged and went to the front door.

"Now what do we do?" Davis asked.

"You're asking me now?" Keough said. "Or do you want to call Commander Fowler and ask him?"

"This is just as much your fault as it is ours," Johnson said, turning to face Keough. "Even more. You and Ralph were here longer."

Davis turned on Johnson and said, "Now you're gonna lay this on me?"

"Whataya mean, 'lay this on me'?"

"Well, you and Keough didn't cover the back—"

"There's no point in throwing blame around!" Harriet shouted, shocking the three men into silence.

"She's right," Keough said. "Besides, we've got the apartment on Lakeshore Drive covered, and his home in St. Louis."

"So which one do you think he's going to?" Davis asked.

"I don't know," Keough said. "Maybe the apartment first, and then St. Louis."

"You think he's going to take her home with him?" Johnson asked.

"If you found your long-lost sister living in squalor like this, what would you do?"

"Honestly?" Johnson asked. "I'd leave her here, but hey, that's my sister."

"Look, we have an opportunity here," Keough said. "You've got to get a forensics team out here as soon as possible. There might be something in the house we can use as evidence."

"He's right," Davis said. He took out a cell phone. "I'll make the call."

"Don't tell Fowler what happened," Johnson warned him.

"Tell him what happened," Keough countered, then added, "just not everything."

While they were waiting for the forensics team to arrive, Keough and Harriet went through one of the holes in the back fence to see where it led. They came out on another residential street.

"Not easy to get a cab here," Keough said.

"Maybe this was where she kept her car parked," Harriet offered.

"Yeah, maybe," he said. "Come on, let's get back. The forensics people probably know what they're doing, but . . ."

They went back through the fence and approached the house.

"How long you going to beat yourself up about this?" she asked.

They stopped before going back into the house.

"I ignored basic police procedure, Harriet."

"Gimme a break, Joe," she said.

"What do you mean?"

"You always do that!" she said. "Why should this case be any different? You just got caught this time, that's all."

"I don't always—"

"Yeah, you do."

He stared at her for a few moments; then she said, "We'd better get inside."

They started up the back stairs, and Keough muttered, "*Always* is a pretty strong word."

Ninety-two

COMMANDER FOWLER SHOWED up shortly after the forensic unit. Along with him came a patrol supervisor and several marked cars. Before long, the house was as bright as daylight, inside and out. There were uniformed police holding the curious neighbors back. Officers assigned to the task force were questioning some of them about the woman who lived in the house, getting as much information as possible. The task force detectives were looking for information inside the house. The forensic people gave Keough and Harriet some attention when they first arrived, but as soon as their own superior officers showed up, the two of them were pretty much shunted off to the side.

"You did a good job finding the doctor, and the house," Fowler said. "Now let us do our job."

As he walked away, Harriet nudged Keough and said, "Why don't you tell him about the two mayors?"

"Shut up."

As Keough and Harriet had stepped outside to get some air, Keough's cell sounded.

"Joe!" Nicole sounded excited. "I've got them!"

"What? Nicole, what do you mean you've got them?"

"Delacorte came back to the apartment with a woman."

"That's his twin."

"His twin . . . sister?" Now she was more excited. "A female serial killer?"

"She grew up virtually impoverished, Nicole," he said, "and abused."

"She's classic," Nicole said, "and he's not, and they're twins. This is . . . amazing."

"Nicole . . . where are you? Your cell is cutting out."

"I've been trying to tell you," she said. "I'm on I-Fifty-five, heading south."

"What are you doing there?"

"I'm following them," she said. "They're heading for St. Louis!"

"But . . . but his car's here."

"There must have . . . another . . . in . . . garage," she said, and then her signal cut out completely.

"Where did you get a car?" he shouted, but she was gone.

"What's going on?" Harriet demanded.

"She's following Delacorte and his sister," Keough said.

"Where?"

"Apparently, they're heading back to St. Louis by car." He shoved his cell phone into his pocket. "Damn it, she was only supposed to watch."

"He couldn't fly back," Harriet said; "he didn't have a ticket for her."

"The question is," Keough said, "Did he see us out here? Does he know we're onto him?"

"If he doesn't, he will when he gets home," Harriet said. "You tore that place apart, didn't you?"

"Christ," Keough said, digging the cell out again. "We've got to get that house put back the way it was—*before* he gets there. And then I've got to get to St. Louis."

"And what about me? You're going to make me stay in Chicago?"

"You'd better stay here and see what they come up with, Harriet," Keough said. "We're going to need all the evidence we can get."

Ninety-three

KEOUGH TRIED NICOLE again, but there was no signal. Damn the FBI and their cheap cell phones. If he hadn't paid for his own, he'd have one of those cheap ones, as well.

He'd managed to call ahead and clear the way with the state police again, and he'd also gotten ahold of Jeter and told him to start putting the Delacorte house together again—fast.

"Why don't we just grab them when they get here?" Jeter asked.

"Did you find anything in the house that connects him to any of the girls?"

"No," Jeter said, "the forensic guys came up empty. No fibers, no nothing. This guy must have really cleaned up after himself."

Keough talked with Jeter for a while, telling him about Sarah Shur, Delacorte's twin sister. Talking helped keep him awake.

"That's amazing," Jeter said. "She grew up abused and poor, he grew up privileged, and they both turned to serial killing at the same time?"

"Apparently."

"What's Nicole going to make of that?"

"She's going to have a field day writing a new chapter in profiling," Keough said.

"Well, make sure she spells your name right."

"Just get that house cleaned up," Keough said.

"Will you be going directly there?"

"Yes. You and Berkery and House keep watch and meet me there."

"Okay," Jeter replied. "See you in a few hours."

Keough was getting groggy as he reached Springfield. He stopped for gas, a bottle of diet Coke, and to wash his face in the dirty men's room of a service station. When he got back in the car and started off again, it was nearly 5:00 A.M. He was surprised when his cell phone rang.

"I thought maybe I'd keep you awake," Harriet said.

"Where are you?"

"My hotel."

"What happened at the house?"

"We found a shoe box full of the angel pins in her basement," Harriet said. "Also some blankets, one with blood on it. They're typing the blood and checking for fibers."

"The same pins?"

"Yes."

"She wasn't as careful as her brother."

"Well," Harriet said, "she's not as smart as he is, is she?"

"Probably not," Keough said. "She's obviously been damn lucky."

"Fowler's getting a warrant for her arrest."

"If he's got enough evidence."

"He says he can get it, and he'll be on a plane to St. Louis in a few hours."

"I'll beat him there," Keough said. "I'm only about an hour and a half away."

"If he grabs the two of them at the same time," she said, "he'll be able to hold her, but not him."

"I know. We'll need to take them both at the same time."

"We still haven't made a case against him," she pointed out.

"I know, but I will," Keough said. "Or . . ."

"Or what?"

"Or maybe I can get him to confess."

Ninety-four

THEY HAD BEEN there. Gabriel knew it as soon as he turned onto the block. He stopped the car.

"What's wrong?" Sariel asked.

"We have to go."

She looked around at the neighborhood and did not see a thing out of place.

"But . . . it's so beautiful," she said. "I can't believe you've lived here all your life."

"I can't believe you lived where you did all your life."

"I didn't know anything else."

No, of course she didn't. . . .

After he entered her house and explained to her who he was and who she was, she hadn't betrayed any surprise.

"You knew," he said then, "as I did, that you were not whole."

"Yes."

She showed him the altar to Lilith, and they exchanged their angel names—Gabriel and Sariel.

"Both archangels," he observed. "We are alike in so many ways."

When he told her he was going to take her away from there, she smiled sweetly and said, "I cannot go. I haven't finished my sacrifices, as you have not finished yours."

He touched her face then and said, "We can finish them together."

And she agreed. . . .

He knew the police had been behind him—all the way to Chicago, to the hospital, the doctor, and now here. He also knew that the back way out—across the yard and through the fence—had been left open for them. He knew all of that, just as he knew as soon as they turned into his block that they had been there.

He could feel it.

"Do we have to leave again?"

"Yes," he said. "I'm going to take you someplace even more beautiful."

"And our sacrifices?"

He touched her face again and said, "Together, you and I will make the greatest sacrifice to Lilith."

Sariel smiled and said, "She will be pleased."

Gabriel returned the smile.

Ninety-five

IT WAS LIGHT out when Keough turned onto the block where Michael Delacorte lived. He pulled his car in behind the one holding Jeter, Berkery, and House. All three men got out to greet him, using the opportunity to stretch.

"You look like shit," Berkery said.

"Yeah, a couple of days without sleep will do that to you. When did he get home?"

"What?"

"Delacorte," Keough said. "When did he get here? And where's Nicole? She was on his tail."

"Joe," Jeter said, "he never got here."

"What are you talking about?" Keough asked, his stomach sinking. Had he truly blown it this time? First letting them get away from the Roseland house, and now this?

"Shit," he said.

"You know," House said hesitantly, "a car did drive down the block, stop, and pull out again."

"When?" Keough asked.

"Maybe a couple of hours ago."

"Why didn't you say something?" Berkery asked.

"I thought it was just somebody who made a wrong turn."

"Damn it," Keough said. "It must have been him. He must have spotted you."

"So where is he off to now?" Jeter asked.

Keough poked the young black detective in the chest and said, "That's what you're going to find out for me."

They all drove back to the task force's office, where they had a security man unlock the door to the building and let them in.

"I'm going to try Nicole again," Keough said. "If we're lucky, she's still tailing them."

He'd been upset at her for taking off on her own like that, but now she was the only chance they had to find out where Delacorte was going with his sister.

"Joe?"

"Nicole, where the hell are you? And why the hell don't you have a better cell phone?"

"It's my battery," she shouted. "He didn't stop at his house, Joe. I thought he was going to stop at his house, but he kept going."

"We know that," he said, talking fast, before her battery went again. "Where are you heading?"

"I don't know," she said. "We're driving west on Forty-four right now . . . know where . . . going . . ."

And the connection died again.

"Damn it!" He started to slam his own phone down on the desk, then caught himself. If he smashed it, he might not get hold of her again.

"You need some coffee," House said. "I'll go make a run."

"Good," Keough said. "Thanks. Marc, you got that computer up and running yet?"

"Almost." Jeter was sitting at Martha's desk, waiting for the computer to boot up.

Keough came up behind Jeter while the computer was clicking and whirring.

"Find me some other home in Delacorte's name, his father's

name, or another place in the company's name. And get me somebody's name from that company. We're going to start waking people up if we have to."

After a couple of hours, Keough was ready to start pulling his hair out. Jeter had found several other places owned by the Delacorte Ball-Bearing Company, but they were in New York and Los Angeles. Gabriel was driving southeast on I-44, so unless he was going to Kansas City to use its airport to fly to New York or L.A., that didn't do them any good.

"I think he's going someplace he can drive," Keough said, "someplace he thinks we can't find, or won't find, until it's too late."

"Too late for what?" Berkery asked.

"I don't know."

"Why don't we just sit tight and wait until they get where they're going?" Berkery asked. "Agent Busby's on their tail, and she's got a cell—"

"With a bad battery," said Keough.

"So she'll find a pay phone."

"Nicole is not a field agent," Keough said; "she's never been a street cop. I don't want to leave her alone in this situation for too long. She'll make a mistake."

"Okay, how about this? We leave Marc here on the computer, you, me, and House get on I-Forty-four and start driving. Somewhere along the way, we'll get directions."

Keough checked his watch. It was 7:00 A.M. and no one was answering the phone at any of the numbers they had for Delacorte Ball-Bearing. They had the names of the officers, and the company counsel, but no home phone numbers. They were going to have to wait until someone arrived at work, which could be 8:30, or as late as 9:00 A.M. In two hours, they could cut down on the miles separating them and Delacorte.

"Okay," Keough said, "I like that suggestion. If they change direction, we can change right along with them."

"Maybe we'll get lucky," Berkery said, "and we won't even have to leave Missouri."

"Marc, you keep at it," said Keough.

"I heard," Jeter said, making a face. He would rather have been going after the serial killers, but considering what had happened between him and the last one they went after together, this was probably a better idea. "How's your cell's battery?"

"It's fine," Keough said, "but just in case, take both John's and Jim's numbers."

Both detectives wrote the numbers down for him.

"As soon as you get ahold of anybody from that company, let me know."

"Gotcha."

"Okay, guys," he said to the other two detectives, "who's got the best car? . . ."

Ninety-six

KEOUGH, BERKERY, AND House were passing Bourbon, Missouri, in Berkery's SUV when Keough's cell phone sounded off.

"Take the exit to Branson," Jeter said.

"What have you got?"

"I was able to get the company lawyer on the phone," Jeter said. "He worked for Delacorte's father, has been with the company over thirty years."

"I don't need his resumé." Keough realized how peevish he sounded, but he'd lost count of how many hours he'd been awake.

"Anyway, he said that Michael had always been the perfect son—high marks in school, no drugs, no trouble whatsoever to his parents. He was shocked when, after his parents died, he sold the company."

"How did the parents die?"

"Car accident. Their brakes gave out on a wet highway."

"The perfect son," Keough repeated, half to himself. "Okay, tell me about Branson."

"There's a place in Branson called Big Cedar Lodge. Big names go there, apparently, and the company keeps a cabin there."

"Where, exactly?"

"He doesn't know," Jeter replied. "He said it's a big sprawling place, and he's never been there. He said the management will know."

"Have you heard from Nicole?"

"No, you?"

"No. What makes us think that's where Gabriel is heading?"

Jeter hesitated, then said, "Instinct? Unless he's going to Oklahoma to use their airport," he added, echoing an earlier thought of Keough's.

Berkery was driving, so Keough was able to give the matter his full attention. Even if they took the Branson exit and it turned out to be wrong, they could always reverse their field. Anyway, they still had some time before they reached it.

"Okay," Keough said, "we'll plan on getting off there and heading to Branson. Get me directions to Big Cedar."

"I've got them," Jeter said. "I logged on to MapQuest and got very specific directions."

Keough, seated in the front next to Berkery, got out his notebook and said, "Go," then took down the directions.

"Marc, keep playing with the computer, see if you can get a bigwig at the company on the phone who might have more insight into Gabriel's—Michael's—personality. Somebody must have seen something wrong with this kid when he was growing up."

"If not, then he goes completely against the profiles."

"Yes, he does." And, Keough thought, perfectly in line with his own theory about serial killers being born with that time bomb in their heads that just goes off at some point.

"Also, stay on the computer. Maybe you'll find a place in Arkansas owned by Delacorte."

"I'll keep looking, but I think if he owns another home somewhere, it's under a different name."

"Let's hope not," Keough said. "This was good work, Marc. Keep in touch."

"You, too."

Keough hung up and passed along the information to Berkery and House.

"So we're headed to Big Cedar on the basis of Jeter's hunch?"

"Instinct," said Keough, correcting him, "and do you have a better idea? We're here on I-Forty-four according to your instincts, aren't we?"

Berkery clenched his jaw and said, "Hunch."

When the phone rang again, it was Nicole.

"Thank God!" Keough said, surprised at the depth of his relief. "Where the hell are you?"

"I can't talk long," she said excitedly. "I'm at a pay phone. They stopped at an outlet mall. Looks like they're buying clothes for both of them, but mostly for the woman."

"Nicole," Keough said, "where are you?"

She was still talking, only half-listening.

"If I had more time, I might be able to buy myself a new cell phone here, but I doubt it," she was saying. "I don't want to lose track of them."

"Nicole—"

"The woman seems really frightened, stays close to the man the whole time."

"Nicole," Keough said loudly, "an outlet mall where?"

She stopped short, shocked into silence, and then said, "Branson."

Ninety-seven

"THERE ARE TWO bedrooms," Gabriel said to Sariel.

While she walked around, craning her neck to look at the arched, high ceilings, stuffed animal heads and pelts mounted on the walls, and the view from the deck, he put all of her new clothes on the bed in one of the rooms.

When he learned that the name she'd chosen for herself in service to Lilith was Sariel—another archangel, like his own—the last piece of the puzzle fell into place. But now that the police were on his trail, he knew it was time to prepare for the final sacrifice.

He had known when he spoke to Detective Keough on the phone that the man would catch him. Once Gabriel made contact, it was inevitable. The only way to continue the sacrifices without being caught would have been to remain completely anonymous. His ego—in the face of the girl being found in the refrigerator—would not allow him to do that. And once he gave in to his ego, he knew he was lost. All he had wanted to do then was have time to find his other half—to find Sariel.

They would find him here, too. The woman following them would make sure of that.

Which reminded him . . .

When he came out into the main room, she was standing in front of the sliding glass doors, looking out.

"I can't believe all this," she said without turning around.

He stood behind her and put his hands on her shoulders. He was surprised at how thin and frail she felt. And yet there was power in her, just as there was in him.

"This is how you should have been living your whole life," he said.

"I never knew this kind of . . . grandness existed."

"It does," he said, "and now you're here." He took his hands from her shoulders and moved away from her. The power in her stimulated him sexually, but she was his sister, and so he felt disgusted with himself.

"I have to go out."

Now she turned, a frightened look on her face.

"You're leaving me alone?"

He kept his body turned, so she would not see his erection and also become disgusted.

"Not for long," he said. "I just have . . . something to do. You take a bath and change into some of the new clothes we bought. When I come back, we'll order room service."

"Room service," she said dreamily. "I've never had room service."

"You can order anything you want," he said as he moved toward the door. "Order as if it's the last meal you will ever eat."

Ninety-eight

JETER'S DIRECTIONS WERE mercifully precise; otherwise, Keough thought, they would have had a hell of a time finding Big Cedar. They drove along the main drag of Branson, with its restaurants, theaters, and other attractions, and it became plain that the lodge was off by itself. Even when they drove through the front entrance, they were still faced with winding roads leading to different buildings, but they maintained a straight course until they reached what he hoped was the main building. They parked and got out, and Berkery pointed out the chalet-type buildings across the river.

"This place must cost a fortune," Jim House said.

"Well, our man's got one," Keough pointed out.

They went inside, found themselves in a huge reception area under a custom-made chandelier of metal and wood. The wooden floor was inlaid with brass wolves and deer.

Keough went to one of the two desk clerks and showed her his ID, which had a federal seal on it. He thought it would be the most impressive of their IDs.

"I'd like to see your manager, please."

"Yes, sir." The clerk was young enough to be not only impressed but also a bit frightened. She hurried away and came back with her boss, a tall, slender man with close-cropped gray hair and a mustache.

"Jeff Cox, manager of the premises. Can I help you gentlemen?"

"I'm Detective Keough; these are Detectives Berkery and House. Can we go to your office?"

"Of course," the man said. "Follow me, please."

He led them behind the desk and down a hall to possibly the plushest hotel manager's office Keough had ever seen. The decor matched that of the lobby. The man's desk was constructed of large logs covered in glass.

"May I see your IDs, please?"

Keough showed his, followed by Berkery and House.

The manager said, "They are St. Louis policemen, but your identification is from the Justice Department?"

"We're a task force looking for a man and a woman who have killed eight children," Keough explained.

"My God," Cox said. "Why are you here?"

"Because we believe we've tracked them to your resort."

The man was struck speechless.

"Mr. Cox, we need to know which cottage or chalet is rented by the Delacorte Ball-Bearing Company.

"The Delacortes?"

"Did you know them?"

"Very well," he said. "They came here often."

"And their son?"

"They brought him here when he was young," he said.

"What about Michael Delacorte as an adult?"

"I really don't know him very well," Cox admitted. "He sold the company some years ago, but I don't recall him coming here as an adult. Of course, he could have come without my knowledge. . . ."

"What about the Delacorte cottage?"

"The Delacortes always took the same one," Cox said, "directly across the lake. You can see it from here; it's one of the largest, and it has a huge deck."

"How do we get over there?" Keough asked.

"Ah, there's a road around the lake, or you can take a boat across, but I believe the cottage is empty at the moment."

"Can you check?"

"I can do that right here on my computer," Cox said, sitting down. He tickled his keyboard for a few seconds, then said, "Yes, according to this, it's empty."

"And Michael Delacorte has not registered in another room?"

He played the keyboard blues again and still came up empty.

"No, nothing."

"We should probably check it out anyway," Berkery suggested.

"I'd have to insist on going with you," Cox said.

Keough turned to Berkery.

"Do we have any bulletproof vests with us?"

"Uh, bulletp—proof?" Cox said.

Keough looked at the manager. "Yes, it could be dangerous. We wouldn't want you to get hurt, Mr. Cox."

"Well," Cox said, "I have seen your identification, so I suppose I could give you a key. . . ."

Cox left the room, and Keough thought back to the hotel manager at Little America the year before. He'd taken three bullets in the chest as shots were fired through the door of one of the rooms. He didn't want that to happen again.

Cox came back into the office and handed Keough a key.

"That will open the front door," he said. "Please let me know what happens."

"Now, all we need is a boat," Keough said.

"A boat?" House asked. "Why don't we just drive?"

"He might hear the car," Keough said.

"A boat would be quieter."

"You can row across in no time," Cox assured them.

"A boat," House muttered.

"What's the matter?" Berkery asked. "Can't you swim?"

"As a matter of fact, no," House said. "Maybe I should drive. . . ."

"That might be a good idea," Keough said. "We don't want to miss them if they drive off while we're rowing across. Jim, get directions from Mr. Cox and drive around, but don't get too close."

"Okay." The look of relief on his face was almost comical.

"Let's go, then," Keough said to Berkery. "Give Jim your keys."

Berkery hesitated, and House said, "I'm not going to scratch your baby."

"Come on, John," Keough said, and Berkery reluctantly handed over the keys.

Keough was almost out the door when something occurred to him.

"Wait."

"What is it?" Berkery asked.

"They might have registered under a phony name," Keough said.

"Or they might be in one of the hotels along the strip," Berkery said. "Who knows? If Agent Busby would just call again—"

"A pseudonym," Keough said. "What would he use?"

"Smith?" House asked.

"Jones?" Berkery suggested.

"Brown?" Cox said, getting in on the act.

"Angel."

"What?" Berkery asked.

"Angel," Keough repeated. "That's what this has all been about, hasn't it?"

He moved back into the room, walking past the two detectives to get to Cox's desk.

"Mr. Cox, can you try the name Angel? See if anyone has registered under that name?"

"Of course." He sat back down at the keyboard and typed it in. "Amazing." He looked up at Keough with admiration on his face. "Impressive police work."

"Hunch," Berkery said.

"Instinct," said House.

"Angel," Jeff Cox said, pointing to the screen, "he paid cash."

"What's the full name he used?" Keough asked, leaning over to look at the screen. He saw it before Cox could say it out loud.

Gabriel Angel.

Ninety-nine

COX HAD A member of the lodge's staff take Keough and Berkery to a boat they could use.

"I've been instructed to row you over." He had arms and shoulders that would get them across faster than either detective.

"No harm in that," Keough said, and Berkery agreed.

The young man got them across and left them at a dock that was a few buildings away from the one they wanted. They were actually on the other side of the regular Delacorte chalet. However, they could see the deck of the building they wanted, so anyone looking out the window could see them, too. Recognizing them—that was another matter.

"Shall I wait, sir?" the man asked.

"No," Keough said, "go on back, and thanks."

The man waved and they pushed the boat off for him. Keough and Berkery produced their guns and started up the dock to dry land.

"I wonder where Nicole is," Keough said.

"Maybe she'll meet up with Jim."

"I just hope she didn't do anything stupid."

"It's because of her we're here, Joe," Berkery said, using Keough's given name for the first time since they'd met.

"I know," he said, "I just want her to be alive so I can congratulate her."

They found their way to the road and looked both ways. There were no cars in sight, not Berkery's SUV and not a car that might have been Nicole's.

"Wait for Jim?" Berkery asked.

"No," Keough said, overtaken by a sense of urgency. "I don't like it that Nicole's not right here. Let's go in."

They moved past the Delacorte chalet and from that point on maintained silence. When they'd worked their way to the front of the building, they split up. They'd agreed in the boat that Keough would take the front and Berkery the back.

Keough moved carefully up the steps to the front door, keeping his eyes on the windows. He suddenly became convinced that he'd followed a trail laid for him by Gabriel. The man was too smart to have rented cars in his own name, used the company apartment in Chicago, and come to the same lodge where the company maintained a chalet. And the name Gabriel Angel was much too obvious.

This meeting, or showdown, had been orchestrated by Gabriel for his own reasons. Keough had to do everything in his power to have the situation resolve itself the way he wanted it to.

Keough approached the front door and tried the doorknob. The fact that it turned easily reinforced his feelings that he'd been led here. He had no choice, though, but to go through the door. They'd come too far to stop now.

He turned the knob and pushed the door open.

"Come in, Detective Keough," Gabriel said. "We've been waiting for you."

By "we," Keough thought he meant himself and his sister, but that changed when he entered and saw Nicole. Gabriel was standing behind her. He had one arm around her waist, and the other was holding a knife to her throat.

And Keough was right back at Little America again, wondering whether or not he should take the shot. . . .

* * *

The girl slid down just enough so that he thought he had a shot, but at the last second, just as he fired, the man hitched her up again, and his bullet hit her just beneath her collarbone. It went straight through her and into the man who was holding her. The one shot knocked them both back, but while she slumped right to the floor, the man remained standing, and he maintained his hold on the knife.

Keough fired again. . . .

"She was already dead, Joe," he heard Harriet telling him later on, after both bodies had been removed. "The paramedic said there would have been more bleeding if she'd been alive."

"Yeah," he'd answered, unable to form any other words.

"She was dead, and you got him," Harriet said. "You had to take the shot. . . . You had to. . . ."

"I know what you're thinking, Detective," Gabriel said. "Should you take a shot, take a chance of hitting your partner?"

Nicole's eyes were wide, but Keough swore it was more from excitement than from fright.

"You are Michael Delacorte, correct?" Keough asked.

"That's right, Michael Delacorte, or, as you know me, Gabriel."

"Where's your sister?"

"She's in the bathtub. You know about her?"

"I know everything."

"I thought you might," he said. "I knew you'd come—well, not you, originally, but after we spoke, I knew. . . . I could sense your resolve."

"I'm flattered."

"You should be," Gabriel said. "I don't consider that I left an easy trail."

This was a different situation from the one in Little America, he told himself. For one thing, Gabriel was a larger man, and he could not quite hide behind Nicole. On the other hand, Nicole was very much alive and on her own feet, so Gabriel was not actually supporting her weight. Keough wished she'd just go limp in his arms.

"But you are here now, and you will be a fitting witness for me."

"Witness to what?" Keough asked.

"Why, the final sacrifice."

"Is that what those little girls were?" Keough asked. "Sacrifices?" He thought if he kept the man talking, Berkery or House might arrive, maybe distract Gabriel.

"Oh yes," he said, "the girls in St. Louis, and the boys in Chicago."

"Your twin sister is every bit as crazy as you are, isn't she?"

"It's amazing, isn't it?" Gabriel asked proudly. The comment did not offend him at all. "How she could be brought up differently from me, and here we end up in the very same place. Ironic. Something for all the scholars and profilers to ponder, wouldn't you say?"

"Yes, I would say," Keough replied.

Gabriel twisted the blade of the knife just a bit and Nicole jumped as the point dug into her flesh. Blood ran in a single trail down her neck.

"Let her go, Michael," Keough said.

"Gabriel," the killer said. "Call me Gabriel. Michael is someone I should not have been."

"And Sarah?"

"The same," he said. "We were both robbed of who we rightfully should have been."

"And you think the killings made up for that in some way?" Keough was sweating now, his hand tacky on the grip of his pistol.

"Of course not," Gabriel said. "Nothing could make up for that."

Gabriel looked completely normal, no hint of craziness in his eyes. It was odd: He looked like most young men Keough had seen in bars or clubs, no hint at all of what was going on inside. And yet how many of them were the same, had the same time bomb waiting inside their heads to go off?

"Gabriel . . . let her go. . . ."

"I intend to," Gabriel said. "How else would the final sacrifice take place?"

Seeing Gabriel's muscles tense, he knew he had to act now or lose control of the situation totally. Pushing Little America from his mind, he took his shot before the other man could move. . . .

Epilogue

KEOUGH STOPPED THE car right in front of the house. Jeter was
next to him. Nicole Busby was back in Washington, excited about
possibly writing a new chapter in serial-killer profiling. Harriet was
still in Chicago. Two days since he'd killed Michael Delacorte—aka
Gabriel—and there were still loose ends to be tied up in both cities.

His bullet had hit Gabriel cleanly, taking him in the throat.
Nicole had jerked herself away from him just in case a second shot
was necessary, but it wasn't. He was dead when he hit the floor.

Keough had been under the impression that Gabriel's "final sacrifice" was supposed to be Nicole, but when she took him into the
bathroom and he saw the body of Sarah Shur in the bloody bath-
water, with candles flickering around her, he realized that the final
sacrifice was not only her but Gabriel himself.

With the death of both serial killers came unanswered questions, but a cache of angel pins had been found in one of the cars in
Michael Delacorte's garage. Both task forces were satisfied that
they had the right perps. Of course, only time would tell. . . .

And then there was the matter of Denise Proctor. . . .

* * *

As Keough and Jeter got out of the car and started walking toward the house, the younger man said, "You're sure about this?"

"Fairly sure," Keough said. "Guess we're about to find out."

Larry Keith had been released for lack of evidence in the death of his stepdaughter, but Keough's subconscious had been working overtime on this case, and once the angel cases were solved, the resolution of this one just seemed to surface.

He was sure he was right.

"Joe, what about Melissa Reid? She hasn't been found yet. Could she be alive?"

"No," Keough said firmly. "Gabriel never would have left her alive when he went to Chicago. She'll be . . . found eventually."

They rang the bell and Larry Keith appeared at the door.

"Oh Christ," he said when he saw them, "I've only been out a few days!"

"Can we come in, Larry?" Keough asked.

"What's this about?"

"What's it always been about?" Keough asked. "Denise."

"I don't have to let you in!"

"Yeah, you do," Keough said. "I have a warrant, Mr. Keith."

Jeter knew that if Keith asked to see the warrant, they were in trouble, but in the end he didn't. He just turned and walked away from the door.

They found Larry Keith and his wife, Denise's mother, sitting at the kitchen table.

"Mrs. Keith."

She looked away.

"Tell us what you came to say, Detective," Keith said.

Keough had gotten a good night's sleep—finally—but he still didn't have the patience he usually had. He decided to get right to the point so he could move on to making some life decisions. His director had told him the night before that solving the dual cases had literally saved their unit and that they were now ready to open a Midwest office. His offer to Harriet and Keough to man it stood.

Keough could leave Washington and move to the city the office would be in—as soon as that decision was made.

"We're here to arrest both of you, Mr. Keith."

"Both of us? For what?"

"Well, Mrs. Keith for murdering her little girl, and you as accessory."

If Mrs. Keith could have turned her head even farther, it might have revolved completely around. Keough didn't think not having any warrants was going to bite them in the ass. He could smell a confession coming.

"You don't know what you're talking about," Keith said.

"I think I do, Larry," Keough said. "You see, I could never figure out why your wife was so intent on your innocence. It was obvious that you beat her. I've seen women put up with men like that, and even love them. However, I've never seen a woman defend a man who had killed her child. That's when I realized that you hadn't killed her." Keough looked at Nancy Keith. "You killed her, Nancy. Didn't you?"

He still couldn't see her face, but a single sob escaped and wracked her body.

"No," Larry Keith said, "I killed her. I did it."

"No, Larry, you hid the body in the refrigerator," Keough said. "But Nancy killed her. My guess, Larry, is that you loved both of them in your own warped way, but when you saw what Nancy had done, you knew you had to cover for her. Denise's mother killed her. What I don't know is why."

Nancy finally turned to look at Keough, her face haggard and anguished. He was totally devoid of pity for her.

Back in his hotel that night, Keough dialed Harriet's cell phone.

"Tied up all your loose ends?" he asked.

"Oh, yeah," she said. She made a groaning sigh, which he knew meant she was taking her shoes off. He was amazed that he knew her that well. "You?"

"Mmm, I guess," he said.

"What's wrong?"

"Nothing," he said, "just a few surprises today."

"Like what?"

He told her about Nancy Keith's confession that she'd killed her daughter in a fit of jealousy.

"Jealousy?"

"She was starting to think that her husband loved her daughter more."

"Sexually?"

"Yes," he said, "that wasn't it at all. Turns out the guy really loved the little girl, he just had no idea how to show it. Now she's dead and both adults are in jail."

"Wow," she said, "that really does tie up loose ends."

"Yeah, but there's one more thing."

"You mean the new office?" she asked. "I think it should be in St. Louis, since you already know the city and we both know I don't want it to be in Chicago."

"That sounds okay, but that's not what I meant."

"What, then?"

Keough walked over to Jack Roswell's chess set and stared down at it. He hadn't told Harriet about it, or about the way Jack's daughter had treated him when he went to her house to offer his condolences. That was why he'd been shocked when she'd showed up at the task force's office earlier that morning. . . .

"Mrs. Wilkens," he'd said, surprised when she walked in.

"I read in the newspaper that you were here," she said, standing with her hands clutching her purse in front of her. They were red and rough, which was probably only part of the reason she was so unhappy. But then, who was he to assume she was unhappy just because she was married, had two small children and a deceased father. Jack had talked about her all the time as if she was unhappy, although pretending to be happy. But maybe Jack was wrong, too.

The only thing he knew for sure from looking at her was that she was uncomfortable.

"Mrs. Wilkens, can I help you with something?"

"I'm sorry, Detective Keough, I'm not used to—I'm just—" Irritably, she brushed a lank lock of hair from her face. "I'm here to apologize."

"For what?"

"For the way I treated you when you came by the house. That was . . . wrong of me, and incredibly insensitive. I should have realized you had just heard of my father's passing. He was your friend, and it must have been a shock."

"It was," he said, "but you were right to be upset with me. I should have stayed in touch."

"Mr. Keough," she said, "please let me have my apology."

Keough stared at her, and in that moment felt ashamed. If Jack had ever mentioned her first name to him, he'd forgotten it.

"All right, Mrs. Wilkens," he said. "I accept your apology . . . and I want to thank you for that chess set. It means a lot to me."

"Good," she said, "I'm glad. He wanted you to have it."

They stood there looking at each other for a few moments, and then she turned and left. When he realized that she had made no attempt to tell him her first name, he didn't feel ashamed anymore.

"Joe?"

"Hmm?"

"Were you were going to tell me what else happened today?" Harriet asked.

"No," he said, picking up the white queen. "No, I wasn't, but thanks for asking."

ALONE WITH THE DEAD

ROBERT J. RANDISI

New York City is in the grip of a nightmare. A twisted serial killer called the Lover is stalking young women, leaving his calling card with their dead bodies—a single rose. And there's a copycat out there too, determined to do his idol one better. But the Lover isn't flattered. He's furious that some rank amateur is muddying his good name. As the nightmare grows ever more intense, one detective begins to suspect the truth. As his superiors close ranks on him, he realizes that his only ally may be the Lover himself.

___4435-8 $4.99 US/$5.99 CAN

ANDREW HARPER

RED ANGEL

The Darden State Hospital for the Criminally Insane holds hundreds of dangerous criminals. Trey Campbell works in the psych wing of Ward D, home to the most violent murderers, where he finds a young man who is in communication with a serial killer who has just begun terrorizing Southern California—a killer known only as the Red Angel.

Campbell has 24 hours to find the Red Angel and face the terror at the heart of a human monster. To do so, he must trust the only one who can provide information—Michael Scoleri, a psychotic murderer himself, who may be the only link to the elusive and cunning Red Angel. Will it take a killer to catch a killer?
